Arms of the Ozarks

by

Betty Hamilton

DORRANCE
PUBLISHING CO
EST. 1920
PITTSBURGH, PENNSYLVANIA 15238

Dorrance Publishing Co
585 Alpha Drive
Suite 103
Pittsburgh, PA 15238
Visit our website at www.dorrancebookstore.com

ISBN: 978-1-6461-0678-3
eISBN: 978-1-6461-0609-7

I would like to dedicate this book to George Reeves. A dear and wonderful friend without him this book would not have been possible. Thank you George for all your wonderful work I appreciate you.

Also to George's sister and my dearest and best friend Susan Reeves that always stands with me even when I don't deserve it. What a wonderful family the Reeves. I love you all, thank you so much for being there for me.

Arms of the Ozarks

Chapter 1

Linda Kay woke up with tears streaming down her face; she knew something was wrong. She had no idea what it was, but her heart was breaking. There was a heavy sinking feeling in the pit of her stomach. This wasn't the first time that something like this has happened: it was a warning of something to come. She got up and retrieved a Kleenex and wiped the tears from her eyes. She was trying to figure out what could be wrong. She may not know what the problem is or how long it was going to last. What she did know was that pain and hurt was on its way, and she didn't know how to stop it. Sometimes her insight to things seemed like a blessing, and other times it seemed to be a burden. Linda Kay used to talk to her grandmother and her mother about these bad feelings that would come over her. They also were able to have pre-warning of events that were to come. Sometimes you knew within hours, and other times it was days before you knew what was happening. This wasn't always easy to understand, but she always knew the instant she figured out what the problem was. Immediately, she would get a sense of relief. She still had to face the pain of whatever the problem was, but she at least knew what she was facing. Although on some occasions, she was able to take care of the problem before it occurred, and those are the one she calls her blessings. This one was such a deep seeded feeling that she felt like devastation was on its way. There was nothing she could do to avoid it.

Some people believe in ghosts; some don't. Some people believe in the paranormal, and others do not. Some people believe there are spirits around us; others do not. Some people say, "Your guardian angel is always with you." The answer to these questions is simple: I don't know. I only know what happens to me, and that's all I can answer, I do not have an explanation. I just know what I see, what I think, and what I feel. Right now, I am very rattled and upset, I know I have to get myself calmed down and try to think rationally.

Linda Kay dressed quickly and headed for the 7-Eleven; it was only a couple of blocks from her house, and she needed a cup of coffee bad. There was no way she could make coffee at home because everything she owned had been packed up. This was her last night at this house. She also knew there would be no sleeping for the rest of the night. All she could do was hope and pray that she could shake this dreaded feeling that seemed to take over her every instinct.

Linda Kay was shaking slightly as she walked in the 7-Eleven; she bought a large cup of coffee. She drank that cup while talking to the clerk about nothing in particular. They both just needed the company. Before she left, she had a thermos filled with hot steaming coffee.

She returned home trying to center her psyche and calm herself down; after all, tomorrow was a big day. Linda Kay was very confused; it seemed as if she had just enough psychic ability to cause her problems. Times like this, she never had enough to give her all the answers. There were other times that she could tell someone what was going on and what was going to happen. Those were the times that were much easier for her to deal with. There had been a few times that she received a message that she did not want to tell the person she was talking with.

On those occasions, she did keep the answers to herself. Other times, it seemed she was left in torment until the situation passed, and this felt like one of those times.

As the sun broke through, Linda Kay knew it was going to be a bright, beautiful day, and *After all, it's my birthday,* she thought. It was time to be happy and to celebrate, not just her birthday but also a new beginning. She tried hard to shove last night's episode to the back of her mind and pretend it didn't happen. She just wanted to enjoy every minute of the day.

I don't know whether to say I'm moving forward, or am I going back in time? It's a decision that I made when my grandfather passed away several months back. I have been looking forward to this day for some time. Even though it wasn't an easy decision to make because anytime you make a change in your life it's hard. You never know what awaits you in the unknown. But in my heart of hearts, I feel like I made the best decision for me.

I have plans. As soon as my best friend Elizabeth Reeves gets here, we're heading for the country where everything is peaceful and quiet. My grandfather left me a log cabin back in the woods close to the Buffalo River. I remember the wonderful times I used to have there, hours on end of running and playing. Floating the Buffalo River with my mom and my grandparents, I always felt so carefree and innocent during those years. My grandparents had always spoiled me with love. They made sure that I was always courteous to others and that I minded my manners at all times. I knew I could always go to them and they would be there for me. My mom was a beautiful and wonderful person, and I loved her more than words could say. In my way of thinking, grandparents are special in a totally different way. That was a time in my life that I have lost forever, but I hold it dearly in my memory. There's no going back to those beautiful days. I can only look forward to the new memories that I can make there. I could always feel the love that permeated through the walls of that log cabin. My desire is to keep that loving feeling flowing through the cabin walls and it will stay with me forever.

Elizabeth is helping me move today. She's tried for a long time to talk me into staying here, but I'd rather go back to my roots. So instead I talked her into taking a week's vacation and going with me. I hope she will find it as enjoyable as I do. We have promised to visit each other often. Her friendship is something I would never want to lose.

I feel that I need what I left behind; I know that my country lifestyle isn't for everyone. I believe it is for me. Everything seems to go at a slow and steady pace there. People stop and take the time to say hello; they ask about you and your family. What's ironic about it is they really care. Everyone there knows everyone else and has most of their life, so when they ask how you and your family are doing it comes from the heart. The worst part about a small town is that everyone there also knows all about your business. I suppose there are positives and negatives no matter where you live. Myself, I prefer that laid-back atmosphere I find in the country. If you live in the country long enough, I think you will also find the time to enjoy your surroundings. Starting your morning with a beautiful sunrise, and ending your evening with a spectacular sunset. Before long, you will be taking in the beauty of the world around you.

I'm an author, and I'm looking forward to the familiar smells and sounds of the country where I can relax and do my writing. There's a lot of peace and tranquility in those old mountains. Besides, I love that old log cabin; that's where my heart is, and that's where I belong. My mom and I lived a few miles from my grandparents, but my greatest treat was the hours I spent at that log cabin.

I will miss a lot of wonderful hours that I spend with Elizabeth. She's my closest and dearest friend.

Linda Kay had a smile on her face as she thought about Elizabeth.

She is a beautiful and independent person; she stands about 5'6" and has a creamy complexion, and she is slim figured. She wears her auburn hair short and lets it frame her face. That seems to accent her deep green eyes. There's something about those dimples in her smile that captures your interest. She carries herself with elegance and has a very vibrant personality.

I'm only about 5'4" with large dark blue eyes. I have a heart-shaped face, and I'm also slim in figure. My hair is a dark blonde and lies in soft curls down my back.

I try to stay strong and keep a smile on my face. I try to maintain a positive attitude about life and see the bright side of an otherwise bleak situation. Sometimes, I find it hard to try and live up to those expectations. And there are times that I have let myself slip and become angry and become a person that I don't even like. I chastise myself and try again to be the person I want to be. I do know that I love God's creatures, whether it is man or beast, and I wish I could make the whole world happy, but I've found that everyone has to find their own happiness.

I love to write to get into my fantasy world and develop something that will help others to escape the humdrum of everyday life and take a journey with me through the unknown.

Elizabeth interrupted Linda Kay's thoughts as she popped her head in the door.

"I know I'm a little early. Sheila got called into work this morning, I told her you wouldn't mind if she dropped me off early. I thought it was very sweet of her to bring me over, so I can leave my car at home. Wow, this place sounds empty and hollow with all your things gone. When did the moving van leave?"

I had to laugh at the way she was jumping from one subject to the next, but I love that bubbly personality.

"The movers left here about an hour ago. I've got my SUV packed solid; now that you're here, I guess we're ready to go."

"Linda Kay, are you sure I can't talk you into staying here? I'm going to be so lonesome with you gone, and what's going to happen to me if you're not here to keep me out of trouble?"

"I don't think I have a lot to worry about where you are concerned. Yes, I'm sure this move is right for me. Besides, you'll be coming to see me quite often. And just wait till you have your first experience of floating the Buffalo River. You're going to be in for a treat. It won't be long after that till you will be looking for a log cabin of your own."

They were laughing as they walked out the door arm in arm and climbed into the SUV.

CHAPTER 2

THE MOVE WASN'T BUT A COUPLE OF HOURS AWAY. They made the most of the trip, they talked, they laughed, and they sang along with the radio. Elizabeth cracked up laughing as she said, "I think it's a good thing that we didn't make singing our career; we would starve to death."

"You are so totally right. I remember when I was a kid wanting to be a singer so bad. I had my grandparents sitting and listening to me for hours on end. They always told me how great I was, but I always knew I couldn't carry a tune in a bucket."

At last, Linda Kay said, "Okay, just ahead is the general store; that's where I'm going to meet the movers, and they will follow us the rest of the way to the log cabin. Hey, look, there they are now, so it won't be long, and you'll see where I spent most of my childhood."

As they meandered down the dirt road, Elizabeth was astonished at the way the dirt plumed in the air behind the SUV.

"Is it always this dusty driving down these roads?"

"Just in the summertime; in the winter, it's mostly ice and mud puddles. I'm afraid it is just one of the things you have to get used to."

"I don't know about that. I like my paved road." Elizabeth looked around at the countryside and realized that they hadn't passed any other cabins for a while. She also hadn't seen anyone else around. Elizabeth asked, "You will be awfully alone out here, you know. I haven't seen anyone in quite a while. Won't you be afraid to stay out here by yourself?"

"No, not really I've never known of anyone having a problem in these back woods that they needed to be afraid of. Of course, you can have the everyday problems of, 'My car wouldn't start,' or "My washing machine overflowed.' What you will really find here is such a beautiful peace and tranquility. That's what I found here in these woods when I stayed with my grandparents. Just wait and see, you will be able to feel the love in that old log cabin. My grandfather built that cabin for my grandmother the year they got married. He had inherited the property from his parents, as they had from his grandparents. That property was very important to his family; they all loved it and cared for. I think you'll love the old home place. It's big it's roomy and spacious. It has an upstairs with the veranda that you can walk out on to watch the sunrise or to see the sunset. There is always a beautiful scene that awaits you from there."

"Right now, with no houses or anyone around, it seems a bit eerie to me. I guess I'm just a city slicker through and through."

"After a while, it's something you get used to and just consider it to be normal. You have more time to think and to enjoy your surroundings."

At last, Linda Kay pulled into the driveway of the big beautiful old log cabin. It looked picturesque as if it should be on a postcard. She turned off the ignition and just sat there with a stunned look on her face as if she was in some kind of a trance. Her heart began to beat fast, and panic rose within her throat. She knew without a doubt she had just run into what had caused the panic in her dreams last night. It was right here waiting for her; now she was going to have to face it head on. That dreaded awful feeling had washed over her once again, pulling on her senses to be on alert: there was something wrong here. Things began to flash before her eyes, and she knew trouble awaited her. She could tell by the way she felt, this was only part of what was to be. A shiver ran through her body at the fear of the unknown.

Elizabeth brought her back to the here and now.

"Linda Kay, are you okay? What's wrong with you?"

Linda Kay was nervous as she looked at Elizabeth.

"Someone has been in my cabin. I can feel it; it's not a good feeling. I just know something is wrong. I might as well face it. Let's go see how much damage was done." As they walked, Linda Kay looked around the property, and a shiver ran down her spine. "I can feel the negativity of things that are lurking around my property."

In the back of her mind, she was thinking about the fact that she had been woken up the night before with that dreaded feeling surrounding her very being. She now knew where part of that dread had come from. She also knew that feeling wasn't going away; she knew that wasn't all of it there was more to come. She didn't know how she could ever explain that to Elizabeth where she could understand. She hoped she wouldn't have to.

Elizabeth looked at Linda Kay questionably.

"You're confusing me. I don't understand what you're talking about. How do you know somebody's been in your house? You haven't even gone inside yet."

"I just know in my heart, I just know it, what more can I say? You'll see when we get inside."

They could tell immediately when they walked in the house; it was nasty, stuff scattered, and there were some dirty dishes in the kitchen, some trash… Everything was left in a mess. It was not the way she had left the house after her grandfather's funeral. It broke her heart to think that someone would come into her grandparents' place and disrespect it in such a manner. A tear dropped from her cheek, and she wiped it away with the back of her hand. She took in a deep breath and tried to calm down and wiped more tears from her face. She didn't have time to deal with her hurt right now, but deal with it she would.

She fought to keep the anger down and put a pleasant look on her face, so she could take care of the things she needed to do now. She had the movers outside ready to bring boxes in the house. None of this was their fault, and they didn't need her bad attitude. As they carried boxes into the house, she told them which room to put them in. Everyone worked diligently until the last the moving van had been unloaded.

Elizabeth knew Linda Kay was hurting, so she tried to back away, giving Linda Kay her own space to try and deal with what she had to face. The movers had just left, their job finally completed. Linda Kay immediately tore open one of the boxes that they had left in the living room. She pulled out a large oyster shell and laid it on the table and continued to search through the box until at last she pulled out a small bag of sand and poured it into the shell. She removed a small charcoal disc and laid it on top of the sand, the disc begins to spit and sputter as she lit it. She pulled out a small bag of sage which she laid on top of the burning disc. Last but not least, she took out a large feather and looked around the room. When she found the right spot, she walked to the corner of the room and began waving the smoke into the air.

Elizabeth couldn't contain her curiosity any longer; she had to know: "What is that stuff, and what are you going to do with it?"

"Don't worry. It's really nothing, but I'm going to sage the house and get rid of all negative energy that has been brought into this house. You'll see when I'm done, everything will feel better and smell better, and you will feel more relaxed."

Elizabeth looked at her as if she had lost her ever loving mind, but all she said was, "Okay… if you say so."

Linda Kay went through the house blessing it as she went. She was smoking every corner, opening the closet doors and opening the drawers seeing to it that everything was smoked. Except for one door she totally passed by. Elizabeth looked at it and saw there was a padlock on the door.

She asked, "Linda Kay, does this door go outside?"

Linda Kay looked at the door and smiled, "No, that was my mom's old bedroom, and when she passed away my grandmother had it locked up. Her room was left exactly like it was the last time my mom was in there."

"I thought you said you and your mom lived a few miles from here."

"I did, but sometimes my mom and I would come and stay a few days at a time; my mom still used her old bedroom when we were here."

"That makes sense, but sometimes, don't you want to go in there and be around some of your mom's things? Just to touch them, and remember her touch?"

"Yes, I used to think about it quite often. I thought it would be a great comfort to me, but my grandmother was so hurt, she just wanted everything preserved the way my mother had left it. I wanted my grandmother to have all the comfort she could get. So, I left it alone, we all have to grieve in our own way."

"Do you think you will ever open that door now, or leave it locked up like it is?"

"I really don't know. I try not to think about it, but some days, I find it almost irresistible. Sometimes I think there's nothing I would like more than to be able to touch some of my mom's things. Who knows? One day I may open the door. Sometimes I feel like part of my mother was trapped in that room, and she needs to be set free. Other times, I think maybe my grandmother was right, and my mother's memory is being preserved, locked away where no one can disturb it."

"Linda Kay, I've known you for quite a while, and I hope you don't mind, but out of all this time, you've never mentioned your dad. Why do you never talk about him?"

"No, I don't mind you asking at all. You see, I never knew my dad. He was in an accident when my mother was pregnant with me. I was told he died immediately, so you see, I just never knew him. I've heard a lot of good things about him, but I don't really have a connection with him. There were a lot of times in my life that I wished I had a dad, but it was just something that I always lived without and never gave it much of a thought.

"Okay, it looks like to me, I've smoked the rooms well, covering everything. That should get rid of all the negative energy that was brought in here."

"You think that's going to do it?"

"Yes, I really do think it's going to work. Once I get this place all cleaned up, I will smoke it once again, just to make me feel better."

Linda Kay and Elizabeth worked diligently for the rest of the day and into the night, unpacking and cleaning the house and getting everything just perfect. Elizabeth had to admit, the smell of sage throughout the house smelled wonderful, making her feel more relaxed and comfortable as she worked.

They were both so tired, they gladly ate a sandwich and drank a glass of milk. They went upstairs, took their baths, and went to bed. There was excitement in Elizabeth's heart, thinking about the float trip she was going to go on in the morning. That is, if they didn't sleep too late. After all, they were both exhausted. She crawled into bed with a smile and hope in her heart.

Linda Kay took what used to be her grandmother and grandfather's old bedroom. She put Elizabeth in the bedroom that she had always slept in as a child. She left the other bedroom empty to make into her office.

The bed felt so comfortable to Linda Kay, it was as if every muscle in her body relaxed going loose and limp, letting her fall immediately into a deep and wonderful sleep. She had only been asleep about an hour when she was awakened by the sound of her grandfather's voice. She could hear her grandfather saying, "Baby girl, be alert; be aware that someone is in the darkness and waits outside, stand guard, baby."

Linda Kay immediately took heed to her grandfather's warning.

Linda Kay's grandfather had come to her before, but never in a manner like this. She knew to pay attention to what he was telling her. She immediately jumped out of bed and ran to the window. Linda Kay looked at her clock. It was after three o'clock in the morning, and she didn't even try to be quiet as she ran from the windows to the French doors. She knew she had no choice; she would have to wake Elizabeth up.

Suddenly, Elizabeth knocked lightly on her bedroom door before opening the door and entering. She was still rubbing sleep out of her eyes as she mumbled, "Are you okay what's going on in here?"

Chapter 3

"*Yeah, I'm okay but* I think you need to come on in, I need to talk to you."

Elizabeth walked to the foot of Linda Kay's bed and slowly sat down never taking her eyes off Linda Kay.

"Can't it wait? We can talk in the morning. I am awfully sleepy..."

"No, this can't wait. I need to talk to you now."

"You know you're scaring me, don't you? Is there something wrong?"

"I don't mean to scare you. You have been my friend for many a year now, and I love you dearly, and what I'm going to tell you, I should have told you a long time ago. I was always afraid to tell anyone. I'm a writer and what people think of me could influence the outcome of the sales of my books. I love writing, I love telling my stories, and I don't want what I believe to influence how other people look at me. I consider you my best friend. I definitely never want you to think badly of me. There are things happening right now that leave me no choice but to confess to you what I believe and what I understand to be true. I hope that you can understand and will stand by me."

"Wow, that's deep, do you really have such little faith in me that you can't trust me with your inner thoughts? That kind of hurts my feelings because I always felt like I could tell you anything, and I thought you felt the same way about me. If we can't trust one another as best friends, we might as well give up; we'll never be able to trust anyone."

"I've always told you everything, Elizabeth, and I do trust you more than you'll ever know. There was one thing that I never confessed to you or anyone else, and I'm sorry about that, but I have to confess it now. I wish we had more time to talk about things, but I'm going to have to tell you fast. There are things we need to do, and we are going to need to do them quickly. I just hope you trust and believe me. We can talk everything over later. Right now, I just need you to listen to me. We have a problem, so what I'm going to tell, I just need you to pay attention and do what I ask you to do.

"All my life, I have been able to hear things; it's like a voice or recorder in my head that warns me of things that are going on. Sometimes I even get a message of love from a family member that has passed on. What I hear and what I receive comes out of nowhere. I never know when I'm going to receive a message. I never know what I'm going to get, but I have learned over the years to pay close attention to that voice. It is there for a reason, it's there for me, and it is real. What disturbed you tonight was the fact that I just received one of those messages. I was up running around the room looking out the windows causing a commotion because I was trying to see what's going on outside. I'm sorry, but I would have had to wake you up anyway. So, I'm glad you're awake.

"Tonight, the message came from my grandfather and he told me to be careful there is someone lurking outside in the dark waiting and watching. We've got to find out who it is; we've got to make sure the cabin is secure, and we've got to make sure that we are protected."

"I've heard of things like that, I never knew if they were true or not. I never put anybody down for saying what they believed to be true because I don't know. Just because it's something I don't know doesn't make it not true. You're my best friend; if you tell me it's so, I believe you, so let's do what we need to do and protect ourselves. Besides that, you promised me a float trip on the Buffalo River tomorrow. So, you better protect me tonight because you're not going to get out of it that easy."

Linda Kay reached over and hugged Elizabeth's neck as she said, "Thank you. You have no idea how much I wanted to tell you this over the years. Most of all, thank you for standing with me; it's something I will never forget.

"Let's get all the windows checked and make sure they're locked. I want to make sure the house is locked up tight. It's something I've never checked out here before. I always felt comfortable and safe; you just never had to lock your doors. We've got to look out all the windows and see if we can spot anyone on the property, and whatever you do don't go outside. Don't open the doors. I really don't know who's out there or what they want."

They took off through the house checking every window and door, making sure they were securely locked in. They met in the living room.

Linda Kay asked, "Did you see anything outside while you were checking the windows?"

"No, but I found the back door unlocked and one window unlocked."

"I found two windows unlocked, both downstairs, but everything is secure now. I think we need to go back upstairs. We can get a better view of what's going on outside from up there."

"Linda Kay, everything seems to be quiet. I don't know if there's a problem out there or not, I just know I'm pretty nervous. I think I'm going to fix us a cup of coffee if you don't mind. I'm a ball of nerves, and I need something to calm me down."

"Coffee sounds wonderful. We're going to be up the rest of the night. I could use something to calm my nerves also. Besides. maybe the coffee will help keep us awake. I'll help you."

"I can do this. It won't take me long because, believe me, I don't want to be down here by myself." Elizabeth wasn't really sure there was anything wrong, but just in case, she told Linda Kay, "I would feel better if you were on the lookout. I'll bring the coffee up to you, go on up and start watching. I'll be there shortly, and if I get too scared, I'll be up without the coffee."

"Thanks," Linda Kay said as she turned and swiftly headed back upstairs because she understood her grandfather's warning. She was sure danger lurked just outside. As Linda Kay walked into the bedroom, she turned the light out and walked over to the window. She was trying to examine every shadow and shape that she saw in the dark of night. The moon was just bright enough that she could make out the silhouette of the beautiful mountains that outlined the back of her property. It was as if the mountains were stretching out their lovely arms to protect these beautiful Ozark Mountains. She gasped as she looked at the sky; it had been such a long time since she had seen the stars in the Ozarks. It was one of the most beautiful sights that God has created. The stars danced overhead like diamonds shimmering in the night, just waiting for you to capture all their beauty. It broke her heart to think that a man lurked in the dark waiting to cause damage in this beautiful world. She pulled her mind back to the present, searching until she saw movement in the shadows of the trees.

As Elizabeth walked through the door carrying a tray, she set it on the desk, turned around and flipped on the light saying, "Why are you standing here in the dark?"

Linda Kay started shouting, "Turn off the light, turn off the light, quick turn off the light."

Elizabeth was stunned unable to move just for a moment then it registered in her mind what Linda Kay was saying. She immediately did as she was told and flipped the light off but as she did, she questioned, "Why do you want to stand here in the dark?"

"Come here, and I'll show you what I see. Look outside. You can see outside, but someone on the outside cannot see in here because it's too dark. If you turn the light on someone outside can see in here, but I cannot see outside."

"Well, of course. That only makes sense, I'm sorry I wasn't thinking."

"That's okay, but what I want you to do is look at the base of that tree over there—" she pointed to the left.

Elizabeth spotted where she wanted her to look, just in time to see the movement at the base of the tree.

"Oh my goodness, did you see that Linda Kay? Someone is out there."

"I know. I've been watching him. I guess it could be a girl, but whoever it is I have been watching them. They seem to be moving closer to the house a little at a time. I don't know if they're trying to figure out who we are because they thought they could get back in tonight. Maybe they're harmless, but I have my doubts. From what Grandpa said, danger lurks. I don't know anything else to do but to keep a watch on him and pray he doesn't try to come in."

"Linda Kay, I brought a big knife out of the kitchen drawer back up here with me. Don't we have anything better than that to protect ourselves with?"

"The only thing that I have is a taser/flashlight combination, but it's in the car. I've been thinking maybe I should try to retrieve it."

"I don't know about that, Linda Kay, you told me a while ago not to open the doors. And I agree with you. Now you tell me you want to go outside. What are you thinking?"

"I don't want to go, but I feel like I need to we have to have something to protect ourselves with."

"Linda Kay, we know there is one person in the back yard. What we don't know is if there is more than one person out there. I think it would be better to stay locked in the house. We need to keep a watch to see what's going on and make it through the night."

"I've got to get my flashlight tonight, Elizabeth; we don't have any other protection. As far as I know, I've gotten rid of all my grandfather's hand guns before I locked the house up. There's nothing here. Tomorrow, I'll go online and order us both a taser. Then I'll have one in the car and one in the house.

"You know, especially in the summertime I do a lot of traveling alone. Spring is a time of the year I always try to set up my book signings. I set them up in his many states as possible. I always felt a little safer knowing I had the taser in case of emergency. I never liked traveling alone, so I always keep the taser in the glove box of my car. It's not going to help us right now if I leave it in the car. I wish I had brought it in the house, but I never thought there would be a need for it here. Come on, follow me downstairs."

"Are you nuts? What about a gun? Don't you have a gun?"

"No, I don't have a gun; I told you I got rid of them when I cleaned out the house. Look, I know how to shoot a gun, I know how to clean a gun, I know how to take the gun apart and put it back together. I can shoot a snake; I can shoot an animal that is trying to hurt me. I don't think I could ever shoot a human; I don't think I could live over it. Would I tase someone that's trying to hurt me, of course. I would in a heartbeat."

"If you had a gun, they wouldn't have to get that close to you, don't you understand?"

"Yes, I totally understand. I also understand that if I were to kill somebody, it's all over, there's nothing I could do to revive them, it's the end of things. Then I would have to live with myself knowing what I had done. I don't think I could survive that. Maybe it would be better if they killed me than it would be for me to try and live with the fact that I had killed someone. I don't think I could do that. No, a gun is just not for me. As for as someone who has the guts to fire a gun and protect themselves or others, I have no problem with that. I understand why they would do it. It's just me personally that could not live with the outcome. Call me chicken, yeah, I am, but it still doesn't change the facts."

"Okay, tasers it is. That would sure be better than nothing right now. I don't like being this vulnerable."

"Thank you. Now please come with me downstairs. Lock the door behind me. I want you to watch me out the window. If something happens, don't open the door; just call the sheriff's department. Otherwise, when I get back to the door let me in."

Elizabeth was having a hard time following Linda Kay through the dark, as she was clinging to the shadows. It was as if she was running from one dark shadow to another trying to seek protection in the night. At last, Linda Kay made it to the car, but before she could open the door, something hit her in the back. She was shoved so hard that it knocked her to the ground. All Elizabeth could make out was the shadow of someone running away from the car staying in the shadows and hiding in the night; she couldn't get any kind of description of who it was. Without thinking about what Linda Kay had told her she threw the door open and ran outside to try to get to Linda Kay.

She helped Linda Kay to upright herself and get back on her feet. "Come on, I'll help you back inside."

"Not without the taser, I've come this far I'm not going back without it." She opened the car door and reached in the glove box and retrieved her taser.

Elizabeth asked, "Are you sure you're okay?"

"Yes, I'm fine; I skinned my knees up, but I will look at them when we get inside, but I'll be just fine." Linda Kay turned the flashlight on and began shining the light around in the yard trying to see into the shadows. At the same time, she was hurrying, wanting nothing more than to get back into the safety of her house. "I don't like being out here and being this vulnerable."

As soon as they entered the house, Elizabeth slammed and locked the door. She then stared at Linda Kay.

"I can't believe how stupid I am! That door was standing open. What if I just locked us in here with some predator? Let's check the house once more. I want to make sure we haven't locked someone in the house with us."

They could both feel their hearts beating in their throats as panic rose over whether or not there was an intruder in the house. Once they were satisfied that every nook and cranny had been checked and they found no one, Linda Kay went to the restroom to clean and doctor her knees.

Once again, they settled in at Linda Kay's bedroom window.

Linda Kay said, "Why don't you pull a chair over here next to me, and we will drink our coffee and keep a watch on what is going on outside."

They watched as time slowly ticked by, the butcher knife and a taser lay between the two of them, their only source of protection as the night slowly drifted by. As time went on Linda Kay and Elizabeth seemed to take turns yawning and stretching trying to stay awake. It was about an hour until daybreak when the shadow seemed to back its way deeper into the woods and scurry away. Neither Linda Kay nor Elizabeth could see where they went. They spent a good hour watching, staying on alert. Daybreak was just trying to shine through when exhaustion at last took them over. They laid down on Linda Kay's bed and immediately fell into a deep sleep.

CHAPTER 4

IT WAS LATE WHEN LINDA KAY WOKE UP, stretching and yawning. Then reality from last night hit her. *Oh my goodness, I should have never fallen asleep!* Then panic, over whether or not Elizabeth was okay overwhelmed her. She began frantically shaking Elizabeth, waking her up.

"Thank goodness you're okay, I'm really sorry; I shouldn't have fallen asleep last night. Since we're okay, let's get up. We need to check everything out. At least we both made it through the night without any harm. I think we need to make some preparations for tonight; I just don't want to be that vulnerable again. It would take too long to order tasers. What I think we need to do is go to Harrison today and purchase what we need. The intruder may never come back again, but if they do, I want to know that I've got some kind of protection."

They dressed quickly in comfortable clothing. Linda Kay said, "If we hurry, I don't see any reason why we should change our plans. We can go to Harrison and still have time to float the Buffalo River today. How does that sound to you?"

"Yes, you know I've been looking forward to trying that float trip."

They walked into the kitchen, and fixed themselves some coffee and a bowl of cereal. They were in a hurry and didn't want to take the time to cook a big breakfast. They still had a lot they wanted to do.

"As soon as we finish eating, let's check the house over and make sure it's still locked up. Then we can run to Harrison and pick up what we want. On the way back, we'll stop and float the Buffalo."

Elizabeth looked up from her bowl of cereal and began staring at the back door.

"Linda Kay, that door knob, it looks funny from here."

Linda Kay got up from the table, walked to the back door.

"Yeah, I'd say you're right. It's about to fall off. I don't know if someone got in the house with us last night or not. This just doesn't make any sense. I can't continue to put up with this; it's scaring the crap out of me. I've got to do something before nightfall. I'm not trying to rush you, but when you finish eating, I want to get started to Harrison. I think I should buy some new locks and get them installed today. I feel like we really need to take precautions before nightfall. While we're at it, I might as well go by the Sheriff's office and talk to them. I want someone to be aware of what's going on. I hope you won't be too upset with me if we put off floating the Buffalo. We're not canceling it; I would just like to put it off until tomorrow. That's one trip I want us to enjoy and not be rushed."

Elizabeth jumped up from the table, rinsed their bowls in the sink and said, "I'm ready, let's go. I just want out of this place; it's scary to me, too. Maybe we should be thinking about going home."

Linda Kay didn't drive dangerously, but she was speeding as she turned off the dirt road and onto the highway. She headed for the Sheriff's Department first. She was rather hesitant because what could she really tell the sheriff.

My door knob is broken and I think I saw someone in the woods last night. Someone pushed me down… The sheriff will probably just say I tripped over a rock. She knew it was going to be egg on her face when she went, but she was going anyway. She wanted someone to know they were having problems out there, in case something was to happen to them.

The sheriff's name was Travis Matthews. Linda Kay hadn't talked to Travis in a long time, but she hoped they could reconnect with their friendship. Linda Kay pulled into the parking lot and put the car in park.

She turned to Elizabeth, "Are you going in with me? I don't think I'm going to get very far. I figure they're just going to laugh at, me but I'm going to tell them anyway."

"Of course, I'm going with you. They may not believe us, but I'll be there to back you up. I was the one that checked that back door last night; I know it was locked, and I know there was nothing wrong with that door knob."

They slowly got out of the car and walked in the Sheriff's Department. Linda Kay asked to talk to Sheriff Travis, and they were shown to his office without delay.

The Sheriff immediately jumped up.

"Linda Kay, it has been so long since I have seen you. You look beautiful, as always. It's great to see you!" He walked from around the desk and gave her a quick hug. "I heard you were back and was hoping to get out to see you soon. I was really sorry to hear about your grandfather; he was a wonderful man."

"It's good to see you, too. I saw you at my grandfather's funeral, but I just didn't get a chance to talk with you. I'd like for you to meet a good friend of mine; this is Elizabeth Reeves. Elizabeth, this is Travis Matthews. We have been friends for a long time. We went to school together and ran in the same circle."

Sheriff Travis extended his hand out to Elizabeth, as they shook hands, they exchanged pleasantries.

"Travis, I wish I could say I was here just so we can catch up on old times, but that's not so, I'm here in a professional manner."

"I'm sorry to hear that, but have a seat and tell me what your problem is."

Linda Kay proceeded to tell the Sheriff everything that had been going on from the time she pulled into her driveway and found the mess inside the cabin. She didn't bother to tell him that she woke up the night before she left to come home with a warning that something was wrong. She also left out the fact that her grandfather had woken her up last night to warn her of the dangers that lurked outside her home. Those were a couple of facts that she would never tell the Sheriff.

"Well, I understand that you're a bit upset, but that's an old cabin. It's been here all my life... Maybe it was just in need of a new door knob. Maybe a screw fell out of it or something; I really don't think you have a whole lot to worry about. I'll tell you what, I'll drive by your place tonight just to check it out, if somebody's out there, I'm sure that will deter them. I don't think you'll have any more problems. It sounds like whoever had been going in your house will now know that you're home. They probably won't ever bother you again. You know, I think you'll find that this is still a beautiful and peaceful county. I just haven't had a lot of complaints from that area. But I'm very happy that you decided to move back."

With that Sheriff Travis stood up, letting Linda Kay and Elizabeth know that their conversation had come to a close.

As they climbed back in the car Elizabeth said, "Well, I think that was a waste of time. As for as the Sheriff driving by, that's just plain goofy. Who is that supposed to scare? I don't know about here, but I do know at home, as soon as the Sheriff got around the corner, varmints would be right back out to play. At least we told the Sheriff about it. Who knows the Sheriff might drive by tonight?"

"Yeah I took it; he thinks it's our imagination. I think we need to go to Harrison and pick up some good locks. While we are there, I want to see what kind of an alarm system we can get. Hopefully something good enough that we can get by with until I can get a reliable service installed. I also want to go to a sporting goods store. I want to see if there're any tasers in stock."

"That sounds good to me. While you're looking for tasers, I will be looking for a gun. I want to be locked, loaded, and prepared.

"If that's what you want do, I don't have a problem."

As they entered the sporting goods store, Elizabeth and Linda Kay split up, each going their own direction. At last, Elizabeth had picked her out a .38 that she thought would be good for her to handle. Then she found out that she had to go through all kinds of red tape to try to buy the gun, and it probably would be three weeks before she would actually get the gun. She told him, "Forget it. I will be back in my hometown by then. I'll just wait and get one there."

She walked up to Linda Kay and said, "Well I hope you had better luck than I did. I'm looking forward to a nice taser."

Linda Kay had to snicker.

"Take too long to get a gun?"

"You knew it would. Why didn't you just tell me?"

"Some lessons are better learned on your own. Now come on, let's finish our shopping and head back." Linda Kay told Elizabeth that she had one more stop she wanted to make.

"What else are we going to do?"

"There's a handyman that's only a few miles from my house. I want to see if he can come over and hook up the home alarm system that I bought. I know it's not a great one, but right now it is better than nothing. I'm going to call and see if I can't get one installed with cameras. I don't know if there's a company that will service us as far out as we are. I never thought about needing it out here, but I guess I do. Anyway, if I can get it, I'd like to have better service."

Linda Kay was in luck. Trinity was at home and told her he would be more than happy to follow her back to the house and help her set everything up. That was a big relief off Linda Kay's mind. She wasn't sure she could install the door locks properly. She had bought deadbolts for the front and back doors. She knew both doors would need to be drilled for the locks, and that was something she didn't want to tackle herself.

After everything was installed, Linda Kay and Elizabeth both gave a sigh of relief. They felt like they could relax for the rest of the evening and get a good night's sleep. They settled for soup and sandwiches and to just sit back and watch TV. They were promising each other that they would cook a good meal tomorrow night. They were both ready to give it up early; they had a long hard day after a really rough night. They checked the alarm system and all the windows, making sure everything was locked up tight, giving them peace of mind. Their plans were to get up early the next morning and by 10 o'clock head for the Buffalo River. They wanted to spend the day enjoying the river.

Chapter 5

Linda Kay woke up and sat straight up in bed, her heart beating fast. She knew someone was out there again. Her grandfather was there telling her that, "Darkness awaits, someone lurks outside, protect yourself," and with that, her grandfather was gone. Linda Kay jumped up and grabbed her robe and slipped it on. She grabbed her taser and cell phone off the nightstand and slipped them into the pocket of her robe. She tapped on Elizabeth's door, before flinging it open telling her to get up, get up now.

"Get your taser, come on, Elizabeth."

Elizabeth became immediately alert she looked around at her clock, 12 o'clock midnight. She didn't think twice about it, she picked up her taser and followed Linda Kay back to her bedroom, where they started the search for the danger that lurked in the woods. The moon was much brighter tonight, lighting up the yard, but sending the shadows deeper into the background. There was a light breeze outside softly blowing the leaves on the trees, shifting the shadows from one spot to another. The stars were bright and danced across the sky. If it wasn't for the evil that was lurking in the dark, it would be a beautiful night, one to be enjoyed by lovers everywhere. Linda Kay and Elizabeth sat there looking out the window trying to take in every shadow trying to find what was lurking in the night.

Linda Kay told Elizabeth, "Look at that mountain ridge. Isn't it beautiful? It seems to be saying that the Ozarks is opening its arms to care for these mountains during the night. It says it's standing guard protecting this land."

"It is beautiful, I don't know that I would've ever thought about it that way, but now that you mention it, I totally understand what you're saying. If it wasn't for the evil that's waiting outside, I would love to sit and talk about all of its wonder. Right now, my heart is pounding in my chest from fear, and my insides are shaking. Linda Kay, you have to go home with me. We have no other choice. If we live through this night, I think we should leave in the morning. We can come back another time and pack this place up. In the meantime, you can stay at my apartment with me."

Linda Kay had just shifted her sight back along the tree line when all at once someone darted out from between the trees and started running across the yard. But as they ran around the other side of the house they could no longer see where they had gone. Linda Kay and Elizabeth began running from room to room trying to see where the man had run to. Then all at once, there was a loud crash from the living room. Immediately the siren went off with a loud piercing sound. The sound was obnoxious, but at least it answered Linda Kay's question, would it wake her in the night? Yes, it would have definitely woken her up. Linda Kay knew the crash was the sound of a window busting open.

They both froze in their tracks, afraid to move, tears began to fall from Elizabeth's eyes and run down her cheeks. Linda Kay was just as frightened, but she knew she had to take care of Elizabeth. She put her arm around her and gave her a hug as she said, "Come on, let's check it out."

Linda Kay had to put on a brave façade; otherwise she was afraid Elizabeth was going to fall apart. They very cautiously began to descend the stairs. As they stepped down on the landing, they could feel a slight breeze blowing in the living room. You could smell that wonderful clean smell of the night air in the Ozarks, leaving Linda Kay with absolutely no doubt her living room window had been shattered. She turned on her flashlight and shined it around the room; she didn't see anyone, but she did see a large rock with a note wrapped around it laying in the middle of the floor. Linda Kay turned on the living room light. There was no need to hide in the dark; they knew she was there, and they knew she had found the note. She first walked over and shut off the alarm. This system didn't alert the police station, it only alerted her, so no one could sneak up on her in the night. What she needed to know is what they wanted and why they were tormenting her. She slowly bent down and picked up the rock and slipped the note from around it. She took a moment, looked up at Elizabeth with questioning eyes, finally Elizabeth nodded for her to go ahead. She slowly opened the note and began to read:

"Go away, leave now while you can."

Linda Kay took her cell phone out of her pocket as she looked up at Elizabeth.

"I'm sure this is a waste of time, but I feel like I have no other choice."

The phone was answered on the other end of the line saying, "Sheriff's office."

Linda Kay inhaled deeply before telling what had happened. She was told that someone would be out there shortly, and they disconnected the line. Linda Kay returned the phone to her robe pocket. With a sigh she looked at Elizabeth and said, "I feel quite confident that was a waste of time."

"What are we going to do? I can't go back to sleep with that hole in the window."

Linda Kay looked at Elizabeth saying, "I'm so sorry I got you into this mess. I never thought anything like this would happen. I really don't know what to do. I don't know if there will be any help coming from the Sheriff's Department. I have my doubts that they believe what I'm telling them. We just have to take care of each other for the rest of the night. Tomorrow, I'm going to have this window replaced, and then we're going to float the Buffalo, we're going to have a good time, and then you're going to pack your suitcase, and you're going home where you will be safe. That's about as far as I can plan."

"You know I'm not going back without you. I can't leave you here in this madness. I don't trust your Sheriff's Department. You can lay out here for a month, and who would be here to help you? This is crazy!"

"I'm going with you. I've got to take you home. But Elizabeth, understand I've got to come right back. So, don't be ridiculous, you know you have to get back to work. As you know, this property belonged to my great-grandfather, and it was passed down through the family. Now it is under my care, my watch, I can't turn my back on it. I've got to fight for what's right, and it's only right that I take care of it. I will be okay; you'll see everything will be fine. Now let me get the broom and dust pan, and I'll clean this mess up. Would you mind fixing us some coffee?"

"Of course, I'll fix us some coffee but I really wish you'd stay in the room with me while I do it."

Linda Kay just looked at her for a moment and said, "You are totally right. We don't need to be separated. As soon as I get this mess cleaned up, we will make some coffee."

"Thank you so much, I don't mean to be such a baby, but I am really scared. I don't know what they will do… Do they intend to kill us? Or do you think they're just playing with you? It's as if they're trying to scare you off. Well, let me tell you what, I'm scared, and I'm ready to run and you need to go with me."

"Yes, I understand. I'm as scared as you are, but were going to make it through the night, and tomorrow will be better. Now I'm going to get the dustpan and the broom." She smiled up at Elizabeth and stuck out her hand and said, "Want to go with me, come on?"

Elizabeth just reached out and took her hand without hesitation and they walked together into the kitchen to get the broom and dust pan.

While they were in the kitchen, Elizabeth ran over and flipped the switch on the coffee pot. She then got two cups out of the cabinet set them on the counter. She turned and got two pods of coffee and set them next to the cups. Okay this will be ready when we come back to put the dustpan away. The two went back to the living room and started cleaning the glass up that had scattered all over the living room floor. Linda Kay had a perplexed look in her eyes as she began looking around the room.

Elizabeth asked, "Okay, tell me, what you are looking for?"

"I would feel much better if I could find something to cover this window with. It being open like that, it makes me feel vulnerable."

In the end Linda Kay wasn't real happy; all they found was a cardboard box that they could cut up and tack to the frame of the window. Linda Kay knew that it wasn't any real protection, but psychologically, it calmed her mind a little. They went back to the kitchen, put everything away and fixed themselves a cup of coffee. They were each deep into their own thoughts, trying to find peace and calm where they could. When they came back to the living room, they set their coffee on the coffee table. Sleep was out of the question for the rest of the night.

Linda Kay inhaled a deep breath saying, "I've got the craziest feeling that they are still out there watching us."

She slowly walked over to the window looking out, searching, and trying to find whoever it was out there invading her space when all at once, there was another big crash, and this time the rock hit Linda Kay in the forehead, knocking her to the floor. Blood was gushing from her head. Her body was covered in broken glass. Elizabeth stood in the middle of the floor screaming for help, praying to God: *Please help us!*

Linda Kay sat up, telling Elizabeth, "Calm down and please get me a hand towel out of the bathroom." She could try and stop the bleeding. "Stay away from the windows and stay low; I'm sure whoever it is, they're still out there, watching and waiting. Who knows what they'll try next…"

Linda Kay could tell that Elizabeth was close to going into shock. She told her, "I need you to stay calm, pull yourself together. Would you get the first-aid kit and help me put a bandage on my head?"

"You're right, Linda Kay, I'm so sorry. Of course, I'm going to help you. I'm sorry I was being selfish, thinking only of myself; that was wrong of me. I was so frightened, I just wasn't thinking."

"Elizabeth, I understand, please just calm down you've done nothing wrong, just help me to get this bleeding to stop and put a bandage on my head, we're going to be fine. We're going to protect each other through the night, and tomorrow, I'm getting you out of here. You can come back and visit me after all this has settled down and I know what's going on, but in the meantime, I just want us to be safe."

"What about you, Linda Kay? Will you please go home with me?"

"No, I can't go, not until this problem is solved. I told you my grandfather left me in charge, and I will never abandon this place."

Then out of nowhere, they saw headlights coming up the driveway. Elizabeth had no idea who it was or what to do; anxiety was taking over her very existence. Had her prayer been answered? Had help arrived? Was it just more devastation lurking, waiting for the chance to once again attack? Her heart was pounding hard in her chest as the fear engulfed her. She knew she had to get Linda Kay the help she needed.

Someone started banging hard on the front door. Elizabeth froze, tears running down both her cheeks. She was frightened beyond words. The banging did not stop; she swallowed hard, trying to muster up the courage to ask, "who is it?" But she seemed to be glued to the floor. Her tongue thick and dry, stuck to the roof of her mouth. At last, she heard someone ask who is it, in a voice that she did not recognize, as she realized it was her asking the question. She didn't know if whoever it was could understand her or not, her voice was shaking and very hard to understand.

"Sheriff's office, open this door!" There was more banging on the door, and someone shouted. "Now, open this door now."

Elizabeth was like a zombie as she walked toward the door unaware of what she was really doing, she opened the door without question or thought.

CHAPTER 6

THE SHERIFF TOOK ONE LOOK AT ELIZABETH AND KNEW that she was in a state of shock. He hastily took one step toward Elizabeth, when she started pointing and a high-pitched noise escaped from her throat. The sheriff swiftly turned and saw Linda Kay sitting on the couch with blood pouring from her forehead.

Linda Kay looked up at the sheriff and said, "I'll be fine, Travis; I just need Elizabeth to go get the first-aid kit out of the bathroom. Then she can help me to stop this bleeding. Other than that, I'll be fine."

The sheriff turned to Elizabeth and said, "Would you please go get the first-aid kit and a hand towel for Linda Kay? It would be appreciated." The sheriff thought about going and getting it himself, but he knew he had to get Elizabeth's mind working on something besides the shock she was enduring. Elizabeth stared at the sheriff for a few seconds before she slowly started to move towards the bathroom. It was as if Elizabeth was thinking in slow motion.

Sheriff Travis picked up the phone and called Trinity. Trinity answered the phone very groggy, "What do you want?"

"Trinity, this is Sheriff Travis. I need you to come to Linda Kay's property as soon as possible and do what you can tonight to secure a couple windows that have been knocked out. When daylight gets here, replace those windows. I don't want to leave the place unsecured tonight."

Trinity became more alert.

"I understand she had some problems yesterday. I'll be right over, and I promise you, her place won't be left unattended, and Sheriff, I'm carrying my .45."

"I got your back, come on. Just don't get carried away with that .45. Remember we're in the house."

Sheriff Travis returned the phone to the cradle and patted Linda Kay's hand as he said, "Linda Kay, why don't I take you to the hospital and see about having that sewed up?"

"No, I don't need stitches I just need you to clean the wound and put a butterfly band-aid on it. I will be fine. I don't need a doctor."

Elizabeth sat down next to Linda Kay and started cleaning her cut. She ended up putting three small butterflies on her forehead.

The sheriff asked Linda Kay, "What made you decide to come back here? I always thought you'd stay a city slicker once you moved away. You have made such a great name for yourself. I would think you would want to remain in the spotlight. There's no fancy restaurant here; no place to hold a big book signing. There's no media or fancy parties to be seen at, I don't understand why you would give all that up."

"It's just not in my blood. I need the peace and the quiet. I love the tranquility of the country; I need that to do my best writing. I will have the city to go back to from time to time to do book signings and make appearances, but I'm coming back to the country. This will be my home. The only thing wrong is I haven't found any of the peace and tranquility since I came back. I'm beginning to wonder if it still exists. What's happened to this place? I've never locked the door here before. I expected things to be like they used to be. I want to be able to sit on the veranda and watch the sun go down. I don't want to be afraid to sit on my own porch at night."

"I'm really glad you decided to come back, you have a lot of friends and people that love you here. I have to tell you there has been a lot of a change since you left. Not all of them good, the corruption of drugs has brought disorder and devastation into our little town. I'm doing everything I can to get it cleaned up, but sometimes, it feels like I'm overwhelmed. But I'm not going to give up, this is my hometown, and I love it here. In the end, they're going to find this is one little town they are not going to be able to survive in. You're right, Linda Kay, there's definitely something wrong. I don't know what going on out here but I will figure it out. The sheriff's department will be keeping a watch on your house until we catch whoever did this. The main thing is to keep you safe until we get it figured out. This is not an area where I've had a problem with drugs. I really have my doubts that the problem lies there. You weren't having any problems before you came here, were you?"

"No, I wasn't having any problems at all. I just decided to come home for the peace and quiet, so I could write. I really didn't feel safe in the city, and other than Elizabeth, I didn't have any close friends. There it was all work and show and tell. I was tired of everybody being a fake to me. You know that I have no family left; for the last few years all I had was my grandfather. I just wanted to feel close to my family and to get back to my roots where I really belong. Travis, I'm so tired. I'm feeling a little dizzy and lightheaded. Please just let me lay my head down just for minute. We can talk later."

"I'm sorry, Linda Kay; I need you to stay with me. If you continue feeling dizzy and lightheaded, I have no choice but to take you to the hospital."

"No, I'll be fine, I think it's just my nerves. We have been scared ever since we got here. I'm just tired. We haven't had much rest; we're too busy trying to stay alive."

"I understand what you're saying, but I can't take a chance, if you're dizzy and lightheaded, you're going to have to go to the hospital.

I'm going to give you a couple of aspirin and see how you feel in a few minutes."

The sheriff went to the bathroom retrieved a couple of aspirin and got a glass of water, returned and handed them Linda Kay.

"Now sit back and try to relax. There are a lot of old memories for us to talk about. We also have a lot of things that you need to be caught up on. Do you remember telling me how you want to go float the Buffalo River?"

"Yes, I still hope to get to do that, but it's looking slim now. As soon as Elizabeth's okay, I'm going to send her home. She doesn't need to be here in this mess."

"Well, I hope you do get to go; I think you would enjoy it, but there is something that I would like to tell you. I know you remember George Gilbert, he's volunteering, doing floating tours during the summer. I thought you might really enjoy seeing him again. You know he also became a writer, only where you write fiction, he writes biographies. But the two of you always did have a lot in common."

Just hearing his name made Linda's heart flutter. She had spent a long time trying to forget George. There was always a connection that wouldn't be broken. Linda Kay could still feel the scars on her heart from trying to break that connection. It would be nice to see him again if they could keep it on a friendship basis. Could they do that? Linda Kay didn't know if she could. There was a spot in her heart for him that no one else could ever fill. She knew at some point being in this little town, they would run in to one another. She would have to put on her brave face.

Sheriff Travis interrupted her thoughts as he said, "Trinity's here, I'll get the door."

Trinity came in carrying some panes of glass.

"I'm sure I have some glass here that will fit her windows. It won't take me long, Sheriff, and I'll have them replaced. If I'm stepping out of line here, someone let me know please, but I brought my wife Mary with me, so she could help take care of Linda Kay and Elizabeth. I figure by now the two of them would like to have some restful sleep. Mary and I will see to it that everything is taken care of and all they have to worry about is getting some rest."

"Oh, Trinity, that would be wonderful if you're sure; I don't want to disrupt your family, but we are really tired, and we're scared, and we really do need some rest."

Trinity walked over and gave Linda Kay a hug.

"You know that Mary and I have always cared about you, and we're not going to turn our back on you now; we're here for the long haul. Now, you get some rest, and tomorrow, we're going to get to the bottom of this. No one should have to live this way, and when we find out who is messing with you, that scoundrel will pay. In the meantime, I can promise you this; nobody will bother you on my watch."

Mary and Trinity had only been married a little over a year, but they had both been born and raised in this little town, so they had known each other their whole life. Mary was a very pretty girl. She was a year younger than Linda Kay. She had been raised with a very strong sense of responsibility. She watched over Linda Kay and Elizabeth like a mother hen. She fixed them a breakfast of soft food. She carried it upstairs and watched over them until she saw to it that they ate. Once she got them settled back down, she carried their trays back downstairs and cleaned up the kitchen. She stayed on high alert not only to protect herself, but for the girls she had promised to watch over. She stayed with them and diligently sought to their every need through the night, while Trinity watched over the property making sure that no intruders would bother them.

They were fortunate. The night went by without any further incident. Trinity was sure that whoever had been out there, knew he was watching and they were waiting for him to back off. They would find out Trinity had no intentions of backing off. Mary and Trinity stayed all day the next day watching over the property, making sure that no one caused them a problem. Linda Kay and Elizabeth got their much-needed rest. They had actually slept longer than Mary thought they would. She had checked on them several times, and they were sleeping peacefully. She did not have the heart to wake them up to eat; that would just have to wait. The sheriff had called Trinity and told him he wouldn't be able to search Linda Kay's property today.

"It looks as if the drug gangs got in a tug-of-war, now I've got to go to the east side of the county to try and settle it. Let's try to set it for tomorrow as soon as I can get this other mess wrapped up."

CHAPTER 7

LINDA KAY AND ELIZABETH BOTH HAD SLEPT MOST OF THE DAY. Linda Kay's intent was when they got up to go ahead and take Elizabeth home. The day had gotten away from them, and Linda Kay really didn't want to take Elizabeth home this late in the day. That would leave Linda Kay driving home by herself late at night. With everything that had been going on, she wanted no part of that.

Elizabeth agreed with Linda Kay, so they stayed home and ate a delicious meal that Mary had fixed for them. They spent the rest of the day relaxing and watching movies on TV. Trinity and Mary finally joined Elizabeth and Linda Kay, and they started catching up on old times.

Trinity was telling about the time that George had got an old tube of lipstick of his mother's. He then met up with Trinity in George's grandfather's field. Well, it was a lazy day; they didn't have a lot to do, so they decided to paint his grandfather's mule's lips with that beautiful shade of red lipstick. Will, George's grandfather, was just sure that old mule had got into the Poke berries and was going to die. Well, he tried doctoring that old mule up with all kinds of home remedies. George didn't have the heart or the guts to tell his grandfather that he had painted old Kate's lips with his mother's lipstick. So instead he watched his grandpa worry for days over whether that old mule was going to live or die.

Linda Kay said, "Do you remember the time that George put that big scoop of chicken poop under the front seat of Mr. Martin's car? You'd think he would know better than to mess with the principal's car, but oh no, not George. Man, that principal was mad; the whole school was in trouble for a while. George lucked out on that nobody squealed on him."

Elizabeth laughed as she said, "I've often wondered what kids in the country found to do for fun; I think I just found out."

It was about 2:30 in the afternoon when Trinity asked, "Linda Kay, would you mind if I laid down and slept for a few hours?"

Mary chimed in and said, "I want to get him up by 8:00."

"I'm going to keep a watch on your house another night. The sheriff wasn't able to get over here today to start the search on your property, so this way, you can get another good night's sleep, and I promise you nobody is going to bother you."

"Trinity, I really do appreciate it, but you don't have to do that; we'll be all right here one more night. Then I am going to take Elizabeth home, but I'd rather leave early enough in the day that I can get back before dark."

"Linda Kay, until this person is caught, you will not be left alone on this property again. So, you girls, play cards, watch TV, make a quilt, or just plain gossip—I don't care, enjoy your time while I get a little sleep. I will be up tonight and see to it that you will be safe."

Mary woke Trinity up at 8:00. She had his supper ready and waiting for him. They all sat around and drank coffee and enjoyed each other's company until it was time for Trinity to start his watch on the property. Everybody else called it an early night and headed for bed with high hopes of sweet dreams.

CHAPTER 8

LINDA KAY WOKE UP STRETCHING AND YAWNING. She felt like she had the best sleep that she had in a long time. She rolled over and looked at the clock and realized how early it was. She couldn't contain herself any longer. She took off to Elizabeth's room saying, "Come with me, and come with me quick I want to show you something."

Elizabeth sit straight up in bed; she had a startled look on her face.

"What's wrong, is he back?" She started to shake once again, and tears began to fill her eyes.

"No, no, it's nothing like that. Come on, I've got something to show you. You're going to love it, come on, go with me."

Elizabeth grabbed her robe and put it on as they walked out of her room and back into Linda Kay's room. Linda Kay was having a hard time containing her enthusiasm as she opened the doors to the veranda. They stepped outside, and both were in awe at the beautiful sunrise that was there in front of them.

Words seemed to slip from Elizabeth.

"Wow, Linda Kay, that is the most beautiful sunrise of ever seen, and look at those mountains in the background.

Linda Kay inhaled deeply taking in a breath of the fresh morning air. She had a big smile on her face.

"Yeah it is beautiful, this is what I remember growing up here, these beautiful times."

They stood there in silence for a few minutes, just looking out over the horizon staring out at the sunrise, gathering up all the beauty and storing it to their memory.

All at once, a painful look comes across Elizabeth's face.

"Elizabeth, are you okay is there something wrong?"

"I'm okay, I understand how beautiful it is here, but to tell you the truth, I'm still scared. I don't know what the next minute is going to bring, and the thoughts of that frightens me. Linda Kay, you could have been killed yesterday, do you understand that? Why don't you just say, 'okay, I give up,' and come back home with me? If the sheriff ever figures out what's going on up here and it's safe, we can always come back to visit. Please, please, Linda Kay, come home with me."

Linda Kay inhaled deeply and blew it out slowly.

"In a way I wish I could, in another I don't. Sure, I want to be safe, and I want to be happy. I want to live free. If I run, I'll never be free. My grandfather left this place to me to love and protect it. There's no way I can turn my back on it and let someone destroy all the beautiful memories that are planted here." Linda Kay placed her hands on Elizabeth's shoulders. "Right now, I do have a suggestion, I think we need to eat breakfast and go float the Buffalo. When we get back, I am going to help you pack your things. Then I'm going to take you home with a smile on your face. I will probably spend one night with you, and come back tomorrow. I want you to take with you the memory of this beautiful sunrise and the diamonds you saw dancing in the sky at night and the memory of floating the Buffalo River. As soon as I get things settled down here, I'll call you, and you'll be anxious to come back and visit. There are a lot of good neighbors, good friends, and good times that you haven't experienced yet."

Elizabeth inhaled deeply a breath of frustration.

"I don't know that I can leave you here, it's dangerous, and I worry about you. Please think about it today, and come home with me."

"Let's not worry about it right now. We're going to have a good breakfast, then we're going to float the Buffalo, we can discuss the rest of this later, I don't want anything to spoil our day."

Linda Kay put an arm on Elizabeth's shoulder and guided her to the kitchen. As they walked in the kitchen door, they were met by Mary; she had a big smile on her face as she said, "Good morning, you two are looking awfully spry so early in the morning. Why don't you have a seat, and I'll get started making breakfast?"

Linda Kay said, "Oh no, not this morning. I'm fixing breakfast, and you're going to sit at the table and talk to us while I do it."

Mary looked nervous, "But I'm supposed to be taking care of you, I just couldn't do that."

"You were supposed to take care of me yesterday, and that you did, but this is today, and today, you are my guest, have a seat."

Linda Kay pulled a large bowl out of the cabinet and started making biscuits. She worked diligently, and it wasn't long before she set a beautiful breakfast of scrambled eggs with onions and cheese, jalapeno bacon, chocolate gravy, and biscuits on the table.

"Mary, would you call Trinity in, let's eat while it's hot."

Everyone enjoyed the breakfast and were happy to help clear the table. This time, Mary stepped in and said, "The two of you go get dressed. Do whatever, y'all want to; I'll clean up the kitchen."

By the time Linda Kay and Elizabeth were dressed and ready to go, Trinity met them at the door and told them that the sheriff would be there later today.

"The sheriff wants permission to search your property. He said that there's an old cave on the back of your property, and he wants it checked out."

"I had forgotten about that cave, that's where I used to play house when I was a kid. That's another thing I would love to show you. It's always so cool and comfortable in there. The air only smelled so clean and crisp. The cave was actually huge, but I was only allowed to play in one section. I had big roomy areas to play in. In my mind's eye, I always divided it up into sections, and I didn't just have a big room in there, I had a mansion. I wouldn't mind strolling down memory lane, so when you come back, let's make that one of the first things on the agenda for me to show you." She turned back to Trinity, "I don't have a problem with anything or anywhere he wants to search. I just hope he can catch whoever is tormenting us and trying to get me off my property."

"You don't have to worry; I'll be keeping a watch on the property tonight," Trinity told Linda Kay. "I'm going to come by and check on your house often today. Tonight, I will call you and let you know when I'm going to be on your property. We're going to get to the bottom of this; you're not going to have to put up with this kind of torment much longer, I promise."

"Thank you, Trinity; you and your wife have done so much for me. There's no way that I can say thank you and have you to understand how much it means to me. After the float trip, I'm going to take Elizabeth home. I will probably spend the night with her and come back early in the morning, that way I will not be driving after dark by myself."

"That sounds like a good plan, but you don't have to worry, I'll still be watching your house whether you're here or whether you're gone. Now go float the Buffalo and have a wonderful day. We will talk to you later this evening. We'll make sure everything is locked up before we leave. You don't have a thing to worry about."

At last, Linda Kay and Elizabeth sat in the SUV ready to head for the Buffalo River. Elizabeth was excited and bubbly. She had heard so much about floating the Buffalo, and at last, she was going to get to experience all the wonders of it for herself. She would then be able to put her own spin on what that float trip feels like. She would have so much to tell her friends once she returned home. She looked up at Linda Kay, anxious to exchange her thoughts. Instead she stopped in mid-thought and said, "Maybe you need to tell me what's on your mind."

As Linda Kay sat down in the SUV, that dreaded feeling came over her body once again. It was quick, and it was fleeting this time, but it left her stunned and numb just for minute. She didn't understand it, but the feeling passed quickly. So, she also let it go, determined that this was going to be a beautiful day. She wanted so much to send Elizabeth home with wonderful thoughts of the Ozarks. She also wanted Elizabeth to come back and visit her often. She couldn't stand the thoughts of losing contact with her best friend.

Linda Kay smiled up at her.

"I'm sorry I was just in my own head. Do you remember the guy that I told you about? The one that I dated all through high school and was close friends with all through junior high school and elementary? Well, I found out that he also became a writer who writes biographies. Most of all, I found out during the summer he volunteers as a tour guide doing float trips on the Buffalo. I have to admit, I'm scared that I will run into him today, and by the same token, I'm excited at the thought that I might see him again. I don't know exactly what to think. I'll admit to you, I still love that guy more than anything, and I'm scared that we won't be able to go on as friends. There's just too much water under the bridge, too much hurt and heartache. We broke up with a lot of anger between us; I don't think I could go through that again. I guess the only way to find out is to face it, so let's go."

Linda Kay put the SUV in reverse and backed out of the driveway.

Chapter 9

As Linda Kay pulled into the lot for canoe rentals, her heart began to pound with excitement about the past and what the future was going to bring. They slowly climbed out of the SUV and walked toward the rental. All it once, Linda Kay came to a stop her mouth agape. Elizabeth followed her field of vision and spotted the handsome man that just walked out of the building. He was tall with thick, black curly hair and a beautiful tan. He had a red hue to his skin tone; you could see the Indian heritage flowing from him. He was very well built with high cheekbones and full beautiful lips. Elizabeth knew without being told that was George Gilbert. She turned and took Linda Kay by the hand and began pulling her forward.

"Come on, you'll be all right. By the way, you're right he is gorgeous."

All it once, this deep baritone voice shouted out, "Linda Kay, you look beautiful as ever." He rushed and took hold of her and hugged her close. "It's so great to see you, tell me everything you've been doing." Truthfully, he knew she'd become a writer; he read everything she had ever published. If anything, he loved her more and more as time went by. He wouldn't say that aloud, for he knew that would send Linda Kay running.

Linda Kay tried to slow her heartbeat as she said, "From what I understand, about the same as you, I became a writer, although I'm a fiction writer.

"Wow, that sounds exciting I'm sure your books are very good. I promise I'll be critiquing them all. But right now, I take it you want to go on a float trip, right?"

"Let me introduce you to my dear friend Elizabeth; Elizabeth this is an old friend, George."

George stuck his hand out to Elizabeth and said, "It's nice to meet you."

Elizabeth smiled up at him as she said, "It's nice to meet you, too."

"Yes, we do want to go on a float trip, Elizabeth has never been on a trip, and I think we need a guide." She rubbed the top of her head as she said, "I don't think I want to try it again."

George cracked up laughing; he was bending over holding his side from laughter. Linda Kay couldn't help it; she had to start laughing herself, but poor Elizabeth just stood there and looked at them as if they had lost their minds. Finally, George got a little more solemn and told Elizabeth the story about the time Linda Kay assured him that she could guide the canoe.

"She wanted in the back of the canoe and to be in control. So. I gave in and said okay. She did pretty well for a while. Then we started around a bend in the river, and I held a limb back out of the way so we could get by. I hollered back to Linda Kay 'Duck!' before I let go of the limb. Linda Kay sticks her head up in the air and said, "Where?" Well, I start feeling all this jumping around in the back of the canoe and told her to be still before she tipped us over. Well I look around and find that she was not in the canoe, but under the canoe banging her head on the bottom of it. I bet now if I say duck, your head will go down not up."

Elizabeth laughed.

"Oh that is funny. Linda Kay, you never told me about that, I do hope you weren't hurt, but that's hilarious. I agree with you; we need a guide."

George looked at Linda Kay, his eyes were sparkling and dancing with laughter as he said, "I'm sorry, Linda Kay, but I had to tell it." He chuckled once more before he said, "if y'all will come with me, I'll get you all set up to float the Buffalo."

"Let's go, I think a change of subject is in order."

George looked at Linda Kay as he said, "Stand right here I'll be back in just a minute". He walked behind the counter and started fiddling around with stuff. At last, George returned and said, "Okay here's your tickets everything is all set. Go get on the bus; it will be leaving soon."

Elizabeth wanted to know, "Why are we getting on a bus? I don't understand this, I thought we would be going to the water and getting in a canoe?"

"The bus is going to take us and the canoes down to the water where we can get in."

"Oh, now I feel kind of foolish."

"Well don't, you're a newbie. Next time it'll be old hat to you."

The actual ride from the rental place to the water took approximately 30 minutes because once they turned off the highway, they were on a dirt road with curves and bends that slowed their pace. That was okay because the canoe rental staff kept everyone entertained. They laughed and talked and enjoyed the ride. Elizabeth almost hated to see it come to an end.

Once they got to the river, it didn't take but a minute to unload the canoes off the trailer. Everyone claimed their canoe, put them in the water, and they were ready to go. For the first time, Elizabeth felt free, and excitement was taking over, she was looking so forward to this canoe trip, a whole new adventure for her.

Once again that dreaded feeling creeped through Linda Kay, and once again, she dismissed it quickly. She knew better than to dismiss those feelings, but this float trip was so important to her, she knew that she should shove the feelings back, ignoring them as if they never existed. She would think about that later. Right now, it was going to be a beautiful day, and she wasn't going to let anything interfere with that. In her heart of hearts, she knew better, but this was the one day she did not want to give up.

Linda Kay hollered out, "George, who's our guide for the day? Where is he?"

"I'll be right there," he finished up the conversation he was having with the bus driver before going to Linda Kay as he bowed and said, "George Gilbert, at your service, ma'am."

"You're going to be our guide?"

"Yes, that was the intent after all, this is what I do. Is that not satisfactory with you?"

Linda Kay's face flashed red just for a second before she placed a smile on her face.

"Yes, of course, that will be just fine. I was unaware that you were to be our guide, it will be like old times. I'm sure we will have a lot of fun."

Linda Kay was thinking, *I don't know if I can handle spending the day with him. There are so many memories most of them beautiful and good about a time that I would love to have back' but I know in my heart of hearts that it can never be. I just hope that we can be friends; I have to give it all I can and try not to hurt for the past.* She looked up at George and thought, *Oh Lord; he still makes my heart flutter with desire. Please help me to get through this day.* She tried to put on a mask of indifference and hoped that she could convince everyone that it was the truth.

Elizabeth thought the trip was absolutely wonderful. She looked over at Linda Kay.

"I think I get it, this trip it is amazing. You go through places that the cliffs and bluffs are beautiful then you go through places that everything is so peaceful and tranquil so enjoyable that it's unreal. Then you round the bend and everything is chaotic, and you have to fight to keep control of the canoe. Your adrenaline runs high, and you turn and you go back to tranquility. It makes you realize how quick life's journey changes."

George warned them that they were coming to the rapids.

"This could be rough; you never know how bad or how gentle the rapids are going to be. Check your life vest; make sure it's secure and fastened properly. Hang on securely until after we get through the rapids. Try to sit upright and stay in the center of the canoe. Otherwise we can get off balance and be tipped over.

"Wow, now you're starting to scare me."

"I'm not trying to scare you, Elizabeth, I actually think it's the most fun of the whole trip. I just want you to understand these rapids could be bad and the rules that it takes to get through them without losing our canoe."

"I will do my best to do exactly like you ask, even if my heart is about to pound out of my chest. But you and Linda Kay have survived it numerous times from the past, so I guess I'll make it once in the future."

George shouted, "Here it is! Hang on."

The canoe started to buck; twist and turn Elizabeth fought hard trying to do exactly like George had said. She had never been on such a ride in her life. While the canoe continued to twist and buck, water was flying over the sides of the canoe. Elizabeth began to panic, her heart pounding she began to cry, but no one could hear over the surging water. Everyone was so drenched, you couldn't tell if tears were falling or not. Every minute seemed to drag on and on; every minute seemed to be hours. Elizabeth was saying a silent prayer asking God to please help them to get out of the mess they had gotten themselves into. She tried hard to do exactly as George had told her, but she found it very difficult. She couldn't help herself. It was as if her reflexes were taking over wanting to protect herself. She began floundering around and tried to pull herself into the floor of the canoe as if she could hide from this wild and crazy ride. If she could only do that, she would be okay.

All at once, they were no longer in the canoe; they had been dumped into the river. Elizabeth was gulping and swallowing the river water while thrashing trying to get to the bank. George got a hold of Elizabeth and managed to get her to the bank. When he turned, he saw that Linda Kay was in distress, she was trapped in the heavy part of the rapids, and he had to try and get to her. No matter what he had to do, he had to save Linda Kay she had always been the love of his life, and that had not changed to this day. This was his only chance to try to make things right once again. He couldn't screw it up now; he had to get to Linda Kay.

The water pushed and turned, toppling George as he struggled to get to her. The water was actually pushing George to Linda Kay. George also knew that she was in the thick of the rapids, and once he got to her, he didn't see a way out, he just knew he had to get to her. Linda Kay was fighting to at least maintain her position, trying desperately to get out of the rapids and get to the bank, but the fight seemed to be futile. Her strength was running out; she knew she was not going to be able to hang on much longer. As George got closer, he was able to grab her blouse and hang on. The violence of the rapids was preventing George from getting a better hold on Linda Kay. Linda Kay and George both were taking in water, causing them to choke with each breath they tried to take.

Things were looking hopeless when all at once George spotted a log that was about to slam into him. George reached out and grabbed the log and pulled it close to him, he hugged it tight with one arm. At the same time, he had his hand twisted in Linda Kay's blouse refusing to let go. George tried hard to calm himself so he could work with the rapids and not against them. George worked and tugged on Linda Kay's blouse, working with the flow of the rapids in order to move Linda Kay closer to him. At last, he got Linda Kay to where he could wrap his arm around her waist. He lifted her enough that her shoulders and arms were draped over the log. He wrapped himself around her, holding her tight against the log. Linda Kay was just lying there lifeless, loose, and limp. George knew that if he let go of her he would lose her once again to the rapids. George used his head and began patting her on the back with his head bouncing up and down in a rhythmic pattern. At last he heard Linda Kay cough and sputter as she spit up water. He laid his head against her back and gave thanks to God.

She's okay, for the moment. He prayed that God would see them safely out of the mess that they had gotten themselves in, and, *Thank you God for the many blessings that you have given me in my life amen.*

George and Linda Kay both held on tight to the log and let it carry on whichever way it wanted to go with hopes that they would soon drift out of the rapids. Time seemed to go slowly as they bounced up and down and back and forth.

At last, the roughness of the ride began to slow. Even though the water was still rough and hit them with a vengeance, it began to slow. For the first time in quite a while George had hopes that they might make it out of this mess alive. He hugged Linda Kay tighter against the log promising that he would never let go of her until he got her to safety. He realized just how much he loved her, and the thought of losing her forever was more than he could stand.

CHAPTER 10

AT LAST THEY WERE IN SLOW WATERS DRIFTING ALONG. George started looking for some land that maybe they could get to. George and Elizabeth both were exhausted and needed to rest. They couldn't go on like this much longer. George thought he knew every inch of the water in this area. He had been floating this Buffalo River since he was a small child. But he had no idea of where he was. It was as if they had been washed into completely different waters. Right now, George was just too tired. He laid his head against the log, shut his eyes just for a moment, but when he opened his eyes again, it was almost dark.

There was land right there in front of them, the water was shallow enough that he could walk to shore. He shook Linda Kay, waking her up.

"Come on; go with me, we need to try to get to safety before dark. I need to find some place where we can rest for the night."

Linda Kay was weak and unsteady on her feet. George put his arm around her and helped her to the bank. He set her down, leaning her back against the tree, telling her, "I'll be right back. Just rest I'm not going far."

George was afraid to wander too far from Linda Kay. He knew

nothing about where they had landed. It was too late to try to search the area; night would be on them soon. His goal was to get them some shelter for the night. George started dragging branches and limbs pilling them up. In his search for more branches, he stumbled across a gully that looks like it was a natural drainage for runoff when it rained. He began shoving dried leaves on to the floor of the gully. It was plenty deep enough that they could sit or lie down without being too cramped. He then took the branches and piled them over the top of the gully where they could be sheltered for the night. He worked diligently and as fast as he could to complete the shelter before dark.

George hurried back to get Linda Kay, taking her to the shelter for the night. George helped Linda Kay down into the gully. Following her, he pulled the last of the branches over the opening of the gully. George could hear Linda Kay trying to stifle a cry.

"Linda Kay, are you okay? Is there something I can do?"

"No, I'm concerned about Elizabeth, where is she? What could've happened to her? Did she make it to safety?

"Elizabeth will be fine; I got her to the bank. Someone will come by and pick her up. I promise you, she was safe when I left her. You know as well as I do the next canoe by will pick her up and get her to safety. I just wish we were there with her.

"Linda Kay, I've got to be honest with you, I have no idea where we are. I thought I knew these waters as well as anyone. But apparently, I don't know as much as I thought I did.

All I can do is promise you as soon as it gets daylight, we will start looking for a way off this island. In the meantime, we're on dry land, and I will take care of you until we get home."

"Thank goodness for that, you've done everything you can do, and I do appreciate it George, thank you. I don't want you to think I'm complaining; I'm not. You've done everything for me you could. If it hadn't been for you, I would've drowned in that water. I didn't stand a chance by myself. My problem is, I'm scared of this island. I don't like it here. I don't like the feel of this place. It feels all wrong, as if danger is hovering all around us. I don't know how to explain that to you, I just know it's not right. I feel like we're in danger. I don't know... Maybe I'm just tired, and I'm scared. I hope that's what it is anyway. George, do you think we stand a chance of making it to a different island?"

"Now, no way. It's too dark and our log floated away while we were trying to make it to shore. I'm sorry Linda Kay, but this is the island we're stuck with for now.

George scooted down next to Linda Kay and put his arm around her.

"You're going to be okay, Linda Kay, I'm here, and I'll watch over you tonight. Now lie down and try to get some sleep; as soon as it's daylight, I'll search the island, and we'll find a way out of here. I really don't want you to worry, you just get some rest. Leave the worrying to me, I'll find us the way home."

Linda Kay and George scooted around to where they could lay down, and he was able to hold her close while they slept. Linda Kay slept fretful through the night. Once she woke and could feel George lying there beside her, she would take comfort once again and rest. Nightmares were trying to creep in around the corner of her dreams. When she started to fret, George would pull her closer, scaring the nightmare away.

George took short naps through the night. When he slept, he kept one ear open, listening to every sound from the outside. His main goal was to protect Linda Kay; he had to see to it that she got home safely and unharmed. He knew that they would no longer be together, but it never changed the way he felt about her. He could only admit to himself how much he loved her and the most he could hope for was that she would let them be friends, even if it was just casual friends. There was no way that he would ever push her or try to persuade her to come back to him. She had been hurt, and he didn't know if she could ever forget or forgive. He had tried to explain it to her but she wouldn't listen. So this time, if they ever got back together, it would have to be on her terms, not his. He was just thankful for the time he got to hold her that night.

CHAPTER 11

ELIZABETH HAD NO CHOICE BUT TO STAND ON THE SHORE watching her friend as she struggled and fought for survival. She prayed that George would be able to catch up with her and keep her from drowning. Elizabeth's heart was beating fast; panic and fear was taking over her entire being. She was alone on a bank of the Buffalo River and helpless. All she could do was to pray. She didn't know what would happen to her if she lost her Linda Kay. They had become so close over the last few years, sharing everything. Elizabeth just didn't know how she could survive without her. At the same time, watching Linda Kay struggle with everything she had, she was afraid her friend was about to die. She felt totally helpless and undone. Panic was beginning to take over; she was hollering and screaming for help, begging for someone, anyone. Yet she knew in her heart there was nothing she could do but watch. The sight of her friends struggling kept popping before her eyes. It played over and over in her head, each time leaving Elizabeth with the loneliness knowing there was nothing she could do but stand there and watch.

She cried until she was completely spent. The last thing Elizabeth saw was Linda Kay and George being swept around the curve of that big mountain out of her sight. Linda Kay was still fighting for survival, and George desperately trying to get to her. Now she stood there on the banks of the river, scared and nervous in a state of shock. She didn't know what to do. She was left alone with nowhere to go for help. Worst of all was the fact that she didn't know if George or Linda Kay were dead or alive. Her heart ached, and her head was pounding as she prayed, *Lord please send me help.*

Elizabeth had no idea how long she had been standing on those banks alone and frightened. It seemed to her that it had been a lifetime and the walls of her life were crumbling down.

When she spotted another canoe coming in her direction, she started hollering and crying out for help. She waved her arms frantically in the air. The couple in the canoe gladly pulled to the bank, questioning, "What's wrong, ma'am, do you need some assistance? How did you get left on this bank, and where is your canoe?"

Elizabeth was crying again, making it difficult for them to understand, but at last between sobs, she managed to tell them what had happened. They told her to get in the canoe, and they would take her in. She really started to cry then.

"I'm scared to get in the canoe. I never want to get in another canoe. How else can I get back?"

"I'm so sorry, ma'am, the best way out of here is in this canoe. The only other way out of here is walking through the woods for miles and miles. If you don't know your way, you could be lost for days. I honestly don't think you are from around here, ma'am. Your chances would not be good of coming out of those woods. You would have to have plenty of food and water to survive, and ma'am, you don't have either."

The couple was very compassionate with Elizabeth; they spent the time that it took to convince her to get in the canoe and let them help her to safety.

The man that was guiding the canoe said his name was Charles; the woman's name Latisha. Latisha promised Elizabeth that she would hold onto her, and they would get safely back. Elizabeth didn't want to do it but felt it was her only choice, and she needed to try to get help for Linda Kay and George. She reluctantly climbed into the canoe and took up her position.

It wasn't long before Charlie hollered, "Okay, we're going to start into the rapids now. Stay calm, stay in the center of the canoe and stay upright. We're going to be okay. The rapids must have somewhat calmed down. We will see you safely back to the canoe rental."

Elizabeth didn't realize that she had been holding her breath until they reached calm water, and the air began to escape from her lungs. Some of the tension began to go out of her body until once again the realization that she had lost Linda Kay hit her hard. Again, she began to sob uncontrollably. Latisha told Elizabeth to stay calm; as soon as they got back to the canoe rental, they would organize a search party.

"All the locals around here know Linda Kay and George. They will all be out searching for them," Latisha said.

With that Elizabeth felt excited at the thoughts of getting a search party together. Maybe, just maybe Linda Kay and George were okay, and someone would find them standing on the bank like she had been. Finally, they reached the canoe rental, and a search party was immediately put together. People from all around began showing up with their canoes to go in search for Linda Kay and George.

Someone had called in Sheriff Travis, and before Elizabeth knew what was going on Sheriff Travis was there, and she was going over and over what had happened. To the best of her knowledge, she told him everything. Her lips trembled as she told him how she had lost sight of Linda Kay and George as they rounded the cliffs, and she could no longer see her dear friend. In the end, Charlie was the one able to give them a better location of where to start their search.

Elizabeth was so distraught and at times uncontrollable. Sheriff Travis once again relied on his old and close friend Trinity. He sighed as he took out his cell phone and gave him a call

"Hey, buddy, I won't be coming back out there to search the property tonight. We now have worse problems."

"There are still no problems on Linda Kay's property; I'm still here keeping a watch. Take your time, and do what you need to, and then we'll get this problem solved."

"We have a real problem at the canoe rental." He then relayed everything that had happened to Trinity and asked, "Is there any way that you and Mary could come in and pick up Elizabeth and Linda Kay's vehicle and take them back to Linda Kay's? I hate to ask, but if you can't get Elizabeth in to see a doctor, would you please take her to the hospital. She's totally hysterical; she's going to have to have something to calm her down. With the state of mind that she is in, she's going to need someone with her. I hate to ask, but I don't know where else to turn. This poor woman has got to have help."

"You know we'll be there as soon as we can we're on our way."

"Thank you so much, Trinity, I really appreciate you."

The sheriff then had one of the deputies to keep an eye on Elizabeth until Trinity could get there. The sheriff headed out in the canoe in search of Linda Kay and George.

CHAPTER 12

AS SOON AS DAYLIGHT STARTED BREAKING THROUGH George began to stir around. He was anxious to explore the area to try to find better accommodations. Most of all, he was in the hopes of finding a way home. He had never seen Linda Kay so distraught. Where they had landed seemed to be frightening her; he hoped that today he could at least take away that frustration and help her to relax until he could get her safely home.

George looked down at Linda Kay and brushed the hair out of her eyes and was thinking just how beautiful she looked lying there. He wanted so bad to kiss her to hold her in his arms and never let her go again. He shook that thought off as she started to rouse. He lightly called her name.

"Are you ready to get up? We need to go exploring and see if we can figure out where we are. Maybe we can find a way out of here so we can get home."

At the mention of home, Linda Kay sat up; she had a tear in her eye as she looked at George.

"I really want to go home. I don't know if this is an island or dry land. I believe it's an island. I just feel that there's something destructive here, it frightens me. I don't know how to explain it any better than that."

George had no idea what she was talking about, but he wasn't going to laugh at her although he really thought what she was saying was pretty funny. Where was she getting these wild ideas, he really didn't know, really didn't understand what she was talking about, but he wasn't going to push the issue. George took a deep breath, trying to compose himself because he wanted to talk to her in a calm and pleasant manner.

"I've never seen you like this. What makes you so nervous about this place? Please try to help me, I really do want to try and make you as comfortable as possible while we're here."

Linda Kay looked up at George her eyes were damp with tears, and it melted his heart as she said, "I know I'm a bit distraught, I don't really know how to explain it. I just feel like there's some kind of entity on this island that's from the dark side. We need to run from here as fast and as far as we can."

"I don't know anything about that, but I'm sure we will be okay. I will be right here with you. You don't have to worry; let me do that for you. Now come on let's go see if we can find a way home. I don't think anything would make either one of us any happier than to get home."

"You're right; I guess I'm just being silly. I just got so scared yesterday; maybe that just stayed with me. I don't know, I just want to feel safe once again, and I haven't felt safe since I come back to this town."

"Yeah, I've heard that someone has been sneaking around your house, frightening you. But from the cut on your forehead, I would say you have plenty of reason to be frightened. When we get home, I promise you, I'll find out who it is, and they won't ever bother you again." He smiled down at her. "For now, let me help you out of this trench. I want to find something to eat and a way home. What do you say? let's work hard and get home."

There was that beautiful smile again; they needed to get home quick. She didn't think she had the defenses to fight that beautiful smile; it always could take her breath away. She had always wished that she could capture it and keep it with her at all times. Now it was just too close for comfort.

They walked side-by-side close to the water's edge for a long time.

At last, George said, "Well, I guess I have to agree with you. I also think we're on an island. I think we're going to have to start walking through the center of the island in order to search for some shelter for tonight and some food. I'm hungry. Keep an eye out for some berries or something that we might be able to eat."

They continued walking, searching the island looking for food or shelter. The woods were thick; the brush was overgrown. In places, they disturbed mosquitoes that seemed to be almost as big as horse flies. Okay—maybe I'm exaggerating a bit, but they were big, and they stung like the devil when they bite.

At last, Linda Kay said, "No more, I'm exhausted. I've got to take a break. I just can't walk any farther."

"There's a clearing right up there; maybe we can get away from some of these mosquitoes and find a place to sit down and take a break. Can you make it that much further?"

"Yes, I'll make it. George, why don't we just go back to sleep in the same place that we slept last night? I am just too tired go on. We've accomplished absolutely nothing today, and we have walked for hours. There's nothing here. We need to find another big log and just float to a different island. I want away from here."

George inhaled deeply trying to push away his frustration; he couldn't blame that on Linda Kay. After all, he was tired, and he was hungry, and he was getting very frustrated with the fact that he had found absolutely no way to get off this stupid island. As he let out his breath, he tried in a very positive manner to explain to Linda Kay that where they had slept the night before had been a natural drainage ditch. If it were to start to rain during the night, they could be washed right back out into the river.

"Besides, Linda Kay we haven't found anything to eat, we're going to have to find something soon. You know after a while it gets past just being hungry and then slowly but surely our bodies will start to slow down. We have to find a source of food. No, I think we better go a little farther. We've got to give it a couple more hours. We need a safer place to sleep. We will have to turn around and go back before too much longer because it will to be getting dark by the time we get back. I hope to have better shelter for the night. I'm afraid if it starts to rain in the middle of the night, we will have to get out of that trench. Then we would have no place to go for protection. It's not good enough, Linda Kay; we've got to find better.

George looked around as they took their seats in the clearing.

"Doesn't this look odd to you?"

"What do you mean?"

"It just looks like this clearing had a purpose; it was used for some particular reason at one time."

"I see what you mean; it is odd to have this clearing pop-up out of nowhere. But I don't know what it could've been; maybe at one time someone's house was here. I can only tell you there's nothing here now."

George put both of his hands on the ground and leaned back bracing himself with his arms. All it once he hollered and jerked back, up looking at his hand as blood began to drip from his palm.

Linda Kay started hollering.

"What happened? Did you get bit? Was it a snake?"

"No, it wasn't anything like that; something stabbed in my hand." George picked up a stick and started digging the ground around where he had placed his hand. As he dug, he began to see glass appear through the sand and dirt. He kept digging until he got the glass lose; it was a large piece of glass that looked like it had been a jug at one time.

"Oh, Linda Kay, this is wonderful." George kept digging with hopes of finding more. To him, this could be a gold mine. He found another piece of glass and stacked it on the large piece. He had a big smile on his face when he looked up at Linda Kay.

Linda Kay just didn't get it,

"Of course, that's wonderful; your hand is bleeding, and you've got a piece of broken glass. Oh yeah, that sounds real wonderful to me." Linda Kay didn't mean to sound as sarcastic as she did when she said, "Just what's so wonderful about a piece of glass?"

"This is going to be perfect to help me start a fire. We need a fire, and I had absolutely nothing to start one with and now I do. One thing, someone might see it, and it could bring help. Another thing, it could scare a predator off. We don't exactly have anything to protect ourselves with, that's why I'm so happy for this piece of glass."

"Okay, that makes sense. I'm sorry George. I guess my nerves are a little short, but you sure did not deserve my attitude. I don't know how you're going to do it, but I'm happy that you know what you're doing. I'm sorry, I'm so grumpy I'm tired and I'm hungry. I definitely trust you, and I hope you accept my apology"

"Of course, I forgive you. I understand; my nerves are a little on edge, too." George began looking around once more, and he said, "That's it, this used to be a dumpsite at one time someone lived around here. Come on, let's keep looking."

Linda Kay jumped up with a spring in her step and high hopes in her voice.

"Do you think someone may still be living around here? Maybe we could find some food. To tell the truth, my stomach is beginning to rumble." She didn't want to admit how hungry she really was.

"No, I don't want to disappoint you but this dumpsite hasn't been used for a long time. I don't think anyone is still around here. This dump has been covered up too long. It hasn't been used in years. But I still want to look around, we might find something useful."

They hadn't walked too much farther before they took a turn around some trees, and right in front of them stood an old homestead. It looked to be not much more than a shack, but it was something. It had seen better days, many years back. George wasn't sure how sturdy the structure was. He wanted to check it out and make sure it was structurally sound before Linda Kay went inside.

"I don't know if we'll be able to take shelter there tonight are not. I'll check it out and see if it looks to be safe. Linda Kay, I want you to stay right here and wait for me while I go check it out."

"I don't like it here; it feels bad. I'm afraid for you to go in that building. Can't we just leave?"

"You know I can't just leave it; Linda Kay, I know you don't like it here. I don't like it here either; I don't want to be here. I want to go home. I'm doing the very best I can to help us get through until we find a way off of this island. Would you please try to take control of your temper? I think we can do with a little less whining. There might be something there that will help us to survive. We've got to find some food soon. I don't know what's inside that building, maybe nothing, but I'm going to find out. Now wait for me here where you will be safe."

George had never spoken to Linda Kay in that manner. She was dumbfounded; she also knew he was right. She didn't act that way. What in the world is wrong with her? She wrapped her arms around her waist. Her nerves began to shake; she was on edge , and she didn't know how much more of this she could take. She didn't know how to put into words how this place frightened her. She just knew the worst thing she could have ever done was to ignore that voice that sent her a message of danger. It was too late now, but she swore if there was a future for her, she would never ignore that voice again. She knew the minute they landed on this island that this was the place she had been warned about in her dream. There was a negative presence on this island that sent a shiver down her spine. She could feel the evil that surrounded the area, begging to let loose with destruction and havoc. The closer they got to the house, the stronger the negative feeling became. Linda Kay felt that she was close to where a negative energy started. She just wanted to run and try to find a place safely away from here. Tears were beginning to drip down her cheek as she heard George shout calling her name in excitement.

"Linda Kay, Linda Kay, come here quickly, see what I found. Come on its wonderful"

Linda Kay was hesitant, but after a moment, she mustered the courage to follow the sound of his voice. She met him coming around the back of the house.

"Oh Linda Kay come look what I found."

A little way out in the backyard was a small garden. George didn't know how long it'd been there. Just everything that had seeded out seemed to be coming back up. He was so excited there was food; not everything you would want but there's food, but there was something to eat. He met Linda Kay handing her a bright red tomato.

"It is wonderful, Linda Kay, it is so wonderful, the garden seeded out; we've got some food back there. Tomatoes are all I found that we can immediately eat. There are some greens back there; I just don't think they'd be very good without being cooked. I don't know, we may end up eating them raw, but at least we won't starve. Come on let's eat another tomato and then I want to try to start a fire."

George is full of excitement with his find. It's as if he feels like everything will be all right now that we had food. Why can I not get him to understand that the most important thing is getting off this island and away from the evil that lurks here? I know that my face shows disappointment, but it's not in the fact that he's found food. I'm happy for that; we need the nourishment. I just didn't want to spend another minute in this evil place. I don't know how to get George to understand. I know that he will never deliberately lead us into harm's way.

CHAPTER 13

ELIZABETH WAS BESIDE HERSELF; this was the second day, and still no word from Linda Kay or George. She had a sleepless night even though she had been taking the medicine that the doctor had prescribed. The medication seemed to calm her down to a point. Her mind was still in a state of turmoil. She feared the worst but hoped for the best. Still, it left her tossing and turning. She prayed that maybe, just maybe, they had made it to safety somewhere on dry land and were waiting for someone to rescue them.

Elizabeth had been pacing back and forth across the living room floor. She appreciated what Trinity and Mary were doing for her. She didn't feel as vulnerable having the two of them with her. There was no way she could put into words how she felt protected and safe with their presence in the house. She mourned for Linda Kay; there was no way that she could explain that there was nothing that anyone could do to make up for Linda Kay's absence.

Elizabeth was very confused about what she should do. She shook her head as if that would clear away the cobwebs of her thinking. She couldn't seem to make a final decision on what to do. Most of all, she was afraid that Trinity and Mary would be going home. What would she do then? She was terrified of being at Linda Kay's alone. What if someone was waiting for the opportunity to get at Linda Kay and Elizabeth again? After all she had no idea who was waiting outside the house or what their intentions were. All she had was a taser; she had no idea if she would be able to protect herself, and she wasn't sure that she could stay here alone. The thought of that was more than she could deal with. Mary and Trinity were both very nice but they didn't really know her, they sure didn't owe her anything. She wouldn't blame them if they went home.

She didn't want to go home without knowing what happened to Linda Kay. She just couldn't run off and leave her friend behind. How could anyone just turn their back and walk away from their best friend? She loved her dearly; there was no way could she do that. By the same token, if she didn't go home, she was going to lose her job. She couldn't exist without her paycheck, she worked hard for her money, but her savings account was small. A few thousand dollars wasn't going to last all that long if she wasn't working. Once that was spent, what would she do then? No way could she go without a job. Standing there pacing back and forth and crying wasn't going to help. It would not bring Linda Kay back, and it would not support her; she had to come up with some kind of answer quickly.

She was so thankful that Trinity had gotten up every couple of hours in order to keep a watch on Linda Kay's property. Mary told her this morning that she had to go home for a while; there were things there that she had to take care of and should be back by early evening. What if they decided not to come back? What would she do? She had no one else to turn to; she was the stranger in this town.

Elizabeth froze in mid stride of her pacing, as she heard a knock at the door. Her heart began to pound in her chest until at last she heard the Sheriff's voice saying, "Sheriff's office. Open the door, Elizabeth. You're fine."

Elizabeth breathed a sigh of relief at the sound of the familiar voice. She wiped the tears out of her eyes before heading for the door. She was so happy to have some kind of company; she needed companionship right now. When she opened the door, she not only found the Sheriff, but also Trinity and Mary were with him.

"Come on in I'm happy you're here, have a seat and I'll put on some coffee."

As Elizabeth walked to the kitchen her heart was beating double time. She was so afraid that Trinity and Mary would be telling her that they would be going home tonight. Elizabeth was trying hard to conceal how nervous she was as she went back to the living room carrying a tray of coffee and cake.

Sheriff Travis looked up at Elizabeth with a slight smile on his face as he said, "I hope you don't mind, I'm going to jump right in to the reason why we're here.

"Did you find Linda Kay and George? Where are they? Are they okay? Take me to them, please, take me to them."

"I'm sorry Elizabeth that's not why we're here. There is still no news on the whereabouts of Linda Kay or George."

Elizabeth could no longer control her tears; it was as if a dam busted. The tears flowed freely. Mary went to her and consoled her trying to get her to calm down. At last the tears subsided, and she was able to regain control of herself once again. She apologized for falling apart.

"I really am trying to hold it together."

The Sheriff told her she was perfectly all right, and everyone understood why she was so terribly upset. The Sheriff proceeded in a much softer and kinder voice trying to reassure Elizabeth that everything would be all right.

"We know that you have to be going through a big dilemma at this time. We come up with, hopefully a solution to help you get through for a while. We know that you're on vacation, and it's almost time for you to go back to work. At the same time, it would be very difficult to leave here not knowing what happened to Linda Kay. We know you have to be feeling as if your life has been turned inside out. Well, it just so happens that there's a job opening at the post office here in town. The job is 40 hours a week with benefits. I know it's not the kind of work that you're used to doing. It is good pay, and it could help you to survive while you're in a state of confusion. It will give you the time you need to come up with a better decision on what you want to do.

"Danny Matthews is the supervisor's name, and he said that if you were interested, come in this afternoon, and he could discuss it with you. Mary has offered to take you to the post office in order to show you where it is. She will also introduce you to Danny. That way you won't feel like you were just dropped off and left on your own; there is someone there in your corner. We know that this is not what you're used to, but you are Linda Kay's friend, and Linda Kay is a part of this community. If something happens to one of us, it happens to all us. So therefore, we're inviting you into the fold, if you would like to join us."

"Oh my goodness, a job would be very helpful at this point. I have a little savings, but it's not going to take me very far. You are right I can't go off and leave Linda Kay out there. I just can't, and yes, I will lose my job. I hate that because I loved my job, but I love Linda Kay more. The problem is, I don't know the first thing about the post office. I have absolutely no training. I am a fast learner, and I would do the best job possible if I was given the opportunity. But Sheriff Travis, I'm scared here. You know what happened to Linda Kay. I don't know who's lurking in the dark. A good job is not going to solve that problem. What good is a job if I'm dead?"

"Stay calm. That has also been discussed. I think we have come up with a good plan. You're not going to be left alone anymore until this mess is resolved. Trinity and Mary will be staying here with you until we catch the culprit that's been bothering you."

"Having someone here with me sounds wonderful, I'm scared to death being left alone. I don't know who's trying to cause damage to Linda Kay or why; I just know that someone is trying to run us off. I would love to have their help, but I will be happy to pay them. I understand they have their own lives to live, they shouldn't have to try to baby sit me."

"Trinity and I have already discussed it, and this is what we want to do. So, let's not talk about that anymore. I'm sure if the circumstances were reversed, you would help me."

"We've also taken a close look at the blueprints of Linda Kay's property, and we found that on the backside, there's a cave. Linda Kay gave us verbal permission to search this property before you went on the float trip. I had plans to already have that property checked out, but once the float trip went awry all the plans had to be changed. Now I'm ready to get started once again, and this time, we will find out who was harassing you. We don't know that we'll find anything there, but we do feel like if there's something to find, that's where we will find it. What I would like is to also have your permission to check that cave out while you and Mary are gone to the post office. Hopefully by tonight we'll have some positive answers, and if nothing else will be able to give you partial peace of mind. As for as Linda Kay, all I can tell you is that there are still search parties going out, and we haven't given up hope. Elizabeth, in order for you to fit in around here, you have to understand everything's not about what you can pay; a lot of it is about paying it forward. We take care of our own. We understand you're not really one of us, but you're Linda Kay's friend, and Linda Kay is one of us, so what we do for you, we're doing for Linda Kay. Now, do you want to try for the job and give us permission to search this property while you're gone?"

"Of course, it's okay with me; you don't need my permission. Linda Kay had already said y'all could search anywhere you wanted to, and its sure fine with me. As for as the job, I don't know how to say thank you enough. I really do appreciate everything that you are doing to help me get through this nightmare. The main thing, I want is lots and lots of prayers for Linda Kay. Other than that, I appreciate any and every thing you do to help, thank you, and someday I'll be able to pay it forward."

Chapter 14

George picked up the glass and carried it around to the front yard where the sun was shining the brightest through the trees. He placed the glass in the sunniest part of the yard and started gathering small twigs and dried grass and placing them on top of the large piece of glass. Then he picked up the small piece of glass and placed it so that the sun reflected off the glass and back onto the twigs and dried grass.

"Okay Linda Kay, keep an eye on this. When it starts to smoke call me. I'm going to check out the house now and see what else I can find."

The longer Linda Kay stood there the more her nerves began to tighten into a ball. She had been excited about the finding of the food. She was also excited at the thought of getting a fire built. She wasn't sure about staying in the homestead. She just did not like the feel of that place, although if they could stay in that old cabin, they could at least have a roof over their head. She was confused herself; how could she possibly explain something to George that she couldn't explain to herself?

There were so many things to be positive about, but yet she stood there with her arms once again wrapped around her waist trying to stop some of her shaking. She wanted to hide her feelings that this place was evil, but that did her no good. She wanted to scream, "I don't like it here!"

How can I explain that to George? I don't know how to get him to understand. I know there's negative energy here… She began to pray, asking God to help her to clear the energy around there, to give her strength and guidance.

There was a smell that began to waft under her nose. Bringing her attention back to the here and now, she looked around and saw that the kindling was starting to smolder. She started hollering for George to come; "We have a fire trying to start up!"

George came running out of the old homestead. He was so excited, he was grinning from ear to ear.

As soon as George reached Linda Kay, he bent and gave her a kiss on the cheek then knelt and immediately started taking care of the fire.

"Linda Kay, I don't know why the people left here, but they must have left in a hurry; it looks like they left everything. Of course, most of it is so old that it's no longer any good. We can use some of the pieces and parts to remake what we need while we're here. It's going to help us with all kinds of opportunities to try and find our way off this island and back to the mainland. It gives me hope. In the meantime, we have protection from the weather. We're going to be fine.

"Do you really think they left here in a hurry?"

"Why else would they have left the house like it is? It doesn't look like they took anything with them."

"George, would you please, try to understand what I'm telling you, there's something evil here, and I'm scared! We have to find a way off this island. The evil lurks all around us; I'm sure that's why the people left in such a hurry. No one goes off and leaves all their belongings behind for no reason. Think about it, George.

"Okay, Linda Kay, I understand what you're saying, but right now I have to be logical. We need a place to sleep for the night. Let's get this place cleaned up enough that we can stay here. It's too late in the day to find a way off the island; we have to give it up for now. First thing in the morning, we'll begin our search again. I promise you, all day tomorrow we will devote to trying everything we can to find a way home. I want to go home just as bad as you do. Right now, I don't think we could find a better place to stay. At least here we know we have food and shelter for the night. We'll gather food and take with us tomorrow. That will free up our time to do nothing else but finding a way home. Maybe somebody will see the smoke from our fire. Just imagine, someone could show up tonight. I have to stay positive, Linda Kay; maybe someone will show up to rescue us. But whatever the case may be, I promise you, we will search hard tomorrow for a way off this island."

"You're right; I understand what you're saying. Surely we can make it through one night here. I'll do whatever I need to do to help us get through this night."

"Thank you, Linda Kay, for being patient with me. I really am trying to do the best by us that I can. The situation that we're in is a difficult one."

George got a nice size fire built out in the front yard. He then took Linda Kay by the arm and said, "Come on let's go take care of what we need to before nightfall. I'll be right there with you the whole time. I will be there to protect you. Everything will be fine I promise."

Linda Kay was surprised as they walked inside the homestead. If it hadn't been for the dust and dirt and spider webs, she would have sworn someone still lived there. Everything that a family would need was there. What astonished her even more, there were two sleeping areas. One was at the front and the other at the back of the homestead. From the outside of the house, it looked to be a one room shack. Nevertheless, there was one at the front of the homestead, which seemed to be for no more than two people. The one at the back of the house was a larger room and had four small beds lined up against the back wall. She figured this must've been a room for kids. The kitchen was at the front of the house on one side of the room. There was a sitting area on the other side of the room with a large fireplace. That was all the house consisted of, the bathroom was outside in a little building that stood off away from everything else.

George hauled four buckets of water up to the house. He worked diligently priming and trying to loosen the handle on the old pump that was in the kitchen. It took quite some time, but at last water began to flow freely. Then he began to dismantle the stove pipe that went to the old wood-burning stove, so that he could clean it out. He wanted to get a fire set in the stove once again. It was dusky dark by the time the stove was clean and ready to start a fire. He went out to the yard where he had a fire burning and picked up a good chunk of burning wood and transferred it to that old wood-burning stove. It wasn't long before the fire was burning well in the kitchen.

George told Linda Kay, "I know that it's a little too hot to have this fire going all the time, but we need to keep it going. I hope someone will see the smoke rising from the chimney. We really don't need to let fire go out."

Linda Kay worked hard trying to wash down and clean the beds so that they would be clean enough to sleep in. She brushed down the spider webs and swept the place out. She tried hard to ignore the fact that she felt eyes following her around the room as she worked diligently. There were a couple of times she actually felt like someone had touched her. Those were the times she couldn't control herself; she would twist and turn to try and get away from something she couldn't see. She knew it would do no good to try and say anything else to George. He didn't understand. She fought back the tears of anxiety and tried to keep in mind: *This is only one night; I can make it one night.*

Chapter 15

Mary and Elizabeth pulled into the parking lot at the post office. Mary switched off the ignition and leaned back in her seat.

"Oh, Mary, I am so nervous. Are you sure I can do this?"

"Of course you can, you can do anything you want to."

"I hope this goes well. I need something positive in my life right now."

"I'm sure everything's going to go well for you. I think you're really going to like Danny. He's a great guy, just wait and see. I think you'll be pleasantly surprised. What I don't understand is how come some of these girls around here haven't snatched him up yet. He would be a great catch for some lucky girl."

Elizabeth laughed.

"Well the one thing I'm not looking for right now is the responsibility of taking care of some man. I would like to enjoy life before I take on another job. Right now, I just need to figure out how to handle the responsibilities I already have.

Elizabeth was still slow and a little hesitant as she stepped out of the car. She really didn't know if she should take this job or just go home. She hated to give up her job at home. After all, it was what she knew and what she was accustomed to doing. She loved that job. By the same token, she couldn't go off not knowing what had happened to Linda Kay. She tried to think what would Linda Kay do if the roles were reversed? She felt so torn with wanting to go home and wanting to stay. She just didn't know how to make the decision so she said, *God, if I need to stay here let me get this job and if I don't, then I'll know I need to go home.*

Elizabeth put a big smile on her face and tried to take on a positive attitude as she entered the building. After all, she had just put everything in God's hands.

Elizabeth had to work hard at keeping the shocked look off her face when she met Danny. He was drop dead gorgeous, and he was about her age. He was tall, broad shouldered, slim in the hips, and he knew how to wear a pair of jeans. He was tanned, as if he spent a lot of time outdoors. His handsome looks put her in a state of awe. For a moment, she lost her voice and was unable to speak. She swallowed hard to regain her composure as they shook hands and said their hellos to one another.

Once Mary had introduced them, she told Elizabeth that she would be waiting for her in the car. Danny and Elizabeth seemed to connect right away. They went over what her job duties would consist of. Elizabeth explained to him that she had never worked in a post office and that she no experience.

"I will definitely need to be trained. I can only promise you that I will do the best job that I can possibly do. If you give me this opportunity, I would very much appreciate it, and I will assure you that I always hold my job in high regard." She also explained to him the situation that she was in. "At this point, I can't promise you that I will be staying here. Therefore, I cannot promise to be long time employee."

"I totally understand the situation that you're in. I'm willing to accept that the only reason you are considering taking this job is because your life has been turned upside down. Once we know what's happened to Linda Kay, you have the right to change your mind. That makes sense and would be only fair to you. After all, this is a different lifestyle than what you're used to. It's not a lifestyle that's for everyone. I appreciate the fact that you told me that you can't make me a promise of long-time employment. I do appreciate that you will promise to do a good job while you're here. That is one thing I do expect of an employee; I work hard and I will expect the same from you. Don't worry about training; you will receive proper training. Who knows? If you decide to go back home, you might want to stay in this profession. Do you think you could be ready to come to work Monday morning by 7:00?"

"Yes sir, I'll be here, and you'll see I'm a fast learner, and I will do a good job."

"I'm sure you will. That's why I'm willing to take a chance on you. Elizabeth, I have known Linda Kay all my life. Everyone in this town loves her and George dearly. We will do anything that we can do to try and help find them. So, if there's anything I can do to help her, I will be more than happy to do it."

"Thank you, that means so much to me. I don't know how to put into words how much all the kindness this town has shown me. It does make me understand why Linda Kay loves this town so much." Elizabeth shook Danny's hand and once again told him thanks for the opportunity before she turned and walked out the door.

Once Elizabeth had returned to the car she related how excited she was.

"I can't believe I got the job. I'm supposed to start working Monday morning. That means I've got to go home this weekend and get all my business there straightened out. I need to pack all my stuff up and get it put in storage. Close up my apartment and turn in my resignation at my job. Mary I hate to do this, but do you think there's any way I can get you to go with me? I will pay you, of course, but I cannot drive Linda Kay's car and my car back at the same time."

"You start to work Monday morning, right?"

"Yes, I might be able to get one of my friends there to drive my car back but then I'd have to take them back home. I've only got four days to get moved and get ready to go to work."

"I understand, but I think we can come up with a better plan. Trinity can drive us up there in his truck. He can bring back the things you're going to need here. We can help you pack up your apartment and get your things moved into storage. While you take care of talking with your old boss, we can get quite a bit of the work done. We'll get it all done, and you'll be back in time to go to work Monday morning.

Elizabeth looked at Mary with a big smile on her face as she said, "I appreciate you so much Mary. I am really excited about this job. The main thing I liked about it is I feel like he was honest with me. I think he will help me to learn the job properly. I also think he really understands the position that I'm in right now. The only thing wrong was that you didn't tell me before I went in just how drop-dead gorgeous he is. I felt tongue-tied for minute. But there must be something wrong with him, or the girls around here would've scarfed him up long ago."

"To tell you the truth I don't know exactly what his expectations are, but apparently he just didn't find them here. He has dated several of the girls in this area and they seem to be crazy about him, but he just didn't seem to be interested in them.

Elizabeth and Mary chatted happily the rest of the way home. They kept going over and over plans and scenarios on how to get Elizabeth moved and ready for work by Monday morning.

As they pulled back into the driveway at Linda Kay's they knew something was really popping, the yard was full of people running helter-skelter. Elizabeth's heart began to beat fast; panic rose in her throat she didn't know what had happened. She hoped it was good news about Linda Kay and George. Or it could be news about the predator that had been trying to break in to Linda Kay's house and scare them away from the property. She was shaking as she slowly climbed out of the car and tears began to creep down her cheeks in fear of the unknown.

CHAPTER 16

AT LAST GEORGE CAME TO LINDA KAY, "That's enough for now. After all we don't plan on moving in here permanently. I don't know about you, but I'm getting awfully hungry. I'm going to go get us a couple of tomatoes and a few of the greens I don't know how good they will taste, but I figure it's time to give them a try."

George came back in the house letting the door slam behind him. He placed a big smile on his face. Excitement was overflowing out of his voice as he said, "Once again you're not going to believe what I found. Look at this, isn't it wonderful? He placed beautiful looking strawberries on the table. They were behind the greens. The garden is so overgrown I almost missed them again. Isn't this awesome, Linda Kay?

"You are so right, they are beautiful. It won't take me but a minute to wash the greens and the strawberries and cut up the tomato, and supper will be ready."

Linda Kay was trying hard to act as excited as George. George understood her too well; he knew she was hurting he could hear it in her voice.

"Linda Kay, I'm sorry you're hurting. Is there anything I can do to make this better for you?"

"No, not really, I just feel like someone is here with us, watching us. I feel like there are eyes staring at me. I guess I'm just being silly. I'll tell you what; in order to make me feel safer, you can come over here and help me fix supper," she tried to laugh, making light of the situation.

George laughed at that, and some of the tension seemed to disappear. They both begin to relax as they talked about how fortunate they were to have found the little overrun garden. Excitement began to fill their hearts at the thoughts of adding strawberries to their meal along with the other food. They ate slowly, savoring every bite, until at last they had eaten their fill.

When they finished eating, Linda Kay asked George if they could walk down to the river.

"I suppose we can, but I don't want to stay out too long. It's almost dark outside. It won't be long before all the night critters will be coming out. I really don't know what that would be in this area. I'd prefer that we stay on the safe side of things until we learn what to expect in the night, considering we don't know much about this island or how safe it is. I would feel better if we were settled in before dark."

Linda Kay grabbed a bar of lye soap.

"I'll hurry, but I really want to wash up before I go to bed. My clothes need to be washed, so I'm just going to get in the river like I am and wash my clothes while I take a bath."

"Now that sounds like a plan. If you don't mind, I'll join you. Let's hurry."

He took Linda Kay's hand, and they almost skipped as they went down to the river.

It felt so good to relax. They were tired and sore, their muscles ached. The water in the Buffalo River began to relax their muscles, and before they knew it, time seemed to have slipped away from them, and the moon was reflecting off of the water and highlighting their silhouettes. They had been laughing and talking, but all of a sudden Linda Kay felt the longing to have George's arms around her once again. She had to break the spell of that lovely moon before all the pain and sorrow that she had felt before came creeping back in. There was no place for her to go to get away from George, she had to be very careful and guard her feelings. Linda Kay knew there would never be a day that she didn't love George, but she knew for her protection, she had to keep up a façade of indifference.

"I think we better get out of here pretty quick. We've let the night sneak up on us. Maybe we should get back to the shelter."

She started walking out of the water.

"Wait just one moment, look at the sky and how gorgeous it is. We need a good memory to help us get through the night. It seems like the moon just pierces through your soul cleansing you of all worry and despair and leaves you full of hope and dreams."

Linda Kay looked up at the sky said, "You're right. It is so beautiful."

The moon was so full; it lit up the sky with love and wonder. The stars were bright and danced their way across the sky. Then they reflect off the water to let us know that this should be a world full of love and peace…

She tried to hide the tears that were welling in her eyes. She didn't know if she was going to be able to handle this because the love she felt for George had never died, but neither had the hurt that now filled her heart.

"Don't forget the soap."

George could feel the bite in her words. All at once, everything had changed and there was now that bridge between them once again. George couldn't understand what had happened, but he got out of the water with the invisible wall between them as they went back to the homestead.

As soon as they walked up on the porch, Linda Kay felt that evil once again. It began to fill her soul. She had the impulse to lash out and let go of all the anger and hurt that she felt, but she knew in her heart of hearts that it wasn't really her. She began praying to herself, saying the Lord's Prayer, trying to clear the air of all the anger that lived within those walls. She felt so alone because she knew George did not understand what she had been trying to tell him.

Linda Kay went straight to the back room and took off her wet clothes. She wrapped herself in a muslin sheet. She took her clothes back to the kitchen and laid them out next to the stove to dry. She felt like she could feel someone watching her, and it gave her the creeps.

Help me Lord; I want to make it through this night.

She lay in bed and tossed and turned as sleep escaped her. She finally gave up and went back to the kitchen and retrieved her clothes. She felt better now that her clothes were dry, and she put them back on. It made her feel safer somehow now that she was dressed once again. She felt like those piercing eyes started to back away. Soon she began to relax, and sleep crept in.

Dreams begin to dance in her head, she saw four beautiful little girls. They seem to age from about 10 years old to maybe three years old. They were outside running and playing, laughing having a wonderful time. It was back in time, when kids played outside; they made mud-pies and lived in a make-believe world. Kids would play piggy in the pen wants a signal and hiding go seek. They seemed so carefree and happy. Linda Kay could feel herself smiling along with them. It was as if she was standing beside them, watching them play the whole time.

All at once, a large man appeared in the doorway, his brow furled and deep lines of hurt crossed his face. Linda Kay became frightened. Her heart began to pound in her chest. It was as if he was wearing a shield of alarm. The girls immediately stopped playing. Fear was written across their faces. He set down on the steps and called the children to him. He wrapped his big arms around them and hugged them tightly. Linda Kay could see that he was a gentle man, full of love for those little girls. She also knew there was something wrong as tears slid down his face. Then he told the children their mother had just passed away. She had gone to heaven. Now they would have to be in charge of the house.

The sad thing was Linda Kay could feel all the pain that the children were feeling. She also felt the suffering and how devastated they were. How much they longed for the love that their mother had always shown them. She began to cry and moan in her sleep until George gently woke her up letting her know that she was safe and she was with him.

"Linda Kay, what's the matter? How can I help you? Please talk to me. I hate to see you hurting like this. Please let me help."

"I was having a dream it was about this place; I could see the house, everything was like it is today. Of course, everything was clean and the garden was pretty, not overrun, and at first everything was filled with love. The little girls were fun-loving and happy they had a wonderful childhood with parents who loved them dearly. The oldest little girl seemed to be maybe 10 years old. Her name was Mamie. The second girl was maybe eight years old; her name was Bernice. The third little girl was maybe six years old, and her name was Nell. The youngest was maybe three years old, and her name was Ruth.

"A large handsome man came out of the house. Devastation was written all over his face you could see the lines of mental anguish forming across his forehead. There was no doubt in my mind it was the girls' father. He walked over and set down on the steps before calling the girls to him. He put his arms out to pull the girls in close to him as he told them that their mother had gone to heaven to be with Jesus. 'It's going to be a lot harder on us without your mama here with us, but we'll make it. You know that she loved you girls more than anything, and so do I. I will do everything I can for you.'

"I can feel their pain and their hurt. It all happened right here in this house, their mother died in that front bedroom. There's a lot of mourning that went on in this house, but there was also a lot of love here. But that's not the evil that I feel surrounding this property something else bad happened here. Right now, what I feel is the anguish and the devastation that those beautiful little girls had to endure."

George put his arm around her and pulled her close.

"It was just a dream, you're nervous about being in this place, and that's probably what caused the dream. I'm here with you everything is going to be okay. Now lie down and try to go back to sleep I'll stay with you until you're comfortable. You've been through so much the last couple of days. Maybe all the stress was just playing on your mind. I'm right here with you now; you will be okay, so relax and go to sleep."

Linda Kay wasn't sure if he was trying to convince her or himself. She looked deeply into George's eyes and said, "I believe it was real. I believe it happened right here in this house just like I told you. I wish you could understand. I just hope that tomorrow we can find a safe way out of here. I want to go home. I'm scared of what is going to happen if we stay around here. I'm telling you there's something that lurks here on this island. And George, I'm not sure that he will let us leave"

George inhaled deeply.

"I'm trying to understand, Linda Kay, I promise you I am trying to understand. Right now it's very late, and we do want to get an early start in the morning. So don't worry about anything else tonight. Just relax and try to sleep."

George stayed with her until dawn started breaking. She had slept fretfully through the rest of the night. He gently shook her and told her it was time to get up. They were going to go search for a way off the island. He wanted nothing more than to get them both to safety. George built the fire up in the wood-burning stove.

Linda Kay walked into the kitchen rubbing her face trying to come awake. She looked around the room then asked George, "why did you do this?"

"I told you we have to keep this fire built up."

"I'm not talking about that I'm talking about why did you smash those strawberries on the wall. That's a horrible mess? Why would you throw all the junk in the floor over there? It looks as if things were just flung in the corner then you went outside and got dirt and threw all over it. That is a sticky mess; I worked hard trying to clean this up yesterday now why would you do this?

"I didn't do that, Linda Kay. I wouldn't do anything like that. I don't know what happened. I wouldn't have a reason to do something like that. I'll help you clean it up before we leave. I don't want something left in here that will cause rodents to come in, just in case we have to come back. Then I want to get ready to go search the island. I'm ready to get out of here."

They worked quickly together, and soon had things back in order. Immediately they started gathering things, so they would be able to search the island

George found a cloth bag in the kitchen. He took it outside and filled it with strawberries and tomatoes for them to eat along the way. Linda Kay had boiled water the day before for them to drink. She filled a canteen that she had found in the kitchen to take with them. They planned to be gone all day if that's what it took; they wanted to find a way home. If luck was with them and they could find a way off this island, they would never have to return here again.

CHAPTER 17

MARY AND ELIZABETH WERE STUNNED standing in the driveway at Linda Kay's looking at everyone scurrying around. Elizabeth wiped the tears from her cheeks and asked Mary, "When you go in the house will you put coffee on? I'm going to try to find someone around here that can tell me what's going on. I'll be just a minute, and then I'll come in and help you."

Mary looked at her with a smile on her face.

"Sure, I have no problem with making the coffee. Before you go in search of what's going on around here, I want you to remember today's a good day. I know whatever's going on around here is going to be good news. Keep that beautiful smile on your face."

She gave Elizabeth a quick hug before heading in the house.

Elizabeth inhaled a deep breath and tried to regain her composure as she started walking around the house in search of the Sheriff. All the while, she tried to keep in mind what Mary had told her: *It's a good day I don't need to be worrying.* She was thinking, *If that's true, why am I so scared?*

At last she heard her name called, when she turned around, she saw the sheriff heading in her direction. She closed her eyes and asked for the strength to get through this. When she opened her eyes again, she swallowed hard trying to get rid of all the fear that surrounded her heart. The closer the sheriff got to Elizabeth the more she began to shake from anxiety and her stomach begin to tie up in knots. As the Sheriff got even closer to Elizabeth, she could see he was wearing a big smile on his face.

Elizabeth began to shout, "It's Linda Kay, and she's okay. Where is she? Was George with her did you rescue both of them?"

The Sheriff inhaled deeply and began shaking his head.

"No, it's not about George and Linda Kay." Her heart sank as the Sheriff said, "We did not find Linda Kay or George the search party is still out."

The tears once again began to overflow from Elizabeth's eyes. She looked up at the Sheriff.

"How can that be? Someone should have found them by now."

The sheriff put an arm on Elizabeth's shoulder, and said, "Come on. Let's go in the house, and I will fill you in on everything that's going on."

As they walked in the house, Mary saw that Elizabeth was crying. She picked up the box of Kleenex and handed it to Elizabeth. She put her arm around her waist as she led her to a chair. Once she had her seated, she told the Sheriff to sit anywhere he liked.

"Is she going to be okay, Sheriff?"

"Yes, she'll be fine as soon as we get her to calm down. She's just been under too much stress, and it's caught up with her. Once she relieves some of the pressure, she is going to be fine."

"I'll bring both of you a cup of coffee. See if you can get her to relax." Mary turned and went back into the kitchen, leaving Elizabeth and the Sheriff alone once again.

At last Elizabeth relaxed her shoulders, wiped her eyes with the Kleenex and blew her nose before looking up at the Sheriff and saying, "I'm sorry I'm a nervous wreck. I really didn't mean to fall apart on you. Please tell me what's going on."

Sheriff Travis looked at her and smiled, "you can start to relax now. I have nothing but good news to tell you. I'm sorry that it's not about Linda Kay and George. What I have to tell you is we got the guy that has been harassing you and Linda. We interrogated him quite some time. I believe him when he told me he was sorry about hitting Linda Kay with the rock. He never intended to hit her, and he sure didn't want to hurt her. That was an accident. He never intended to inflict pain on anyone. You see, he went to school with us his name is Terrence Williams."

Mary was just returning with their coffee, when she overheard the Sheriff tell Elizabeth it was Terrence Williams. A loud gasp escaped from Mary before she could prevent it.

"Oh no, I hate to hear that. Why did he do such a thing?"

"The reason why he wanted everyone off this property is because of that cave that's on the backside of this property. He had what he thought was the perfect set up in that cave. He had a rather large bootlegging business going on. The only thing that went wrong was when Linda Kay and Elizabeth showed up, it run his clientele off. So I can assure you that he didn't want to hurt you. He just wanted the two of them off the property. I can assure you that he won't be causing any more problems on this property or any other property for quite some time.

As Mary looked at the sheriff, a worried frown crossed her face.

"I'm really sorry to hear that. He really is a good guy it's just his head's really been screwed up from the time he lost his wife. You know his mom is going to be totally devastated."

Mary turned and slowly walked back into the kitchen.

Elizabeth looked at the Sheriff and then hung her head.

"Wow, I hate to see Mary upset like that. I don't really understand. She must have known that Terrence guy pretty well. It sounds like good news to me but pretty hurtful for her. It's a big relief off my mind. I don't know if I will ever be able to relax and feel comfortable out here anyway. It's so far out from everyone else. I don't feel like I have any protection. If something were to happen, it could be days before anyone would ever know I was lying out here."

"Please don't feel that way; give it a little time I think you will find it peaceful and lovely. I also think you will find, when you run into someone you know, that they will really be interested in what you have to say, and who you are and that they value you as a person."

"Maybe in time, right now, I just want Linda Kay back and then maybe my world could be put back together. I don't know where everything will go from here. But on a better note, I've also got some good news for you. I got that job at the post office. I start to work Monday morning."

"Elizabeth, I am so happy for you I think you'll enjoy working there. You couldn't work for a better boss."

Mary came in the room carrying a tray of cookies and set them on the coffee table and said, "I hope you enjoy". She turned to leave then paused for a moment and turned back around "I hope you don't think I'm interfering or butting in. I overheard what you said about staying here, and I understand why you would be scared. I know of a cabin not far from the post office. You could buy it really cheap, it's not as big as this one, but it could be a nice cabin. Only problem is, and the reason why you can get it so cheap is, it does need some work. But you could stay here while it was being worked on. If you decided not to stay after the cabin was finished you would be able to sell it for profit. It's something to think about. Now if you'll pardon me, I'll be out of your way, sorry for the intrusion."

Elizabeth said, "Get another cup and come sit down with us. I would like to hear more about that cabin."

"Are you sure? I don't want to disturb you."

"You will not be disturbing us. I have something I want to ask you. Now run, get your coffee, we'll wait for you."

"Okay, I'll be right back."

Once they were all settled down, the Sheriff told Mary that he understood about her being so upset over Terrence it had upset him to.

Mary shook her head.

"You know that really breaks my heart. He's really a good guy. I know he's had a hard time; things didn't go exactly like he thought they should. I just really hate to hear it about it being him. I would love to just try and shake some sense into him. But I guess it's too late for that now. I will go spend time with his mama tomorrow, maybe take her something special. She's such a goodhearted woman."

"Everything you said is true, and I hated it myself. He used to be such a good, hard-working man until he lost his wife. After that, he didn't seem to care about anything. He lost his job and just seemed to give up on life. He let himself fall into that trap of looking for too much too fast. You're right; things have been really rough on him the last couple of years. I think when he lost his wife, it did something to him. He hasn't been the same since. I know his mom tries to help him, but it seems she just can't get through to him."

Elizabeth said, "You are making me feel really bad now, especially for his mom. I'm feeling sorry for him. He was the one tormenting me, and I'm feeling sorry for him. I don't know how that makes sense, but I do." She slowly shook her head in disbelief. "I can't believe I'm saying this, but what if no one presses charges against him for anything? Would that help him? And if I don't press charges, what kind of assurance would I have that he wouldn't do it again?"

"This is a dry county, Elizabeth. He was caught with the goods, there's really nothing I can do about that. As far as the damage he did around here and what he did to you and Linda Kay, it's up to you to press charges."

"What do you think Linda Kay would do?

"Right now, Linda Kay's not here, and no one can answer for her. What I need to know is if you want to press charges. There are several charges that you could bring against him; after all you, have gone through a lot. No one would blame you if you want to press charges."

"Let me ask you this, with the charges that you have against him, do you think it will stop his harassing people. I'm telling you, I've never been so scared in all my life. I don't want to go through something like that again. Do you think he would get the help he needs?"

"Yes, because I'm going to follow it up. I feel like as a community we failed him. When he lost his wife, he cried out for help. I don't feel like as a community we stepped up and gave him the kind of help he needed. I don't intend to fail him again. Elizabeth, you have to understand you have to do what you think is right. No one is going to hold that against you."

"I won't press any charges. But understand when Linda Kay comes home, I cannot speak for her, she will have to make her own decision."

"It couldn't be any other way and I promise you this, he will definitely know the sacrifice that you're making for him."

Elizabeth smiled.

"This is a good community you have, you have stuck by me during Linda Kay's absence, and you helped me to get a job. I hope what I'm doing will help Terrence to get his life back in order. Myself, I'd like to give him a good piece of my mind. So therefore, I would like the right to be able to see him. I just want to tell him how I feel and how much he hurt Linda Kay and me. I want him to know what I expect of him. I think he really needs to know how much torture he put us through. After I tell him how I feel, then maybe I can forget and forgive and try to help him myself.

"Right now, I can't say how long I will be here, but as long as I am, I want to do my share to be part of the community. Everyone I've met has been great to me. I understand why Linda Kay loves it here so much. If there's help to be given to Terrence, then I think we should do it.

"Now Mary, what I wanted to ask you was if there's any way I could talk you and Trinity into staying one more night with me? I need one more night to try to calm down. I would like to have the time to talk to Trinity about that cabin you were telling me about. If I can afford it and he can fix it up for me, I think I'd be happier with the move. I don't know that you could call that the busy section of town, but at least it's busier there than it is here. Even if I don't know how long I'm going to stay here, I think I would be happier around more people. So much depends on what we find out about Linda Kay. I really would appreciate having your company tonight. I will also need to think about getting my stuff moved and turn in my resignation at work. Besides I need you to help me pick out what to wear to work Monday, how to fix my hair, how to communicate with people."

Mary started laughing.

"I don't think that would be a problem. I personally think we can have a lot of fun. Well, I don't know how much fun Trinity will have, but you and I'll have a lot of fun."

The Sheriff stood up saying, "Okay, I'm going to leave this to you two. I'm going outside and get everything wound up. I'm sure things will be a lot more pleasant for you around here now. If you have any problems just let me know."

"It will be better when Linda Kay comes home. Please never forget about her I need her home. I feel like she is my family."

"Linda Kay and George are first and foremost on everyone's mind; no one will forget. I didn't want to tell you, but we can only keep the search party out one more day and then we'll have to call it off."

"But what if you haven't found them, what will happen? Who's going to be looking for them, we can't just give up until they are found."

"Elizabeth, if we haven't found them by then, we have no choice but to give up the search. After all, people have to go back to work. They have their families they have to care for. They can't stay on the river, at some point we have to give it up."

Chapter 18

Linda Kay was so excited about looking for a way off the island that she was almost running as she skipped down the steps. Before she could reach the bottom, it felt as if someone had reached out and grabbed her ankle tripping her, causing her to go tumbling over and over. She didn't stop until she hit the ground. George saw her take her tumble as he came around the corner of the house. He ran over to her.

"Oh Linda Kay, are you okay?"

"I don't know my ankle hurts, I'm not sure I'll be able to walk on it. George, I was tripped. Do you hear what I'm telling you? I was tripped. It felt as if someone grabbed my ankle and was holding it there. You're going to have to start believing me, there's something going on here; we've got to get out. Let's find a way off this island now."

George gave her a questionable look before bending down to check her ankle.

"Linda Kay, I'm sure you got your shoe hung on that board that's standing up. Please try not to be so scared all the time. We going to find our way out of here, but I don't think it will be today. I can tell you now, you won't be walking on this ankle today or anytime soon. You have a really bad sprain. I don't think it's broken, but you have to stay off of it. There's no way to put your weight on it. That ankle is just not going to hold you. You really need to keep it propped up. I'll get you back in the house. Then if you want me to, I'll go in search of a way off this island. If I find something, as soon as your ankle gets well, we'll leave"

Linda Kay looked at George with piercing eyes full of anger.

"Are you nuts? There's no way you're going off and leaving me here by myself, that won't happen. Find something that I can use for a crutch I'm going with you; we've got to get off this island today."

George began shaking his head in disbelief.

"You really need to keep that ankle propped up. Would you rather just wait here a few days, then we'll go together?"

"George, did you not hear what I said? I am getting away from this place today. As far away as I can get."

"Well, the first thing we've got to do is get you inside and find something that we can wrap this ankle with." George helped her back in the house being as gentle as possible with her. He set her down and got another chair and placed it in front of her to prop her foot on. He grabbed a muslin sheet and began tearing it into strips. He carefully wrapped her foot and ankle in the muslin strips and then tied it snugly in place.

"Linda Kay, there no way you're going to be able to walk on that foot. So, you've got a choice you're either going to have to stay here by yourself, or we will have to wait until your foot gets better before we can go looking for a way off the island. Think about it, and tell me what you want to do."

"I can tell you one thing for sure I'm not staying here by myself. I meant it when I told you that I had been tripped. I did not just fall, someone or something tripped me. And I want off this island now; I'm telling you this place is evil. Make me or find me something that I can use for a crutch. I am going to look for a way off this island today. I don't care if I have to crawl. Now you can think about that if you want to while you are looking for something that I can use as a crutch."

George looked deep into Linda Kay's eyes and knew she meant every word she said. One way or the other, she would be looking for some way off this island. She could be one of the most stubborn people he had ever met. He knew there was absolutely no need for him to waste his time and energy trying to change her mind.

"Okay, I'll go look and see what I can find that we can use. Please keep your foot propped up while I'm gone. I will not be very far from here. If you need me, holler, and I'll come right back. With that, he turned and started out the door, you could tell by the look on his face he was not happy.

"George?"

"Yes?"

"I'm sorry I made you angry, but thank you for going to look for something I can use. I don't know what I'd do without you."

With that, you could see the look on George's face soften. He was always putty in her hands. There was nothing he could do about that, he loved her more than words could ever say.

"It's okay, I'll do whatever I can to try and get us off this island today." He grinned at her and said, "I'll be right back."

"Thank you"

George shut the door softly as he went outside to search for something to make a crutch for Linda Kay. He walked to the back of the house to what used to be an old toolshed. The door creaked as he opened it. The hinges were rusty like everything else inside. He had to bat away spider webs before he could enter. Sure enough, there was an old hatchet that's so covered in rust. George didn't know if he would ever be able to use it. He picked up an old rusted flat bastard file, and with questionable expectations, he started to work on the hatchet. It took him quite some time, but at last he had it honed to a fine sharp edge. Finally, he set out to look for a forked branch. He searched the trees staying close enough to the house if Linda Kay called for him, he would hear her. He didn't want her getting scared and him not be able to hear her. After all, he had promised her to stay close in case she needed help. George would never tell his thoughts to Linda Kay, but he honestly didn't think they stood a chance of getting off of the island today. The most he had was high hopes of coming up with some way of signaling for help or maybe something that he could make a raft out of. He didn't have hopes of leaving the island anytime soon. There was no way they could walk off the island, and there was no way they were capable of swimming that far. At last he stumbled across the branch that he thought would be perfect to make a crutch out of. He hacked away at it until it last the branch was free. He carried it back to the house so he could get the right measurement on it so it would be a little more comfortable for Linda Kay. Once he finally got it cut to his satisfaction, he wrapped the forked part of the limb with strips of muslin in order to cushion it. At last that task was complete.

Linda Kay was ecstatic. She thought he had done a great job, and with that, she would be able to go with him in their search for a way home.

George looked at her and said, "Linda Kay, it's getting later in the morning now, and I'm getting hungry. I really think we need to eat before we set out on another task."

"You're right, we do need to eat first, but our day is getting away from us. We've got those strawberries you picked this morning. Can we just eat them on the way?"

"Yes, we can eat these, but I will still have to pick more berries before we leave because I'm not going to go without taking some with us. You never know what's going to happen in a place like this, and there's no way I would want to leave without taking food with us. Here is the bag of strawberries. We're going to eat these, and then I'll go pick more for us to take."

Linda Kay was starting to get aggravated again; she didn't want to wait. She wanted to leave now. She was scared of this place. It gave her the creeps, and she didn't want to spend another minute in that house. Why could she not get him to understand that? She didn't understand how anyone could not feel the evil that poured into this place. Linda Kay knew this is one battle that she would lose. It would be a lot quicker to go ahead and eat and let him gather more berries to take with them than to fight about it. She reluctantly agreed with him.

Once they had eaten, George went back to the garden and picked more strawberries, but something kept nagging at him, telling him take more food. It was a feeling that George could not ignore, so he gathered more than he thought they could possibly need.

Linda Kay had a big smile on her face as George said, "Okay let's go, and stay close to me in case you have a problem with that crutch."

George helped her down the steps he turned and stared at her just for a moment. He knew it wouldn't do any good to ask her to wait until morning. So, they set out in search of a way off the island.

CHAPTER 19

MARY WAS WITH ELIZABETH AS THEY ENTERED THE JAILHOUSE.

"Elizabeth, are you sure you want to do this?"

"Yes, I think he needs to know what he did to me and Linda Kay. He needs to know how I felt. He also needs to know that I tried to buy a gun, and if I had got it, he might be dead now. And I would be the one trying to live that down. He may be upset with his life, but that doesn't give him the right to destroy mine. If I'm not going to file charges against him, then I think he should understand exactly what he did to me and to Linda Kay. Yes, I definitely want to meet him, and I definitely want to tell him what's on my mind."

"Okay, I will definitely stand by you. Let's go get our names on the book and see what they say."

"What kind of book?"

"Well, I'm not really sure what it's called I just heard you got to put your name on the book. So, I figured we'll be putting our name on the book."

"Okay, I'm really nervous. I've never done anything like this before. I'll just follow your lead if that's okay."

Mary started snickering.

"What's so funny?"

Mary looked at Elizabeth as if she had lost her mind as she said, "I haven't been in here before, and you want to follow my lead? I'm afraid we're both lost, but that's okay, we'll figure it out." They slowly walked up to the window and asked, "Can we see Terrence Williams?"

"Are you on his list of visitors?"

"What? I don't know what you're talking about. How do we do that?"

The jailer shook his head as he said, "You have to be on his visitors list or you can't see him."

Mary said, "Okay how do we get on his visitors list?"

"He has to put you on the list. If he wants to see, you will be on his list."

"He doesn't know we want to see him, if he did, he might have us on his list. Now, how can we get a message to him and tell him to put us on this list."

"You don't, if he wants to see you he will put you on the list. Now would you move along; I'm busy. I need to help the people behind you."

About that time Mary saw Nathan, a friend of hers, she called out to him and asked if she could speak to him a moment.

"Sure, I'll be right out there."

Mary looked at Nathan and nodded her head toward the man they had just talked to, "That man is so irritating. I hope you can help us. I do appreciate you taking the time to talk with me." She explained what a difficult time they were having trying to see Terrence Williams.

Nathan nodded his head.

"Yeah he can be a stickler for the rules. I'll tell you what I'll do. I'll get a form and take it back there to him. If he wants to see you, I'll have him to fill it out, and I'll put it in his file. Then I'll give you a signal, and you go back to the window again. Tell him you just remembered that you are on his visitors list. It'll take me a few minutes, so y'all have a seat over there and wait."

"Thank you, Nathan. I appreciate it a lot. We'll be waiting." Mary said, "Come on, Elizabeth, let's go over there and have a seat. Plan one didn't work; let's see if plan two works."

It took quite some time, but at last, Mary saw Nathan again, and he gave her a slight nod. She knew they were now on the visitors list.

"Come on Elizabeth, it's time to go back and try again."

They walked up to the window; Mary placed a big smile on her face and said, "Yes, we're here to see Terrence Williams."

"Ma'am, I have already told you if you're not on the visitors list you can't see him. The two of you can leave, now! Please don't waste my time."

"Sir, I believe we are on the visitor's list. We've been thinking about it, and I bet he would put us on that list. Please would you check it for us?"

"You're just wasting my time. If you weren't on the list a while ago, you're not on the list now, so leave."

"Sir, I believe we made a mistake, and we are on the visitors list. If you would just check, I would appreciate it."

He puffed up like an old toad frog before saying, "I will check, and if you're not there, if you don't get out here, I'm going to have you arrested. I'm tired of dealing with you two.

"Fine, if we're not on the visitors list, we will be happy to leave, and we won't bother you anymore."

You could see the anger steaming from the jailer's ears as he pulled out the list with their names on the list. Anger was boiling over as he told them, "Have a seat and I'll have him brought out. I will call you when we're ready for you to go back and see him. You will have to lock your purses in the lock boxes over there on the wall. You can't take anything to the back with you."

They took their seats and happily sat there visiting with one another until at last Elizabeth said, "Wow, I can't believe how long this is taking. We've been waiting for 45 minutes already. How hard can it be to see someone? I'm sorry, Mary; I wouldn't have asked you to do all this if I'd known how much trouble it was going to be. If you wish, we can just leave and maybe try again sometime."

"That's okay; it makes me happy to see him that angry. He's always been snooty. Even when you try to befriend him, he still won't meet you halfway. He always acts as if he is smarter and better than everyone else."

"I didn't want you to spend all your time just sitting here. We haven't seen him yet. Who knows how long that man is going to make us wait?"

"You can count on it, we're going to be here for a while just waiting, it's uncalled for. It's because we made him mad, and he has the power to pay us back. So, we might as well relax and spend our time visiting with one another. Besides, if he doesn't think he's bothering us, then we will get back there quicker."

Elizabeth began talking to Mary about how worried she was because no one had found Linda Kay or George. She began questioning Mary about what would happen if they stop the search.

"What will we do? We can't just quit looking. Or, I can't." Her eyes begin to fill with tears.

"I don't want you getting upset. Come on let's talk about something else; we're going to keep a positive outlook on things. Let's just put it in God's hands, and it will work out the way he wants it to. You know what? I know how to get back there to see Terrence quicker."

"How, I'm ready to get this over with?"

"I can't promise you, but I lay you odds that if we buy us a coke out of that vending machine, as soon as we open them he will call us back."

"What makes you think that?"

"There's a sign right there that says no food or drinks beyond this point. If he sees us get drinks as soon as we open them, we'll have to throw them away. Is it worth the chance of losing a little money to you?"

"Oh definitely, but please let it be my treat."

They were giggling as they walked to the vending machine. They enjoyed listening to the clanking of the coins as they dropped through the slot. As they walked back to their chairs, they popped the top of their cokes. The popping and sizzling sound was music to their ears. Mary had a big grin on her face because out of the corner of her eye she could see the jailer watching her closely. Just as they started to sit down, the jailer told them that he would buzz them back.

"You will have to throw your cans in the trash, or you can't come back."

Mary and Elizabeth looked at each other their eyes dancing with mischievous excitement. They placed their coke cans in the trash as they went through the door.

They were told to take a seat in front of a glassed area. There was a phone on the wall next to them. They were told that once Travis come into the room, they could talk to him over that phone. There was a small room on the other side of the glass. The door opened, and in walked a tall, well-built man with dark hair. He was a nice-looking man, but his face looked tired and worn, and the signs of depression hovered around him. He was wearing an orange jumpsuit that clashed with his complexion, making him take on a sick and waxy look. He sat down in a chair on the other side of the glass and picked up the phone as he motioned for us to pick up the phone on our side of the glass.

Mary whispered to Elizabeth, "That's Terrence" as Elizabeth picked up the phone receiver. At last she was able to talk to Terrence. Tears formed in Elizabeth eyes as she began speaking. She let him know exactly how she had felt while he had been tormenting her and

Linda Kay. She also let him know that Linda Kay was now missing and how her heart was breaking.

"You spoiled the last days I had with my best friend, and I want you to know I feel anger. I feel hurt that because of you our last days together were spent in torment. You soiled our precious memories. If it hadn't been for you, we could've been having a good time." When she looked up and looked him in the eye, she saw he also had tears rolling down his cheeks. That seems to have grabbed a hold of Elizabeth's heart and squeezed. It made her feel guilty that she had just hurt someone that was already hurting. It made her wonder, was she any better than him? Still she couldn't take back the words; she had meant every one of them.

He slowly begins to speak, telling her how sorry he was and that he had made a horrible, horrible mistake. He wished he could do it all over again. He would never do anything like that again. He knew he had made the worst mistake of his life.

"Not because I'm in jail, not because I got caught, but because it was wrong. I never ever would want to hurt Linda Kay or anyone else. I understand if there's no way you could ever forgive me. I would like to say thank you for at least giving me the opportunity to tell you how sorry I really am."

At last Elizabeth told him, "I'm not going to file charges against you for what you did to me and Linda Kay. I really hope that you have learned your lesson."

She stood to leave when he asked her to wait just one minute.

"I want to ask you something, I don't know how long I'm going to be here, but if you get a chance, would you mind every once in a while coming by to see me? I would really like to make up to you for what I've done."

Elizabeth just stared at him for a moment before at last she answered, "I don't see why not."

She replaced the phone on the hook, and she and Mary got up to leave.

As they walked out of the building, Elizabeth was shaken, but she felt better now that she had gotten her feelings off her chest. She turned to Mary with a solemn look on her face as she said, "Thank you so much for coming with me, believe it or not, I do feel better. I don't feel quite as frightened as I did. Also, I understand what you and the Sheriff were saying about him. I do believe he is a good man and maybe with guidance he will do all right. Now I feel like I can get on with my life. All I need now is for Linda Kay to come home."

"It was no problem going with you, besides I had fun just watching the jailer dance around in there trying to stay one step ahead of us. On a different subject, I need to let you know that Trinity wants to get an early start in the morning. We should have everything done and you moved down here in time to go to work Monday morning. Trinity's already checked out a good storage company a few miles from here. We're going to get a rental truck to go get your stuff. Trinity can drive the truck back. You and I can ride in your car on the way back. The storage company here is quite a bit cheaper than one there. Besides, your stuff will be closer to you if you decide to stay. We're going to put the things that you will need here, in the truck first. We will stop on the way home and unload everything else in storage. Then if you decide to get that cabin it won't be so far to go and retrieve your things. I hope those plans are satisfactory. If it's not; we can change them to suit you."

"That sounds like a great plan to me! I can't believe how quickly he was able to put everything together. He really is an amazing person."

Chapter 20

Linda Kay was trying to keep a positive look on her face as they walked and searched for any way to get off this island. She tried to stretch her imagination for any kind of an idea. They had walked for a long time when at last George said, "Come on, let's go over here at the base of that rock mountain where we can get some shade and take a break."

"Thank you, that will be fine with me," but truthfully in her heart of hearts Linda Kay was ecstatic at the thought of getting to take a break. She had not complained, but honestly that crutch was really irritating under her arm. Her foot was throbbing; she hated to admit it even to herself, but George had been right. She should have left it propped up.

George helped Linda Kay to sit down and made her as comfortable as possible.

"After we get a break, I want to try to get around to the other side of this rock cliff. Who knows what we can find there; maybe something positive. Maybe there'll be a way to cross off this island. If we don't find anything there, we're going to have to call it quits for the day. So please don't get upset if I tell you it's time for us to head back toward shelter for the night."

"I know that you have been trying really hard, and I want to thank you for that. I really do appreciate everything you're doing for us. But if possible, I had rather find someplace else to spend the night. I still say there is something very evil on this island. I can feel it, George, even here. It's not just at that house. It's as if it's following us everywhere we go."

There was astonishment in George's voice.

"Linda Kay, look up there, I'm listening to you, and we'll talk about that later. Right now, I need you to look. It's a cave. We need to see if we can find anything in there, can you make it?"

There was frustration in Linda Kay's voice as she said, "Yes, I can make it. But you're right. We are going to talk about this island. I'm not going to forget that subject. Why don't you go on up there and check it out? I'll wait here for you. It's probably just a waste of time, and you'll be back in just a minute."

"You're right, Linda Kay; we do need to talk about this island. I really hate to see you so upset. I would do anything I could to make you feel better and to make this situation better for you. I promise you, we will truthfully discuss it tonight. Right now, before it gets too late, I would like to try and explore that cave. I cannot go off and leave you here. After all, we came out here to explore this whole island and to find a way off of it. What if there's something in that cave that I could build a raft out of? We can't ignore anything we might be passing; it could be our only way out of here. Now will you please help me out?"

"Okay, help me up, let's go."

George grew more and more excited the closer they got to the mouth of the cave. His enthusiasm was catching; Linda Kay began to think, *Maybe we can find a way out of here.*

George inhaled deeply as he said, "I feel like the answer to our prayers will be inside that cave."

Linda Kay was keeping her mouth shut. All she could think about was how bad that crutch was hurting under her arm. She just wanted to stop somewhere and rest. As Linda Kay reached the mouth of the cave she took in a deep breath and backed up.

"Oh no, I'm not going in there; it is way too dark. If there was something in there for us to find, we couldn't see it anyway. No, I'm not going in there. There could be a big bear in there, or a mountain lion."

"Calm down, I don't blame you; it is awfully dark in there. Wait for me right here, I'll be back in just a minute."

As soon as George walked through the mouth of the cave Linda Kay's stomach begin to tie into knots. She had that creepy feeling that something was wrong, and she was being watched. She started looking around for anyone as she turned in circles. She strained her eyes trying to take in all the scenery around her. She knew she wasn't going to be able to see what was bothering her. It didn't stop her from hoping that she would find something human standing there waiting to help them.

She felt the rocks under her feet slightly shift, just as George stepped out of the cave calling her. That dreadful feeling immediately left her then, but she wouldn't ignore that feeling; she would never do that again. She would stay on guard.

George kept his word and was only in the cave a very short time then he comes out carrying a torch.

"What are you going to do with that?"

"It's a torch, and look what else I found."

"It's a rock. You found a rock." George just look around. "Rocks are the one thing that we're not short of."

George took in a deep breath trying to swallow down his aggravation and looked at Linda Kay with piercing eyes. It let her know that he was getting very frustrated with her. It was time for her to back off and try to work with him before he lost his cool. Tension was tight in his voice.

"This is not just a rock. This is a flint rock, and it will help to start a fire. Now if you will move out of my way I will do, what I can to get this torch lit".

The tone in George's voice bit deep, and Linda Kay knew she had pushed him too far. He had done everything in his power to try and appease her, and yet she sounded so unappreciative. She felt the shame as her heart went out to him.

"George, I'm sorry, I was short with you, and for that I apologize. I think both of our nerves are a little on edge. I also think that each other is all we've got right now, and we need to try to be a little kinder to one another. I really want to work with you, not against you. I may need to be reminded of that once in a while. I honestly do know what you have done for me since we've been in this mess, and I do appreciate it. I know I haven't been showing it and once again I'm sorry for that, please forgive me George."

George took hold of her shoulders with his broad hands and looked deep into her eyes.

"You're right Linda Kay; we don't need to be fighting with each other. We need to get along and take care of each other. That's something we have done since kindergarten. I don't think we should change it now. This is when we really need each other. I'm sorry I was being harsh to you; you don't deserve that." He pulled her close to him and hugged her tight as he whispered in her ear, "I never want to hurt you."

He pulled her back looking her in the eyes just for a moment before he reached up and kissed her softly on the forehead. Then he let go of her, turned, and started picking up kindling. Linda Kay stood there with her mouth agape trying to figure out what to do or what to say. At last, she pulled herself together asking, "Is there anything I can do to help?"

"No, you're fine I'm just going try to get a fire started, so we can light this torch. Someone has been in there otherwise, there wouldn't be a torch. There's no telling what we will be able to find. It may be nothing, may be a lot, but we have to check it out. Without this torch, we can't see a thing, it would be a total waste of our time. If these things hadn't been just inside the mouth of the cave, I would've never found them. So, keep your fingers crossed that I get this thing going. If the conditions are right, inside of this cave, maybe we could stay here for the night. We wouldn't have that long walk back to the homestead. Also, tomorrow we won't have quite so far to walk in search of new territory. If we can get to the other side of this island, maybe there would be a way off the island and we can get back to civilization.

"You got it, I'm on your side, and if there's anything I can do to help you just tell me. I'll give it my all, I promise."

She sat back and watched as he began to knock the flint rock against another rock and watch the sparks fly into the kindling. As George continued striking the rocks together, Linda Kay kept her hopes high that he could accomplish what he wanted done. At last, smoke began to rise and then flames followed. George smiled as he placed the rocks back in his pocket picked up the torch and lit it. He then motioned for Linda Kay to follow him.

The torch illuminated the walls of the cave much more than what Linda Kay thought it would. Throughout the cave, there were more torches mounted on the walls. George took another one down handed it to Linda Kay and lit it from his giving them much brighter light. They could see into the nooks and crannies of the cave. There was rubbish that had been left behind by someone a long time ago. There ere a few wooden stakes scattered on the cave floor. Spider webs hung from the walls of the cave. As the light hit the spider webs, it would look like there were raindrops sprinkled through the web. George knew that it was the light reflecting off of the spiders themselves and not the web. He did not bring that to Linda Kay's attention. He remembered just how afraid of spiders she was.

All at once Linda Kay grabbed George's arm saying, "Let's get out of here, fast."

Linda Kay couldn't move very fast with the torch in one hand and a crutch in the other. She placed the torch back on the wall saying, "Come on, let's go, let's go."

"Wait, slow down. You're going to fall, I'll help you." He grabbed hold of Linda Kay's arm trying to help steady her. "What's wrong with you? Why are we running?"

"I don't know; there's something wrong I can feel it. Evil is in here with us. Please, I want out of here." About that time, there was a loud rumble sound, causing them to pause just for a moment to try and figure out the sound. George picked up Linda Kay and started running. Her crutch clattered to the floor. George didn't stop to retrieve it. He was afraid it was a rock slide, and they would be trapped. George had to get them out quickly, so he just kept running. His heart was beating fast, pounding against the wall of his chest. Anxiety over a possible cave-in had George in a state of panic. Once he rounded the corner and could see the mouth of the cave, he knew he was too late. The rocks were tumbling, closing the exit off. He took in a deep breath, trying to think logically. He knew he couldn't go off in a state of hysterics; he had to protect Linda Kay. He set her down gently on the floor telling her he would be back. He ran to retrieve her crutch and the torches.

When he returned to Linda Kay's side, he sat down beside her, "I think maybe it's time for that talk now instead of tonight. I need to try and understand what you're telling me. I need to take heed when you tell me there's an emergency. You're right. There is something strange going on. I don't understand it, and you have a better insight than I do. So, when you tell me something, I promise you, I will immediately take heed. It doesn't matter if I don't understand what you're talking about. I just need to do what you tell me. I know I was a little late in learning this lesson, but I will do everything I can to protect us and to get us out of here safely. I don't know if there's another exit or not, and has it also been sealed up? I don't know. We have to explore the rest of this cave and try to find an exit. We have enough food with us for today, but I think we better ration it."

"Thank you, George, I appreciate you saying that, it's really not my imagination. It's something I feel. I know it is hard to try to explain. It's like a voice in my head that's telling me something's wrong. Most of the time, I don't know what it is, but I know it's out there lurking and waiting for something bad to happen. I wish I could explain it better but I can't, I don't know how. Sometimes I call it a blessing, and other times I call it a curse. I can't really change things. It just gives me a warning that something's coming. We're really going to have to be careful and watch out for one another. And you're right; we have to explore this cave and look for another exit, and I think we better get started."

George helped Linda Kay to her feet and steadied her on her crutch. Before he let go of her, he looked deep into her eyes. It was as if something had a hold of him and wouldn't let him turn loose of her. Her eyes were filled with worry and concern. It broke George's heart to see her so afraid. It hurt him even worse knowing there may not be a thing he could do. They may both die trapped in this cave.

"I know you don't want to hear this; I can't help it. I've got to tell you now, because I don't know if we're going to make it out of here or not. If we don't, there are things I want you to know. I hope you won't to be angry with me, Linda Kay, but I have to tell you that I love you as much as ever. I have never quit loving you, and I never will. Please hear me out; at this point it's something I had to tell you. If something were to happen to us, I want you to know just how wonderful I think you are."

George took his index finger placed it under her chin and lifted her face so he could look into her eyes. Instead, what he saw were tears running down her cheeks.

"Oh, Linda Kay, please don't cry, I never want to hurt you, ever. I'm sorry. I guess I should've never said anything. I can't help how I feel. You are and always have been the love of my life. I still pray that someday you will listen to what happened that day. I'm sorry, Linda Kay; I really didn't mean to mention this. I wanted to wait until you were ready to hear what happened. Now I don't know how long we have, and I just don't want to waste one minute of time."

"I don't know if I ever want to know what was going on that day. You know how I always felt about you. What I saw left me with enough hurt to last me a lifetime. My heart was crushed, and I don't want to go through that again. I'm afraid if we start to talk about what was going on then, I will have to live through the pain once more. Don't ask me to go through that again please, I don't think I could do it."

This time a tear fell from his eyes as he said, "Okay." He kissed her lightly on the lips before saying, "Let's go search the cave."

George's shoulders were slumped in defeat; in his mind, the rejection from Linda Kay was worse than being trapped in the cave with no way of escape. Knowing that their time was now limited was very scary. He knew he had to give it his all. He had to do everything in his power to save Linda Kay that was first and foremost in his mind.

CHAPTER 21

ELIZABETH WAS STANDING ON THE VERANDA looking at the sunrise. It was so beautiful; she thought about Linda Kay standing there with her and how they had shared the beauty of the morning sun before Linda Kay had been whisked away from her. God, she missed her. Elizabeth had made it a ritual to get up every morning and play like she was sharing this time with Linda Kay. She stood out on the veranda and described that beautiful sunrise to Linda Kay every morning. That was how she shares a moment in time with her each morning.

Elizabeth didn't like the conversation she had with the Sheriff yesterday. From the way he had talked, they were going to stop the search for Linda Kay and George today. She didn't know what she could do. Now she had nobody to help her find her best friend. She felt abandoned. Elizabeth felt that she could not live with the fact that they just give up searching for her. What if Linda Kay was out there praying for help? Not knowing if they were dead or alive made it impossible for Elizabeth to turn her back and walk away. Were they out there somewhere in the unknown needing help? Were they starving to death? Had they found any shelter? The questions could go on and on, but the torment of not knowing was tearing Elizabeth's heart apart, she loved her friends so much.

Elizabeth understood that everyone had to get back to their lives. They had families and loved ones to care for. They had jobs to go to or farms to tend. They had to get back to their own lives. Everyone here had been so kind to her, she couldn't fault them for giving up the search. She could understand why Linda Kay loved it here. Linda Kay was also right; the countryside and the mountains were beautiful here. The peace and quiet was tranquil and carried its own kind of beauty. She just wished Linda Kay was here to share it with her. She thought to herself, *That makes it sound like I plan on staying here. I just don't know; maybe I will, and maybe I just have to wait and see what my future holds.*

She had to pull herself back to reality; this was going to be her first day at work. She was excited and scared of the unknown. She slowly turned and walked back inside to get dressed. She did not want to be late for her first day at work.

Elizabeth stopped in front of the post office and put her car in park. She was thinking, *What in the world am I doing here? I know nothing about working in a post office. I hate to go somewhere and make people think I'm stupid.* She knew she wasn't stupid; she was actually a very bright girl. She had just never given it a thought about what went on in a post office. As long as she got her mail, that was all she cared. Now she was just going to have to show how inept she was at this job. She didn't have a choice; she couldn't leave without knowing the whereabouts of Linda Kay. She felt as if she had no choice but to stay here and try to learn a new way of life. After all, the people in this small town had taken the time out of their lives to help her. That was a kindness she couldn't turn her back on without giving back everything she could.

She couldn't believe that she was actually going to look at some property today. She had never thought about buying property. This place has a log cabin on the property. She couldn't envision that being her way of life, but who knows? She really was warming up to this little town. She was still very confused over whether she should or shouldn't buy property. She didn't even know if she was going to stay here. She was told it would be a great investment one way or the other; she wouldn't lose. Anyway, she was going to look at it and then make the decision. Then a quick thought ran through her head: she had only come here for a week vacation. How strange life can be.

Now, she had quit a job that she had loved, and there she was in this strange little town all alone. She took in a deep breath and stepped out of the car straightening her spine, she walked into the post office as if she had all the confidence in the world.

Danny met her at the door and welcomed her. He wanted her to relax; he was aware that she had no experience in working for the post office. She was a bright girl, and he was sure that she would catch on quickly.

"The first thing that I usually do when I come in is to get me a cup of coffee. Come on I'll show you where it is."

Elizabeth diligently followed him. By the time, they had got a cup of coffee; she was starting to relax. Then he started explaining some of the ins and outs of working at the post office. By the end of the day, her mind was whirling with new information. She found it to be an exciting and new experience, but she also knew she had a lot to learn.

She was in the process of leaving when the Sheriff walked in. She looked at him and tears begin to fill her eyes, "Did you hear anything?"

"I'm sorry, but no, we found nothing. What I came to tell you is that we have just called off the search party."

With that, tears streamed down her face.

"What can I do now? I have to find her, tell me how I search for myself. I will do it."

Danny walked up to her and gave her a hug, assuring her that they would figure a way. They would not give up on finding Linda Kay and George. The Sheriff gave his apologies once more before leaving.

Danny asked her, "What are your plans for Saturday?"

"I don't have any plans. I don't know anything to do"

"Why don't we go out Saturday morning and look for Linda Kay and George? I have a canoe; we can take that. I can fix us a picnic lunch, and we can spend the day searching for them. Would you like that?"

Elizabeth's heart began to pound rapidly as she thought back to that awful day in the canoe. At the same time, she knew they would be the only ones looking for them. It was all she could do to keep from crying. She wanted to decline, but in her heart of hearts, she knew she couldn't do that she would have to take every opportunity to search for Linda Kay and George.

"I would love it; I appreciate it more than I can tell you. Please, let me bring the picnic lunch. That way at least I will feel like I've done something."

Danny laughed and said, "I'm really glad you offered to do that because I'm afraid my lunch really wouldn't be very good, edible but not good. I think we should get an early start. What do you say? I pick you up at 7:00 Saturday morning. That way we are to be able to get in the water by 8:00. Will that be okay with you?"

"That sounds wonderful to me. How do you like cold fried chicken?"

"I love it a lot better than a sandwich."

"Good, I'll fry some chicken. I promise you, we won't go hungry, if you promise not to lose the canoe."

"I know you have to be nervous about getting back in a canoe; that's only logical. I promise, you that was a freak accident. It doesn't happen very often. In fact, I only know of one other accident that happened when I was a kid. I really don't think you have to worry, and I promise you will be wearing a life jacket. So, try to relax, and we'll spend the day searching for our friends."

"Thank you so much; I really do appreciate it. Danny, I know this is a change of subject, but I'd like to ask you a question if you don't mind?"

"I don't mind at all, what's your problem?"

"Terrence asked me if I would come and see him sometimes. I told him I would. I had been told that really he's a good person. That he just had a lot of problems. But I'm a little leery on whether I should go. I would appreciate your opinion."

"I think it would be a good idea with everything he has been through. If you tell him to add me to his visitation list, I would love to go see him sometimes. When he lost his wife is when everything changed for him. It was as if no one could reach him. I hope now we will be able to reconnect and become friends again and help him to get his life back on track."

"I'll be happy to do that; he actually seemed rather depressed the last time I went to see him. I'm sure he would appreciate someone he knows coming to see him. It's always nice to have a friend in your corner.

"I got one more thing I'd like to throw at you and see what you think. Mary and Trinity told me about some property that's close to the post office; it's supposed to have a cabin on it. They told me it needed a lot of work. I'm supposed to go look at it this afternoon... Do you think that's a good idea? They told me they thought it would be a good investment if I decide not to stay here."

"I know the property they're talking about. I hadn't thought about it before, but yes, personally, I think it would be a great idea. Even if you decide not to stay, it would be a great investment. The location is wonderful for the people that come and spend their summers here. Yes; I agree, I don't think you can lose. Because I know you can get that property really cheap. The owners just want to get rid of it and stop paying the taxes on it. Their kids are all grown and have their own families to take care of. The couple that owns the property doesn't drive anymore, and they can't really get around very well. So, they really don't have any use for the property anymore. There was a time it was really nice property, and yes, it does need a lot of work, but with some tender loving care, I think it would be a good investment."

"Thank you for everything you're doing for me. I really do appreciate it. I'll see you in the morning, you have a good evening."

With that Elizabeth softly closed the door behind her. She would have just enough time to go by the jail and see Terrence before they cut visitation off for the day.

As nervous as she was, once Terrence was seated in front of her she began to relax. Things seemed to be normal as if this is the way things should be. Terrence was excited at the fact that Danny wanted to come see him. You could see the sparkle in his eyes and the way life begins to seep back into his soul. Elizabeth told him about her new job and just the basics of what was going on in her life. She also told him of the plans to go look for Linda Kay and George. As Elizabeth got ready to leave, Terrence apologized to her once again. Elizabeth let him know that she didn't want him to talk about that anymore; that was the past, and it was time to look toward the future. Elizabeth felt good about herself when she left the jail. She felt like she had enlightened his life.

Now she was going to meet with Mary and Trinity and look at that old log cabin to see what kind of mess she was getting into. She didn't know whether to say she hoped that she would like it or not. She still doesn't know whether she would be staying here or moving on. If she was going to stay here, she really wanted to be closer into town with more people around. So, she was going to look at it without bias. Mary and Trinity were already there when she pulled into the drive. Elizabeth stepped out of the car with a look of devastation written across her face.

"I don't believe this; you told me it needed a lot of work. What this needs is to be torn down and another one jacked under it. What are you thinking?"

Trinity laughed, "I know it's not much to look at now, but I see beauty in all this devastation. I can fix it, and I can offer you a deal that you can't turn down on having it fixed up, I promise. I can tell you this; they're almost ready to pay you to take this property. I can promise you by the time I finish with it that you definitely can get your money back and lot more than what you pay. Here comes Sarah now; she will go over the price with you. Then you do what you think is right."

In the end, Elizabeth signed the paperwork. She was in the process of buying a broken-down home on a shabby-looking piece of property. She was shaking her head as she left; she must have had rocks in her head to do such a thing, but she did it. *I don't know why I let them talk me into it. I made the decision, now have to live with it.*

She had a spring in her step as she headed for the grocery store. She wanted to pick up a few items and get home before dark. She had just about enough time to do that.

She has high hopes that when she went to sleep tonight that she could feel like her life was filled with new excitement and new learning experiences. Her head was filled with all the things she learned about her new job. At the same time, she was scared at the thoughts of spending her savings on that broken-down property. Her heart ached at the loneliness of Linda Kay not being there to share things with. She was filled with high hopes of maybe finding Linda Kay this weekend, and at the same time, she was filled with panic at the thoughts of getting in that canoe. She drifted off to sleep, tears dripping on her pillow.

Chapter 22

Linda Kay was getting very tired they had walked for a long time with no signs of a way out of the cave. She was beginning to feel very depressed at the thoughts of being trapped. Linda Kay knew there was no way she could continue to drag that crutch along. Her arm ached from leaning on the crutch. Her underarm was sore and raw; it was to the point she wanted to scream with every step. As they rounded a corner in the cave, there seemed to be steam rising from the floor. George stopped abruptly and helped Linda Kay to sit on the floor while he went to check out what was going on. He was afraid it might be some kind of poisonous gas, although he couldn't smell anything that made it seem dangerous. He just had a check in his soul that made him very leery of what this could be. As he walked closer, he realized that it was a big hole in the cave floor that was filled with warm water. It was cool in the cave, so with the water being warm, it caused steam to rise. It was an odd-looking situation, and George didn't know if it was some kind of odorless gas or just water.

George returned to Linda Kay, telling her what he had found.

"My advice is that we stay away from that. It may be nothing but water, I just don't know. I'm leery of it. It just seems so odd to me that there would be a large hole filled with water in the middle of this cave. It has to be coming from underground. I'm afraid it could be some kind of poison gas. I'm not saying it is, I'm just saying I'd rather we avoid it. Are you ready to continue our search for a way out of here?"

"I'm sorry, George, but no; I just don't feel like I can go anywhere right now. I have to have a break please bear with me. I really don't want to complain, and I tried very hard to keep my mouth shut. The truth is, I'm in a lot of pain I just can't go any farther. My arm is sore and raw; I can feel the blood running down my side. I can't use that crutch any more until my arm gets well, it's just too sore, and the pain is getting unbearable for me. I can't walk without the crutch, and for now, I can't walk with it. You will just have to go without me. I'm sorry, George, I don't want to be a wimp, and I know it's a burden to you, but I did the best I could. I just can't help it; I can't go any farther without a break.

"I don't know if it's day or night I just know I'm tired and sleepy. Please let me just take a nap, and maybe when you come back, I'll be able to go again."

"I'm not going to push you; I wish you had told me earlier that you were in pain. We would have stopped and let you rest a while. I don't know how much pain you're in if you don't tell me. It will take longer for you to get over the soreness under your arm than if we had stopped and rested a while. So, from now on, please let me know immediately if you're in pain and you need a break. Now let me take a look at that arm."

"You've got to be kidding."

"No, I'm not kidding; I need to know what we're looking at."

Linda Kay took in a deep breath before saying, "Maybe you're right. I know I pushed it too far. I really shouldn't have."

With that, she slipped her arm out of her shirt and raised it high so George could take a look at the damage. He gasped when he saw how raw her skin was; sure enough there had been blood running down her side.

"You're right. You're not going any farther today." He kissed her on top of the head. "I'm going to go just a little farther and see if I spot anything. I promise you, I won't go very far, then I will turn around and come back. After we both have a few hour's rest, I'll resume the search alone. You need some time to let that ankle heal any way. Now lie down and try to get some rest. I will not be gone long, I promise."

George stood up and pivoted to leave when Elizabeth shouted out, "Oh, George, look at that. She pointed to the far wall of the cave; it was a lit with a beautiful rainbow of color. Have you noticed that when the light from your torch hits the walls in here, it makes a beautiful rainbow? The rainbows seem to be scattered all over this part of the cave, it's beautiful."

"Yes, I've noticed it's crystals that are in the wall of the cave. There are some pretty big ones, and when the light reflects off of them, it puts out a beautiful array of color."

"You know that crystals are full of positive energy. I'm thankful they are there; it makes me feel better. I didn't notice any of them before; did you happen to see if they were in the other part of the cave?"

"Actually no, I didn't notice any crystals until we got to this section. Isn't that odd? I wonder if it has anything to do with that pond. Please just stay away from that thing while I'm gone." George hesitated once again and his shoulders slumped. "Linda Kay, I need to talk to you before I go. I'm going to be honest with you, that pond is bothering me. I don't know how close we should be to that thing. My concern is whether or not that is odorless gas or just water. I just feel like I need to get you away from here. I'm like you; I don't know if it's day or night either. I'm just as desperate to find a way out. If I find someplace that looks a little safer, I'm going to come back and get you. I will help you to move to a safer location. I'll be right back. If I don't find anything any better, we will both lie down here and sleep; both of us could use a rest."

"Thank you, George. I appreciate you just letting me rest a while."

George had no more than walked away when Linda Kay lay down and closed her eyes. She immediately drifted off into a deep hard slumber letting dreams play in her head. For the first few minutes, she smiled in her sleep, as if she was a child with no cares or worries.

George was as good as his word. He wasn't gone long before he hurried back to check on Linda Kay. As he drew close, he could hear her moaning and groaning in her sleep. She was having another nightmare. George pulled her close to him, holding her gently and cooed to her that she was okay. He slowly and gently woke her up soothing her constantly. He told her she would be okay; she was having another nightmare.

"Do you want to talk about it? Can you remember what you were dreaming?"

"Yeah, I remember it was about those little girls again. My heart goes out to those little girls. George, you have got to listen to me, those little girls I told you about before; they used to live here on this island. That was their house that we were staying in. This time, the father told them that he had to go away for a while and hunt for food for the winter. He told them that he would be gone maybe two weeks. He told them to stay close to the house and to not let anyone in the house. To 'keep the door locked while I'm gone. I will get back as soon as I can to check on you.

"'Mamie you're the oldest I need you to watch out for your sisters. You know how to use my shotgun, do not play with it. If you need to protect you or your sisters, do not hesitate to use it. I'm leaving it up there where you can get easy access.' He hugged Mamie as he told her how sorry he was to go. If he didn't, they would not have food for the winter. Going hunting was his only choice. As he waved goodbye to the girls, he told them how much he loved them, and he would return as soon as possible.

"George, I'm telling you those little girls were really scared staying by their selves. They really weren't old enough to run a household, but they were going to have to take on the responsibility. I'm telling you, George, if you could see what those kids had to go through on a daily basis it would break your heart, too. They were doing more work than what most adults do today. They were very poor, but they were thankful they had each other. They needed someone to take care of them. I understand, for back in those days the father had no choice but to leave them or else he wouldn't be able to feed them through the winter. He loved his kids a lot, but he had to take care of them the best way he knew how. I don't mean to sound like he's trying to abuse those kids, because he's not. I understand that he was doing all he could to take good care of them. It doesn't change the fact that it's heartbreaking to watch. George, I feel those little girls' pain. I may not know how to put it in words other than to say it's heartbreaking."

"Try not to think so much about them; it was a long time ago. They have moved on now I'm sure they're living different lives they're probably very happy today. Right now, I worry about you; I want to get you out of here. I want to see you happy again. I'm here with you now. I'm doing everything I can to get you to safety once more. Right now, I think we need to rest and take up searching again when we get up. What do you say; you sit up for a little while, and let's eat something from what we have left. Then we'll both get some rest. You won't need to worry anymore tonight I will be right here by your side. Then we'll see what tomorrow brings."

Linda Kay slowly sat up as she said, "I'm almost afraid to eat anything right now. I'm afraid we will get hungrier later."

"I know what you're saying, but the strawberries will begin to get mushy, you know they won't last. I think we should stretch them out as far as we can, but we need to eat them before they rot. The greens are already wilting, so we will need to eat that before it gets too bad. The only other thing we have that is holding up is our tomatoes. With it being cool in the cave, they should last the longest, we will save them for last. We will have to eat our food wisely."

With that, they had a small portion of greens and a couple of strawberries before lying down and closing their eyes. George pulled Linda Kay close to him, as he told her to sleep comfortable.

"I'll be right here to look out for you."

Chapter 23

Elizabeth rose early the next morning and dressed quickly. Her head was in the clouds as she went downstairs for a cup of coffee. Her mind drifting over everything she had learned the day before. She had high hopes that she could remember exactly how to do what she had been taught.

She really liked her boss and hoped he would be pleased with her. She didn't know what it was about Danny, but she was really attracted to him. She remembered the first time she saw him and how tongue-tied she got. She knew she would have to guard her feelings; he was very nice, but she was sure he didn't want to get caught in a trap by some girl. If he did, he could've had his pick of any girl in this town. There were some beautiful girls there, and they all seemed to think a lot of Danny, but that was as far as it went. Everyone was friends with Danny. She had never been one who wanted to take on the responsibility of someone else. She had always wanted to live her own life, so maybe that's the way Danny was. Anyway, she was going to spend time with him this weekend having a very nice time looking for Linda Kay and George.

In a lot of ways, this little town was great to her. She didn't quite understand their ways. But she was learning fast on how to fit in. On the other hand, she had never known such kindness from others. It seemed that each day she was getting more confused. She didn't want to give up her city ways, and at the same time, she never wanted to leave this place. She just wasn't sure she wanted to get that invested here. She knew in her heart that each day that went by she was falling more and more in love with this little town. The slow pace, sacrificing for your neighbors, and the giving of oneself was more than she had ever known. She definitely understood now why Linda Kay said she wanted to come home.

The word home has a totally different meaning in this small town. I would never be able to explain that to someone else. I now understand what Linda Kay meant when she said that the walls of that cabin permeated with love, she thought. All at once, Elizabeth realized how really free she was and just how happy she would be if only Linda Kay was there to share it with her.

Elizabeth left the house early and headed for work. Her head was full of the new things she was learning, and she was too nervous to wait any longer. She was sure she would have to wait for Danny to arrive and unlock the door before she could get in. It would be okay, but she was totally surprised when she got there to find that Danny was already inside working. She knocked on the door, alerting Danny of her arrival.

As he came to unlock the door, he had a big smile on his face.

"Good morning, Elizabeth! I hope you're doing well this morning."

"Do you always wake up in such a good mood? How do you do it?"

"Oh yes, morning is my favorite time of the day. No one has messed with my Wheaties yet. It's the afternoon when everyone puts in their complaints because they didn't get the letter they wanted that my mood shifts."

"Okay, I'll try to remember that one. I've never looked at it that way, but maybe with practice my brain could take on that concept. Oh well, change of subject; I'm ready to see how much I retained from yesterday."

"I hope you can deal with me."

"I'm sure I can."

"I don't know; you have already forgotten the first rule." Elizabeth got a panicked look on her face. Then Danny said, "You didn't head for the coffee pot." They laughed as he said, "Come on, let's get a cup of coffee to get the day started. You learn fast. I don't think we're going to have a problem. You get along well with everyone who comes in. That's one part you didn't have to learn it just comes natural to you. That's a lot of your charm. So, come on back, and we'll get started."

"I hope you don't mind, but at lunch today, I plan on going to sign the final papers on that house. I have never heard of a home loan going through as quickly as this one has. I thought it would be six or eight weeks at least. Hopefully, it won't take too long, and I won't be late coming back from lunch."

"The difference is you're dealing with a small-town bank and realtor office that knows everything about the property around here. They don't have to do a lot of research; they've already got it. They already know everyone that ever owned that property. They also know if anything is owed on the property," Danny laughed as he said, "Welcome to our world. You'll learn that can be a good thing and that could be a bad thing because everyone in this town knows your business. You may be a little late coming back from lunch, but in this case, it won't be a problem; you will be excused."

"I just wish I felt better about the purchase. Have you looked at that property in a while? Trinity says he can make it look good. While I don't want to hurt Trinity's feelings, honestly I have my doubts; that place looks horrible. I may have just bought a pig in a poke and wasted my life savings. It doesn't matter how small my savings was, I had worked hard for it. Now I get to start all over, and that's a little scary to me. I don't know; it may have been the dumbest thing I have ever done."

Danny laughed again.

"You underestimate our Trinity. If he says it will look good, you can carry it to the bank. Otherwise, he would've told you to walk away from it. No, if Trinity tells you he can do it, you're in for a wonderful surprise. Okay, you can follow me. Now we'll start to sort the mail."

It had been a long day, and Elizabeth learned that there was a lot more to this job than what she had originally thought. She found it to be very interesting and appreciated, the opportunity that she had been given. She really was catching on quick and was astonished at what all went in to the postal work.

Before she knew it, it was Wednesday, and she had promised Terrence that she would be there today. Terrence always seemed to be excited about the company and any information she could give him about what was going on with his friends and family. Mostly about his mother; he loved that woman dearly. Elizabeth thought the one thing he regretted most of all was hurting his mom the way he did. He knew in his heart it was time for him to let go of his hurt and take up life and living again. He had discussed that with Elizabeth quite often. It was as if he was trying to seek her approval on which way to go in his life. Elizabeth mentioned to Danny that after work, she was going to visit Terrence.

Danny asked, "Would you mind if I go with you today? I found out yesterday that I have been added to the visitation list."

"No, I wouldn't mind at all. In fact, I think I would feel a lot more comfortable if someone was with me."

Terrence's eyes lit up with excitement when he saw the two of them waiting to talk to him. There was so much joy in Terrence's voice and at the same time so much sadness.

As he asked Danny, "How can I possibly straighten my life out now? You know after I lost Doris, I felt like my life had come to an end, and from there, I screwed everything up. Without Doris by my side, sometimes I think it doesn't matter. I guess I'm just screwed up in the head, but I want you to know I appreciate you coming to see me. Both of you, I really need your friendship; I hope that there's some way I can get my life back together."

Danny put a smile on his face as he told Terrence, "You will be just fine. You will be out going to court any day now. I'm sure that you will get probation. Then you will have Elizabeth and me to knock sense into you if you need it. There will be no more of your silly decisions. The people in this town love you and care about you, and we're all going to be there to kick you in the pants if you misbehave again."

By the time they left, everything felt better, for the first time, Elizabeth had seen signs that Terrence had just smiled from his heart.

Elizabeth looked up again and smiled, "You know I feel good about coming to see him. He needs someone to care about him, and I need to feel as if I have helped someone."

Danny pulled her close to him and gave her a slight hug.

"That is what makes you such a special person."

That lifted Elizabeth's heart and made her feel better as if maybe her life would go on after all.

By the time Friday afternoon rolled around, Elizabeth was excited about the possibility of finding her best friend. At the same time, she was still filled with anxieties about the canoe trip. That night before she crawled into bed, she prayed for her and Danny's safety on the canoe ride. She also prayed that they would find George and Linda Kay waiting to be rescued. She wanted her friend home more than words could ever say.

Elizabeth woke up with a song in her heart and excitement dancing all around her. Her hopes were so high of finding her friend. She just knew today was going to be an absolutely wonderful day. She was just going to have to push the fear of the canoe ride to the back of her mind. She was trying to learn how to take things as they come and deal with them on a one-on-one basis. She no longer wanted to worry about what might happen and what could be in the future. There was enough in the day to day life without searching for things that may never come.

Elizabeth was in the kitchen packing a beautiful picnic lunch when she heard a knocking at the door. Out of habit, for an instant, she froze scared to move before reality hit her, and she reminded herself that she no longer had anything to fear. She headed for the front door with a spring in her step.

As she arrived at the door, she hollered out, "Who is it?"

Okay, some habits were going to be hard to break. Most of the people in this little town, when someone knocked on their door, they would shout out, "Come on in!" with enthusiasm in their voices. Elizabeth may be a city slicker, but she knew not everyone was your neighbor, so she didn't know if she could ever break the habit of finding out who was at her door before she invited someone in.

"It's Danny."

Elizabeth was excited at the sound of Danny's voice as she opened the door with a smile on her face.

"Good morning, you made it here just in time to help me."

"It seems like my timing is always just right to find myself a job, but there is no one I had rather help than a pretty lady like you."

"Come on in the kitchen with me and get yourself a cup of coffee. I'm just finishing up packing us a picnic lunch. The cups are in that cabinet right above the coffee pot. Help yourself"

"Wow, girl, you got enough food in there for three or four people. I bet I can handle it, that cake it looks good. It also looks homemade. Did you make it?"

"Yes, it was my mother's recipe. I hope you like it. All I have left to do is cut the cheese; it won't take me much longer." At last Elizabeth placed cheese into the basket closed the lid and said, "Okay, I guess I'm ready to go."

Danny placed his coffee cup in the sink and walked over and picked up the picnic basket telling Elizabeth he would carry it. Then he was giving her that beautiful smile again. She didn't know what it was about him, but there was definitely something about that smile that made her heart beat faster. He insisted that they both go to the river in his vehicle. He would see her home safely after they completed their search.

The ride to the Buffalo was wonderful and relaxing they talked about their likes and dislikes. They also shared a lot about their inner thoughts. Everything was fine until it was time to get in the canoe, and Elizabeth froze, standing on the shore. She was unable to move; she had shut herself off from everything around her. She stood there; she began to relive that dreadful day that she had lost Linda Kay. All at once, she started to scream begging for help. He stood there in a state of shock wondering what to do. He had to calm her down; he put his arm around her waist and guided her away from the shore. He continued talking and soothing her and telling her it was okay they did not have to go. After some time, Elizabeth began to regain her composure, apologizing desperately for making such a spectacle of herself. She told Danny she was sorry; she really did not mean to embarrass him. It took quite a while for him to calm her down. They sat on the bank of the river until she was completely composed.

Then Danny told her, "Come on I'll take you home. You don't have to go through this. You'd have to do a lot more than that to do something wrong."

"No, I've got to go through with this, otherwise, I'll never be able to do it. I need to go look for Linda Kay myself; otherwise, I'll never be able to deal with it. She's my best friend, and I can't just walk out on her. Whether she's dead or alive, she needs me now, and I can't walk away. I do ask that you stand by me. I need your strength and your guidance at this time. I hope you don't think badly of me Danny, but this is one time I do need someone to lean on."

"Okay, come on take my hand. We'll go together."

When they got back to the water's edge, Danny saw to it she put her life jacket on. He helped her in the canoe and went over the rules of safety. He assured her that at any time she felt uncomfortable, they would dock until she felt better and was able to continue their journey. Danny pushed the canoe into the water and climbed in and they were on their way.

Danny hollered to the front of the canoe Elizabeth, "Keep an eye out for any alcove that George and Linda Kay could've been swept into. If you spot something, alert me right away."

As they started around the cliff where the canoe had capsized, Elizabeth had to fight for control. Her heart began to pound; her pulse began to race, and she grabbed a hold of the sides of the canoe and gripped hard trying desperately to fight for control of herself. She felt sick to her stomach. She didn't want Danny to know how close she was to falling apart again. He had been so kind to put up with her already; he didn't deserve to go through any more of it. She had to be strong for Linda Kay. What if Linda Kay was out there somewhere, waiting for help? Elizabeth had to do whatever it would take to find her. She straightened her spine, swallowed hard, and took on the façade of being strong and able to handle whatever was to come. She wasn't able to fool Danny; he had seen the fear in her eyes.

He pulled over to the bank and said, "Okay it's time for a little break." He knew he had to get Elizabeth calmed down once more before they could continue on. Danny tried to act like he didn't know how upset she was; he let her think he was just ready for a break. As they got out of the canoe, Danny told Elizabeth that if they were to look around they might be able to find some arrowheads.

"I've always thought that they were very fascinating. I often wondered who used them. What had they done with them, did they kill something for food, and had they been used for survival, had they enriched someone's life?"

"That's really exciting to think that someone from the past had used them. The fact that arrowheads were at one time the way of life, it would've been very difficult for people to survive back then without them. Do you mind if I take a few minutes to look around and see what I can collect? I think I would love to do that."

"I would love to join you. I always like looking for arrowheads. To me, it's like traveling back in time."

Once they had collected some rocks and some arrowheads, they got back in the canoe with Elizabeth calm and ready to go forward once again.

CHAPTER 24

LINDA KAY WOKE-UP RUBBING SLEEP FROM HER EYES, she looked around the cave she saw that they still had a torch lit. Reality of where they were come to the forefront of her mind as she remembered that they were trapped in this cave with no way out. She was trying to keep panic out of her voice as she asked George, "How do you feel this morning?"

"Do you really know if it's morning?"

Linda Kay chuckled, "No I really don't know."

George inhaled a deep breath before he said, "I just know that you slept fretful. I was hoping that you could get some rest. We need to finish checking out this cave and see if there's a way out. How's your ankle? Are you going to be able to go on?"

"It's still sore and hurts, but it does feel better. It doesn't throb like it did. George, what are we going to do, is this it? Is this where we're going to die?"

"Linda Kay, you've always been more positive than that. You would never go down without a fight. I can tell you now I'm not ready to give up. I'm going to search the rest of this cave for a way out. If I don't find something this time around, I will keep looking. I will not give up; I will not quit until we are out of here."

"You're right, sorry; I guess I was just having a pity party. All that did for me was to make me ashamed of myself. There's no time like the present to get started searching, and I'm ready to go."

George helped Linda Kay up.

She smiled at him, saying, "Thank you for bringing me back to my senses, and we will get through this together." She squeezed his hand as she took the crutch from him and slid it under her arm.

Once again, they started out on a long search for an escape route. They walked praying for safety as they went, until at last Linda Kay said, "No more today, George, I'm getting tired and I am really hungry."

"I agree with you, I don't really know how long we've been walking but it seems like a long time."

He put his hand around her waist and guided her to the ledge on some of the rocks. He helped her to ease into a sitting position. He then propped the crutch against the rocks close to her. He reached into his knapsack and took out a measly portion of food for today. As he handed Linda Kay her portion, he looked deep into her eyes as he said, "One day soon, we will be out of this cave, and I promise you we will never go hungry again."

"I know, but right now, I'm thankful for what I have."

They ate their meager portions in silence and leaned back against the rock to rest.

Linda Kay jumped up and grabbed her crutch all at once. George set up with panic in his voice, "What's going on? What's wrong with you, Linda Kay?"

"This isn't right! We have to go back to the pool of water. Come on, we need to leave now."

Linda Kay shoved her crutch under her arm and took off, leaving George to follow.

"Wait a minute, what's going on? What are you afraid of? We know there's no way out back there. Why should we go back?"

"Linda Kay turned around to face him.

"The evil is lurking in here with us. I can feel it, ready to pounce once again. I just know we shouldn't have left the pond. Our only chance is to get back to that pond. We need to go, and we need to go now. Come on."

Suddenly rocks were being thrown toward them. A large rock hit George on his shoulder blade, almost knocking him over and causing him to scream out in pain. Linda Kay reached out and took George's hand to help him right himself.

"George, we have to get away from here fast. It's going to kill us with those stones!"

The stones and rocks were being thrown faster, harder, and more abundantly.

"I want to get back as soon as possible, hurry! It's our only chance to survive, George."

George didn't know what was going on, but he had learned from the past. When she said something was wrong, his only choice was to follow her direction. George reached out and put his arm around her waist, so he was able to help her move as fast as they could go. Rocks were still being flung all around them. Linda Kay ducked her head just in time to be able to bend and avoid the rock that soared past her, so close she could hear the sound of it as it whirled past her head.

"If we can make it back, we will be safer at least for a while. I just know that's where we should be."

They kept moving as fast as they could go, and at last the rocks started to slow until, as suddenly as it had started, it came to a stop. George breathed a sigh of relief; thank goodness hopefully that is all over.

"Can we take a break now? I'm really tired. We had walked a long way."

"George, I'm as tired as you are, but our life depends on getting back to that pond. No, I'm not going to stop. We are still in danger. I know we need to go back, and I'm going back now. I'm tired, too, I don't know that I'll make it, but I'm going to give it all I've got. I hope you will go with me."

"Of course, I'm going to go. There's no way I can let you go by yourself. It's just such a long walk back; we have been walking for hours in the other direction."

"Then I'll be walking for hours going back, but going back I am."

By the time they returned to that strange pond, they were both totally and completely exhausted. Linda Kay breathed a sigh of relief. She looked at George as she said, "Okay let me see that shoulder."

"I think it will be okay."

"I can tell you're in a lot of pain. Now let me see what it looks like."

He removed his t-shirt, trying to avoid moving his hurt shoulder. Then he slowly turned, so that she could see the damage that had been done. A loud gasp escaped from Linda Kay before she could stop it.

"George, your shoulder is swollen badly, and I believe we've got to figure out how to put it back into place."

Linda Kay had George to back up to the cave wall. She felt sick at her stomach, but she knew she had no choice; she had to shove hard on his shoulder to pop it back into place.

"I'm sorry, George, this is going to hurt, but I have no choice. It's what I've got to do." And with that, she shoved as hard as she could against his shoulder until she heard a loud pop. George could not help himself; he screamed out in pain. 'I hate to tell you this, but you got a pretty good gash back there. I've got to have something to put on it to stop the bleeding."

George handed her his shirt.

"Use this."

It was very difficult for Linda Kay to apply pressure on his shoulder in order to stop the bleeding. She could see the pain was excruciating to George.

"I'm sorry, George, I have no choice. I have to stop the bleeding; it's definitely going to be painful, but I have to do this."

Once she got the bleeding to stop, she rinsed his shirt in the pool of water. George begged her to stop because he still didn't know if that was just water or an odorless chemical. Linda Kay rinsed all the blood she could out of his shirt before she wrung it out and made a sling for his arm.

Linda Kay was tired and exhausted; she leaned her head back against the rock and closed her eyes. She was so thankful for the coolness of the cave; she lay down on the rocks next to the pool and fell asleep.

She woke up screaming and crying, and George was trying to calm her down to no avail. Even when she became fully awake, she was distraught.

He was having a hard time trying to talk to her.

"Please tell me what's wrong?" He pulled her tight, hugging her close, rubbing her back trying to soothe her.

"I was dreaming about the little girls that lived in the house. They were trying to clean the house. They each took a different chore and were doing the best job they could. They were happy, laughing children who just wanted everything right when their daddy came home. All of the sudden, there was a knock at the door; they all seemed to freeze in place. They remembered what their daddy had told them; 'Don't let anyone in the house while I'm gone.' At last, Mamie got the nerve to say, 'Who is it?' As she ran to retrieve the gun, Bernice begged her to wait.

"'At last there was a deep voice at the door that said, 'I come here to talk to your daddy, where is he?' Again, Mamie answered, 'He's not here right now.' I'm telling you, George, it was as if I was standing in the room with them, but yet I couldn't help them in any way. All I could do was stand there and watch. I could feel how scared they were. One at a time, I could feel their hearts beat, hard and rapid. They were frightened beyond words. I knew how unsure they were of themselves, while trying to answer the man's questions that he was shouting through the door at them. My heart was breaking for them as I stood there helpless and unable to do a thing for them other than to watch the panic and the anguish that those little kids were going through. I am telling you, these kids are real, they were in the house, and this did happen, and it's horrible."

"I understand what you're telling me. Just talk it out, get it off your chest. I'm here with you. I'm not going to leave your side. You will feel better once you tell it all."

Linda Kay laid her head against George's chest. It was as if she was going through the dream once again only this time, she was awake.

"The man demanded to know the whereabouts of their father, and restated, 'I told you I want to talk to him. Well speak up girl; I haven't got all day to fool with you.' Mamie turned around and looked at each of the other kids before she answered, 'He's hunting he'll be back later today.'

"'Well, let me in, so I can sit a spell. You can give me a cool drink of water.'

"'You can get a cool drink of water out of the river, and you can sit by the river while you wait. Now go away and leave us alone.'

"'Girl, you just don't have respect for people. Now you open that door up, and act nice to your neighbors like you're supposed to be.' Then Bernice looked at Mamie and whispered, 'That is the polite thing to do.' And Mamie whispered back, 'I know that it is, but that's not what daddy told us to do. I've got to do what daddy said.' Bernice had a question in her voice as she said, 'You're right, I suppose we do.'

"At last, Mamie answered him, 'I'm sorry sir, but you can't come in until my daddy gets home. So, I have to ask you to please leave, and come back later when my daddy's here.'"

"'You are an insolent child; you will get your due.' With that, they could hear his footsteps as he began to walk away. They all gave a sigh of relief, and after a minute, their hearts began to slow in pace. They began to relax and went back to their chores. Laughing and talking as they worked, putting the stranger's voice behind them. The day wore on without any further events. Yet Mamie stayed on high alert. She took her dad's words to heart, and no matter what she had to do to protect her sisters, she would do it. Mamie would not let any of them go outside for any reason. If they needed to go to the restroom, she made them use the nighttime bucket. They thought Mamie was being mean to them because they just wanted to go outside and play. Yet she told them, no, they would play games inside today. She tried hard to keep them entertained, and at the same time, she felt she had to try to keep them safe. Mamie read a story to them. Then she took down the button jar, and let them play with the all the different buttons. They sorted them into colors and sizes. She even made some paste out of flour and water and let them glue the buttons to paper making different shapes that seemed to keep them occupied for quite a while. She let them play hide and go seek in the house. Even though Mamie knew normally that was against the rules. She reasoned out that this one time, Daddy would forgive her. After all, she just wanted to protect her sisters. Even though Mamie wasn't much more than a child herself, she tried to make decisions.

"The day went along fine until they were getting ready for bed when once again they heard heavy footsteps on the porch. They all froze in place, afraid to even breathe. There was a loud knock on the door that made their hearts began to pound once more. Fear surged through their little bodies. Ruth began to cry, rubbing her eyes, she didn't understand why her sisters were scared, but she understood something was wrong. She grabbed a hold of Nell, hugging her legs tight trying to find comfort. Anxiety and fear filled the room as Mamie picked up the gun ready to defend them.

"'Who is it?'

"'You told me to come back later, it's later, and I'm here, so tell me where your daddy is. I want to talk to him.' This time his words sounded slurred, as if he had been drinking. That really put Mamie on alert. She knew a man that had been drinking could do some stupid stuff. She had overheard her daddy talking about one of their friends who had gotten drunk, and he had ended up in jail. The few times Mamie had seen someone drunk, they had scared her. She really wanted this man to leave now.

"'It's late, go away.'

"'I'm not going away this time I'm coming in. Now are you going to open the door and let me in, or am I going to break in? It really doesn't matter to me but I'm coming in. I'm going to be there to see your daddy. He owes me. I may just take what he owes me out in pleasure. After all, you have been rude and I told you, you're going to get what you deserve. Now save me the trouble and open this door. You're going to be mine.'

"'I will not open the door! You are not welcome in the house, go away and don't bother with coming back. We don't want you here. I'm warning you, do not try to break in my house you will regret it.'

"'What's a snotty nose kid like you going to do? If that's the way you want it, I'll show you who the boss is. Apparently, your daddy didn't raise you with any manners anyway.' There was a loud thudding noise against the door. It reminded Mamie of the thudding sound that was made when her daddy chopped wood. She remembered well when she was little how she would sit on the ground and watch her daddy as he chopped wood at the chopping block. There was no doubt in her mind that someone was using a hatchet chopping at their door. Fear was rising higher among the children, and they all gathered around Mamie. All of them were talking at once. Some told Mamie to shoot; some telling her not to shoot. They were all in a state of panic, and one would grab for the gun this way another grab for the gun from the other side. Everything was chaotic when the door opened, and there stood a giant of a man. Just as the gun went off no one knew exactly how or who pulled the trigger. Everyone was in too much of a panic, no one had control. Now they were all screaming and throwing up the contents of their stomachs. No one knew what to do.

"Mamie gathered everyone up and took them to their bedroom. Telling them all to be quiet, stop the screaming, they needed to talk. It took a few minutes but at last she got them calmed down enough that they were just crying. She asked them to please stay in there and calm down, and she would be back in a few minutes. She went back into the living room took one look at the man lying on the floor and was sick at her stomach again. She grabbed her stomach and ran out the door. She had to step over him in order to get out of the house. That made her stomach lurch even more. She barely made it outside to the yard before she lost the contents of her stomach.

"It took her a minute to gather her courage before she could go back in the house. She looked at the blood soaking into the wood floor as she fixed a pail of water and started trying to scrub as much of the blood up as she could. But for the longest time it seemed as if blood continued to flow from the man soaking into their wood floor. The harder Mamie tried to clean up the mess, the bigger it became. She wouldn't give up. She kept getting buckets of clean water and continued to scrub. Once she got as much cleaned up as possible, she covered his body with a sheet of muslin. Tears streamed from her eyes and ran down her face as she scrubbed and cleaned. The whole time, she was saying a silent prayer. She was asking God to please have mercy on their souls. She tried hard to pull herself together before going back and getting her sisters. She needed help to get the body out of the house.

"They tried pulling, pushing, and tugging but it did no good. The body was just too heavy for them to move. At last, Mamie said, 'I've got to take the muslin sheet off him. We will lay it out on the floor next to him. Then I will need you to help me to roll him on to the sheet.' At last, they grabbed the corners of the sheet and pulled it out the door with the body on it. It wasn't an easy job, but at last they had it out on the porch. Mamie knew they had to get him away from the house. There was a lot of mumbling and groaning, but everyone tried to pitch in and help, including three-year-old Ruth. At last he was off the porch, but that wasn't good enough for Mamie. She insisted that they move him to a stand of trees that was some distance from the house. They complained that their arms hurt, and they were tired, and they didn't want to move him anymore. Mamie wouldn't give up. They continue to tug and pull him across the yard until at last they had him in some trees away from the house.

"No one really slept that night, the girls cried and fretted. All of them scared and not knowing what to do. When daylight broke through, Mamie went outside and tried to dig a hole next to where he lay. The ground was too rocky, she was unable to dig. She just pulled the muslin sheet across his face as she said, 'I'm sorry, Mr.' With her head hanging low, she went back inside and started fixing breakfast for the younger kids. Everyone was grumpy and cranky that day. It was as if that was the day they started losing their childhood. Life was no longer free and happy. There wasn't a song in their voice or laughter from their hearts. They were all carrying a heavy weight in their hearts that no one knew how to put down.

"As it started to get dark things got even worse. Their life changed even more, and it wasn't for the better. For them, their life would never be the same again. There was a scratching at the door, everyone scurried as fast as they could and gathered around Mamie seeking comfort. Once again Mamie said, 'Who is it?' No one answered, but the scratching continued. Mamie didn't want the younger kids to know just how frightened she was. She tried to keep her composure about her as she said in a stern voice, 'Go away.'

"She started to reach for the gun when all at once a saltshaker flew off the kitchen table. It almost hit her in the head as it flew past her and hit the wall and fell to the floor with the crash. Salt scattered everywhere leaving the girls standing there with her mouths agape. Ruth started crying, Nell tried to console her as she asked Mamie, 'What are we going to do?'

"Mamie pulled them closer to her, trying to comfort them in the only way she knew how, when all at once the butter dish flung across the room and splattered against the wall. Mamie's heart was pounding, was about to pound out of her chest. As quickly as she could, she scurried the kids to the bedroom and pushed the door closed behind her. As fast as she could, she slammed the lock into place.

"The kids were all distraught; she tried hard to calm them down and keep herself pulled together at the same time. Things seem to be quieting down from the other room which helped her to calm the kids. They were all so tired from not sleeping the night before, they all fell asleep cuddled together in one bed.

"All at once, there was a loud piercing scream, and Mamie realized it was her. Everyone was awake now, staring at her with questioning eyes. Mamie had a long slash in her gown, blood was pouring from the hole. She slowly lifted her gown; she was bleeding heavily from a deep cut she had across her ribs. The pain was agonizing. She grabbed a muslin sheet off one of the beds and began applying pressure. Mamie realized there was no way they would be able to stay in that house. There was something unseen after them. Whatever it was, totally intended to hurt or to kill them. She was just a child, how was she supposed to deal with something like this? There was no one else to rely on, she had to step up and try to be the adult.

"She told Nell to grab Ruth up in her arms. She then told Bernice to hold onto Nell and to, 'Stay together, no matter what happens. Don't let go of the other person, we're getting out of here.' She unlocked the door to the bedroom, and they all ran for the front door. As they ran things, were being flung around the room, trying to hit them. As fast as Mamie could, she unlocked the front door, and they ran across the yard towards the river bank.

"The kids huddled together as tightly as possible at the edge of the water. Bernice asked Mamie, 'Why not take that man's boat? We can get off the island.'

"'Because we don't know what he would do to us if we got on his boat. If he were to sink the boat, we would probably drown. No, we're better off on land. There's no way we could all get out of that water. I suppose you're right, but what are we going to do, we can't just sit out here. Nell set there rocking Ruth back and forth, trying to soothe her. She was scared and confused, just like the rest of them. Her little body trembled from anxiety; she was in desperate need of a mother's love. Nell had done her very best to mother the child since the loss of their mother. She had never dealt with things like this. It wasn't the everyday needs of a child. Ruth was in need of the real comfort of her mother. It broke Nell's heart to see Ruth in such a state. She did everything she could to pour all the love she had in to that child.

"Bernice again chimed in, 'Well, what are we going to do?' Mamie replied with sternness in her voice, 'We are going to wait here on the beach until daylight. We're going to take everything one step at a time until Daddy gets back and gets us away from here. We'll do whatever we need to and be ready when something happens. Right now, I don't know anything else to do. We can't walk across water. We are trapped until Daddy returns.' You could hear a cold sternness in Mamie's voice that you felt she would carry through the rest of her life. She had been left in charge of her sisters, and she knew she really was incapable of handling something like this. She not only feared for her life, but the lives of her sisters."

Linda Kay was crying and shaking uncontrollably. George rubbed her back and pulled her close as he told her.

"That's enough for now. We'll talk later. You need to rest for now."

"But those little girls, George, they were tormented."

"I understand but right now you need to give it up. We'll talk later."

Chapter 25

Elizabeth stared at a stand of trees in the distance; there was something that looked weird to her. From here, she couldn't see exactly what it was that looked different, but she just felt that they should check it out.

She asked Danny, "Could we please go over there and check out that bank?"

"Of course, I don't see why not let's go."

He turned the canoe and headed in that direction. As they drew closer, it became apparent that there was something odd at the way the trees were spaced at the bank of the shore. They slowly began to round the edges of the bank, and sure enough, there was a gap between the trees that Danny had never been through. He turned the canoe and paddled slowly through the gap, looking around at territory that he had never seen before. After paddling around taking stock of everything that he could see, he pulled up next to the bank and docked the canoe.

"This is all new territory to me I thought maybe we might get out and look around is that okay with you?"

"Absolutely, there's something about this place that seems to draw me to it. I really would like to walk around and see what we can find. Hey Danny, look at this, there's footprints all around here."

"Just because I have never found this spot doesn't mean a lot of other people haven't. If you find a good fishing spot around here, you don't go telling your friends and neighbors. You keep it a secret it's just part of the code of the mountains. Those footprints could be from a lot of different people, so don't get your hopes up. Elizabeth, there are a lot of cutoffs on this river and I'm sure there are a lot of them that I haven't ever seen."

"Okay, I understand what you're saying, but I still would like to go wandering around the island with you. You never know what we might find."

"Sure, let's go." He reached out and took hold of her hand as they started up an incline. It was as if he had given her an electrical shock with the touch of his hand. She almost jerked her hand back she was so startled at the feel of his touch. She swallowed hard; it took her a moment to compose herself before she was able to continue discussing the new surroundings with him. Her mind began to drift, thinking only of how Danny's touch affected her. All at once, they came to a halt. Danny squeezed Elizabeth's hand drawing her attention. She looked up at him and followed his line of sight. There in front of them stood an old homestead.

Elizabeth didn't know what to think. She was not expecting to see and old homestead on this island. It looked totally deserted. Her voice was almost a whisper, "Are we going to check it out?"

"Definitely, we need to be careful, but yeah. I definitely want to check it out."

"I don't know what it is about this place, but it seems a little eerie to me. I feel like there's something I should be picking up on, but I just can't put my finger on it."

Danny laughed, "I guess you're right. It is a little weird feeling in here. I'm surprised this old building hasn't rotted down by now. I can't help it; I wonder how old this building is and who used to live here."

Danny walked up on the porch and slowly opened the door. Elizabeth followed him inside. They continued walking around the house checking everything out. At last Danny said, "George and Linda Kay are not here, so maybe we also need to get out. You're right this place kind of gives me the creeps, let's just go."

Danny didn't want to tell her that this house actually frightened him. It was as if things went on behind these doors that he never wanted to know about. Danny wanted to make light of everything, so he took a hold of Elizabeth's hand.

"Come on, what do you say we go down to the river bank and dig into that picnic lunch. I'm getting hungry."

This time Elizabeth laughed, "Sure I think I'm about ready for some fried chicken."

They found a nice shade close to the bank and spread out a blanket. Danny was pleasantly surprised by the lunch she spread out. They had fried chicken, deviled eggs, sliced tomatoes, pickled okra, and most of all, coconut cake.

They enjoyed each other's company as Elizabeth started telling Danny that Trinity had started to work on her house.

"It's very exciting to me to think I have my own place. I never really thought about owning my own property before. I just really didn't want the responsibility of it. Now I would just like to be closer to work and closer to more people. I love Linda Kay's house, and I love her property. It's beautiful, but I'm just used to people being around me all of the time. I don't like that isolated lonely feeling. At the same time, I'm still quite leery of what Trinity's going to be able to do with my place. I think I would be lucky if he could just get it livable. If he can't, I guess I'll just try to sell it and recoup some of my money."

"I keep telling you, you just haven't seen Trinity's work, I will lay you odds when he's finished with it, you will love it. I bet it will be the best-looking cabin in the area. I have no doubt that place will look like a new home when he's finished."

"Well, that really does help my feelings a lot. After all, if anyone should know, it would be you."

"Try to relax about your cabin; in the end, you will love it. I tell you what, if you don't like it, I will try to help you sell it. Once he gets the property cleaned off, it will look totally different. I know the weeds were so high and everything so overgrown, you couldn't really get to the back of the property. But you just wait and see that is a beautiful piece of property. I can tell you now just for the property alone you can get your money back. Even if there's not a cabin left on the lot you will be okay."

"Okay, I'll be glad to take it your word for it. You're right, I need to quit worrying about it so let's change the subject and have a good time."

It turned out to be an absolutely wonderful day for Elizabeth and Danny. They really enjoyed each other's company, and the time that they spent together. Danny had used every idea that he can come up with too prolong the day. At last, Danny had no choice; it was time to take Elizabeth home. He walked her to the door he couldn't constrain himself any longer. He tilted his head and lightly kissed her good night before thanking her for a beautiful day.

Elizabeth felt like she was floating on air. She didn't know when she had ever had such a wonderful time. That light kiss seemed to make her float up the stairs as she went to get ready for bed. The only thing that upset them both was that there was no sign of George or Linda Kay. Elizabeth felt guilty that she had had such a good time when Linda Kay was still lost. Was she wrong enjoying Danny's company? Should she just move on? She just knew that she did enjoy his company and didn't want to give that up.

Chapter 26

Linda Kay's tears began to dry up as she regained her composure. She once again started telling George about her dream and those beautiful little girls that were in such distress.

"The girls huddled as close together as possible through the rest of the night. They only slept a few minutes at a time. Fear was all around them, making it impossible for them to get any real sleep. As daylight broke through, they were all awake and ready to get up. They still didn't have anywhere to go and nothing to do. It was as if their life had been put on hold waiting for their father's return. They were covered all over in mosquito bites, Mamie warned them to try and not scratch, it would only make it worse.

"Ruth began to cry because she was hungry, and she was too young to understand how dangerous it would be for them to try and get food. There was nothing on the riverbank for them to eat. Bernice went to Mamie and told her she was going to try to sneak back to the garden. 'We're all hungry, and we can't go on like this. It breaks my heart to hear Ruth cry because she's hungry. I have no choice I have to go. If I make it, I'll bring us some food back. Remember, if I don't come back, do not come looking for me. Stay away from there. You'll know it's dangerous, or I would have come back.' A shiver ran down Mamie's back because she knew in her heart that Bernice should never go there. Mamie looked at Bernice with tears forming in her eyes and asked her, 'Please don't go. I don't think it would be a good idea. I'd rather you stay here. No one expects you to go, please just stay here with us.'

"Bernice shook her head. 'No, we have to eat, and we don't know when Daddy will be back. You take care of the other kids. I'll be back shortly. She hugged Mamie's neck, 'I love you, sis," and took off running back up the hill before Mamie had a chance to stop her.

"Mamie tried to hide her face from the others, she didn't want them to see how upset she was, but she couldn't hold her tears back any longer. She loved her sisters so very much; she wished she knew she could protect them. But how do you protect someone from something you can't see or touch? Bernice had been gone a good hour when Mamie give up all hopes of Bernice returning. She was sick at her stomach from worry about her sister. She didn't know what had happened to her. How was she going to explain this to the others? She was very angry with herself for letting Bernice go. She should've stopped her, she could of. In her heart of hearts, she knew if she had come down hard enough on Bernice, she would've stayed there. How could she live with herself knowing that she had let her sister go? She could feel the hardness coming over her. She would never live with such pain again. She put up a wall in her heart; she would never let anyone else get that close to her again. She would never love someone so much that it would ever be this devastating at their passing. She had built her wall in her heart, and she would never let anyone cross it again.

"All at once, she could hear someone running and making agonizing noises as they came. She looked up the hill and there was her sister trying to run down the hill. Her dress was tattered and torn. Her face was twisted in agony. Mamie's heart pounded in her chest. She was full of excitement seeing that her sister was alive. At the same time, her heart broke as she looked at the anguish and torment that was on her sister's face. Mamie began to run to meet her sister. As soon she caught up with her, she threw her arms around her and hugged her tight telling her how much she loved her. But there was something in those words that had already changed. The wall that Mamie had put in her heart blocked the true meaning, not only from Bernice, but from herself. The connection is just not quite there. Then she pulled back looking her sister over, she saw she was covered in gashes and scratch marks. Blood was smeared across her face, arms and legs. Mamie began to cry in hard sobs as she said, 'I'm so sorry I shouldn't have let you go.' But Mamie knew in her heart she would never feel such agonizing pain again. Never again would she let herself care in that manner. Mamie wouldn't know how to tear that wall down even if she had wanted to.

"'That was not your choice that was my choice. I don't regret it. Someone had to go. We could have starved without any food. We don't know how long Daddy will be gone. I know I didn't get enough food, but I got as much as I could. I'm sorry; I just couldn't stand the pain and the fear any longer. I had to run.

"'Mamie, there's no way to hide from whatever or whoever it is. If it wants us, it's going to get us. There is nothing we can do to stop it. Don't tell Nell; there is no need to upsetting her anymore than what she is. Besides, she's working hard at trying to keep Ruth calm and entertained.'

"'Yeah, I was afraid of that. I'm going to ask you something, maybe I shouldn't, but I would like your opinion. Do you think it's the ghost of that man we killed?'

"'Yes, Mamie, I do.'

"Mamie sadly shook her head in agreement. Let's keep that between me and you. Now come on, let me help you down to the water's edge, so I can try to clean you up. There should be some yarrow back here in the woods, as soon as I get you cleaned up, I'll go get some.

Mamie ripped off strips of her petticoat to clean Bernice's cuts. While Bernice untied the skirt of her dress and emptied out what she had managed to gather. She had gotten up some tomatoes, potatoes, radishes, carrots and some strawberries she even managed to get a few ears of corn.

"Mamie looked at Bernice from different angles, 'You look better but not by much. I'm going to get some yarrow, which will make those cuts and sores much better. I won't be gone long.'

"'If it's okay with you, I'll just sit here and relax, until you return. Believe me, I really need the rest.'

"Nell had walked, rocked, and soothed Ruth until at last she had fallen asleep in Nell's arms. She laid her down gently in the shade. Feeling relief that she could have a few minutes for herself, she so wanted some time to talk to her sisters to try and find out what kind of plan they had come up with. They had to survive better than this. Nell was full of questions as she walked over to talk to Bernice. She took one look at her sister and gasped as tears begin to form in her eyes, 'What happened to you? Are you going to be okay? How can I help you Bernice?'

"'I'll be just fine now; you stop that fretting. I had a little bit of trouble getting the food. You know how clumsy I am; I fell and hurt myself, but I'm going to be okay, nothing to worry about, in fact Mamie's gone to get me some yarrow now. You know that will take care of about any problem I have.'

"Nell looked as if she was still full of concern, 'That ghost was after you again wasn't it?'

"'Where in the world do you come up with your ideas?'

"'I'm not totally stupid Bernice, and you're wasting your time trying to hide things from me.'

"'Well, I wanted to keep that knowledge away from you. I don't want you to worry about it. I'm okay, I got away. That's why I didn't get more food than I did. I managed to run. I'm fine I promise. Nell, please be careful talking about ghosts around Ruth; I'm afraid we will frighten her too much.'

"'I understand what you're telling me. Believe it or not, I've got enough sense not to frighten her. Besides if I was to do that, just who do you think is going to take care of her? So of course, I'm not going to frighten her. She's already frightened enough. She doesn't really know what's going, on but she knows we're upset, so therefore she is. I'm talking between me and you, we both know it is a ghost. We're going to have to be on guard, you're not fooling me. I know how you got hurt. What I'd like to know is if you think it's the ghost of the man we killed because that's exactly what I think.'

"'I honestly don't know what it is. I have to agree with you. What else could it be but a ghost? The ghost of the man we killed, I don't know, possibly, after all, we never had a problem like this before. I know one thing: whoever or whatever it is it's very angry. I also know you make it impossible for me to keep a secret from you.' She wiped a tear off of Nell's face and gave her sister a hug. 'Now here comes Mamie, and I need to let her doctor all my cuts and scratches.' Nell turned to let Mamie get closer to Bernice. Mamie was already chewing yarrow root that she would place on Bernice's cuts.

"George, those little girls stayed down there on the banks of the river with no shelter for three days and nights. Mosquitoes were literally eating them up. They were covered in whelps from head to toe. They hadn't had a decent meal to eat in several days. Can you imagine the suffering they were going through? You never saw such happy faces as they had when they saw their Daddy row up to the bank and pull his boat ashore. All but Mamie and suddenly her heart was filled with rage and anger at her dad. How could he put all this responsibility on her? Why wasn't he there for her and her sisters? She had been left with more responsibility than what she could handle. She totally intended to talk to her dad about it, and she had her doubts that she could ever forgive him for what he had done."

CHAPTER 27

"THEIR DADDY WAS NOT HAPPY TO SEE THE SHAPE THEY WERE IN. The girls showed him where they had been scratched and cut by the unseen entity. They explained to him what had happened and how they had shot and killed a man. They told him how they had dragged his body and left it lying among the trees. There was a tear in their daddy's eyes as they told him everything. Their daddy gave them all a hug and told them that everything was going to be okay. He was there now and would take them back to the house, and he would bury the body and see to it that everything was taken care of; they didn't have to worry about anything, it would all be okay.

"Once Mamie saw how hurt her dad was, her heart softened a bit, but the wall of anger was still there. She didn't really know how she felt, only that she no longer felt as a child full of love and happiness.

"So, they all headed back for the house, and Daddy took care of the girls first. She fixed them a tub to take a bath in while he fixed them a good meal. Once they were dressed in clean clothes, he doctored all their cuts and scrapes. He had them to sit at the table, they all held hands as they said a prayer thanking God for their many blessings. Then they ate a wonderful filling meal.

"Their daddy told them to stay in the house as he went out and dug a grave. He then wrapped the body well before burying the man and said a prayer over the body. Mamie could tell by the look on her daddy's face that he knew the man. She asked him, very quietly so that the other children wouldn't hear, how did he know the man?

"Her dad told her that he had met him when he went to town to get supplies. 'His name was Evan. We spent a good while visiting with one another. Once I left his company, an old friend come up to me and told me that I should have avoided him. That he was known to be mean, and he had hurt a lot of people. Not just physically, some he hurt mentally. He hurt them trying to blackmail them, threatening to hurt their family members. A lot of times he got by with it. There were some families that lived around here he took for thousands. I don't know what he thought he was going to get out of me. But sweetheart, I don't ever want you to feel bad about what happened. That man was mean, and he could have hurt you and your sisters beyond your imagination.' He pulled Mamie close and told her how much he loved her and kissed her softly on the top of the head. 'I don't like judging people on gossip alone, so I checked it out with the people that he was supposed to have hurt. They showed me where the man had caused damage to them or their family members. I thanked everyone for his information promised myself to avoid Evan in the future. That was the extent of it, I don't know about that man. And no, I did not owe him money or anything else.'

"Mamie nodded her head that she understood and told her dad she wouldn't say anything to the other kids. As she walked away from her dad, she was wishing she could get her childhood back. After all, Evan had robbed her of that

"Everything seemed to be going fine as they all settled down, and once again, you could hear the children's laughter. It was wonderful having their daddy home. At last, the house starting to come back to life, and it begin to feel like home. Once again, the children knew they were loved, and they would be cared for. Even Mamie felt better, but she did not know how to tear down that wall that she had built around her heart. She wished she could; she was missing the old feelings she wanted them back desperately, but the wall stayed right where she had put it.

"When night appeared, so did the ghost. This time not only did it attack the kids, but also, their daddy's blood was flowing. All of them had cuts, were burned. and stung, putting them all in agonizing pain. Nell cried out in pain, screaming for her dad's help her leg had been cut deep. Her dad had grabbed a towel and applied pressure to her leg as he held, her trying to rock her and soothe her. She felt like a little China doll to him, very fragile as he held her carefully in his arms. Now it was Ruth who was screaming in horrible pain. No one really understood what was happening, how could anything be so cruel that it would hurt a small child?

"This time, it was Daddy who hollered for them to run. Their dad took just enough time to grab the rifle and some shells, and he began to run. He took long strides, as he ran blood was running down his face and it blurred his vision so much that he stumbled and fell. He laid there unable to move for several seconds before once again he grabbed his gun, got to his feet, and began to run. As fast as they could, they all ran to the river. He put the kids in the canoe and rowed away. They never returned to this place. I don't know if they safely made it away from this island or not. What happened to them once they got in the canoe, I just don't know. They never returned to this place. The entity is still on this island full of anger and hatred."

CHAPTER 28

"GEORGE, YOU KNOW IN YOUR HEART, whether you want to admit it or not, that was a ghost that tripped me, causing me to hurt my ankle. Not only that, he also caused the cave-in that trapped us in here. That ghost is here with us, and it's evil through and through. He was an evil man, and when the girls killed him, he became even worse. Even if we were out of this cave, he would still harm us. I don't know that we will ever see the light of day again; it doesn't look like we will. George, whether we're in this cave or not, as long as we're on this island we're in danger. We haven't been able to find a way off, and now we're trapped in this cave. I've been thinking I don't know how much longer we have to live, probably not long. You know the food's about all gone. I don't know how long we'll live after that.

"I hope I don't regret saying this, but I think I want to know your excuse for kissing my ex-best friend Casey. I'm sure you remember her. That's one thing you cannot deny. I saw it myself. Whatever you do, don't try and fool me, I want the truth the whole truth. If you can't do that, I'd rather you not tell me anything at all. You say you have a reason, I doubt it, but if you do, I'd like to know what it is. This will probably be my last chance to ever find out what your excuse is. If I sound angry and hurt, it's because I am. I have tried to act like we were never together, that we never cared for one another. Now time may be running out for us, I need to know the truth before it's too late."

"Yes, I do have an answer, and you needn't worry; I won't lie to you. I have no reason to lie to you. Everything I'm going to tell you is the truth. It's the truth today, and it was the truth then, nothing has changed. I'm going to start with the beginning of that day. I'm sure you remember that our senior prom was to be that night. I had everything planned to make this a very special night for you, until my phone rang, and everything changed. It was my boss, and he told me I had to come to work. There'd been an emergency there, and I had no other choice I had to go to work. I had no option; I had to go in. I needed my job.

"I called Casey and asked her if she would finish putting together the wonderful night I had planned for you. I had a corsage especially made for you, and it needed to be picked-up along with a box of chocolates. I also bought an engagement ring that was to be picked up that day. My intent was to ask you to marry me. Once Casey got to the jeweler's, they didn't want to let her have the ring. It was a lot of confusion and took her a couple of hours before she met their satisfaction. At last, they conceded to let her have the ring.

"When I got off from work, I had just enough time to go by pick everything up from Casey. Get back home and get dressed for the night.

"When I went by Casey's to pick everything up, she was running frantic trying to get herself ready for the night. She had spent most of her day doing things I wanted done. I was in the process of leaving her house. I felt very grateful to her after all, without her I would not be able to have a special night for you. She had done so much, spent most of her day doing the things that I wanted. This was a special night for her also; it was her senior prom night, too. She had given up her day of preparation, so I could make you happy. It was simply a thank you kiss. A kiss like you would give your sister; a kiss like you would give a baby.

There was no passion; it was a quick thank-you kiss, and that was all it was ever intended to be. You walked up just as I kissed her, and that was the end of us and the end of your friendship with Casey. You would never let me explain how she had given up a large part of an important day for her to make you happy. Instead, she lost a great friend, and I lost the love of my life. We tried hard to explain to you, but you would never give us the opportunity. You turned us off and walked out of our lives. I knew that you were going on the float trip with Elizabeth, so I made arrangements that I could be your guide. I just wanted to be around you; maybe we could at least be friends. I have high hopes that we will get out of here. I also have high hopes that you will let me be your friend first and then I have hopes that you will forgive me and let me love you once again."

Tears streamed down Linda Kay's face as she sobbed, "I'm so sorry. I should have trusted you more. That's why I was so confused. I never had any doubts about you before. It was such a shock, and I didn't know what to think. I was afraid to find out what was going on at that point, I was afraid that maybe you loved Casey and not me. I didn't think I could survive if I heard those words. That's why I wouldn't listen to y'all, I was afraid. I am sorry, I feel like I missed out on an awful lot in my life. At the same time, I feel like we are where we should be at the time. Who knows? Maybe we both needed some time to grow before we could think about taking such a giant step as marriage."

George tilted her head up to face him and wiped the tears from her cheeks lowered his head and kissed her deeply. Then he whispered in her ear, "I love you as much today as I ever did, and I will always love you. I still have that ring. When we get out here, I'm going to ask you to marry me.

"I love you, too. I never quit loving you."

George kissed her once more, then he held her tight and told her it was time for her to rest because, "Tomorrow, someway, somehow, we will find a way out of here. After all, we have a lot to live for, and we're going to make it."

CHAPTER 29

ELIZABETH AND DANNY WERE LAUGHING as they left the jail. Everyone seemed to be in a good mood, and they were very happy that Terrence would be going to court in the morning. Of course, there was no guarantee, but they were fairly sure Terrence would be let out on probation. After all, this was his first offense.

Elizabeth turned to Danny.

"I'm going by to check on my property. I want to see what it's looking like. Would you like to go with me?"

"Sure, I'd love to see it. To tell you the truth, I've heard through the grapevine that it's looking good. But there's nothing like seeing it for myself. I'll just follow you, that way you won't have to bring me back."

"That makes sense, okay, I'll meet you there."

As Elizabeth pulled into the driveway her mouth dropped open; she couldn't believe what she was looking at. Her property had been mowed, cleaned and trimmed. It looked as if a landscaper had worked on it and brought it to perfection. It looked like a totally different place.

Danny walked up to her and took a hold of her hand.

"It sure is looking better!"

They slowly started walking around the house. Elizabeth was totally astonished at the transformation of the property. By the time they reached the backside of her property, she was in total awe.

"I can't believe this; it almost looks picturesque. Just look out there, at the view it's awesome. I didn't know when I bought this place that there was anything like this. All of a sudden, I don't really care about the house. I could throw a tent and just sit here and look at the view."

"I had almost forgotten just how beautiful this property was. It's really coming back to life."

"For the first time, I'm getting rather excited about the thoughts of my property. I always said I really didn't want to own property."

Danny shook his head in disbelief.

"Why would anyone not want to own property?"

"I didn't want the responsibility of keeping it up. You've got to keep the yard mowed. You have to make all the repairs. Then there are taxes and insurance I just always thought it would be too much responsibility. I was busy with my job, and I just didn't want to fool with it. But now I'm getting excited. Let's go look inside the house, I really want to see what he has done in there."

"I bet whatever Trinity is doing you're going to like it."

"Well to me this kind of looks like a mess. What is he doing, this is just the two bedrooms. He was supposed to add a bathroom along that wall, so I can understand that being torn out. I don't understand why he's got the roof tore up. What is he doing, I can't figure it out."

"I would say if he's tearing it down, there was some kind of problem up there, and he will fix it."

"I suppose."

Danny turned to Elizabeth and asked, "What do you say we leave now, and we'll come back next week and look at the changes. Right now, I want to know if you have any plans for tonight."

"No, not really."

"The Lyric in Harrison is a historical building they now have live bands playing there. Mostly its local bands sometimes they're really good and sometimes not so much. Tonight, they're supposed to have an Elvis impersonator. I don't know the guy that's performing, just that his name is Cody. From what I understand, he performs all across the country. They say he's really good, would you like to go? We can check it out for ourselves."

"Sounds like fun to me. I'd love to go."

Danny walked Elizabeth back to her car.

"Why don't I pick you up about 7:00?"

"That sounds fine to me. It sounds like we will have a lot of fun. Even if the band's not good, I'd love to see the old building."

"If you like old buildings, they've got one there that's been empty for years. I think it is absolutely beautiful. I don't know who owns it, but I wish it was me. It would need a whole lot of work, but once it was done it would make a beautiful home.

"I love old buildings. They have so much more character. It's as if builders a long time ago built love into their craft. I think the problem is they taken craft out of building. Now they made it a job and what you get is a building. The art, the love and the pride of a job just isn't there anymore. If they try to add character it's done cheaply with a manufactured product. In the end, profit is the bottom line."

"I totally agree with you. If you're not too tired, I've got another idea."

"Oh, and what is that?"

"I could follow you home, so you could leave your car there. We'll go to Harrison and grab us a bite to eat. Then we should have time to look at some of the old homestead's there. Who knows? You may pick up a few good ideas for your place. We still have time to listen to the band."

"That sounds like a good idea to me. Let's go. I'll meet you at my house."

Elizabeth was feeling rather giddy on the way home. Her heart filled with excitement. She really appreciated Danny's friendship; he distracted her thoughts and even made her laugh. It didn't change the fact of how much she loved and missed her friend, but it did help her to get through the day.

In order to save time, they decided just to stop by the Dairy Queen and grab a burger and fries. They were both anxious to get started looking at the old historical buildings in town. Elizabeth oohed and awed over something in every building they looked at. until they went to the last building which happened to be Danny's favorite.

You could hear the hurt in Danny's voice as he said, "Oh no, look at that."

"What's wrong, Danny? I don't get it."

"I'm being selfish. It just hurts my heart to see that for sale sign out front. That's the close of my dreams of someday owning this house. Truthfully, I shouldn't feel that way about it maybe someone who can afford it will fix this house up and turn it back to the glory that it once was. I hope they do. I would hate to see someone come in here and try to change the natural beauty that was put into this home." Danny gave a small laugh as he said, "I guess that's my problem; I'm afraid whoever gets it won't fix it my way."

As they walked around the house Elizabeth realized that this is the one homestead where she loved every part of that building.

"Danny, after looking at this house and the property, I understand exactly how you feel. I'm so sorry you're not able to buy this house and make it your own. I really do understand about losing sight of your dream."

"I wish I could afford this building. It is most beautiful thing I have ever seen. The possibilities are everywhere; this is a mansion in disguise.

It breaks my heart to think about going off and leaving it. I just hope that whoever gets it will treat it with tender loving care."

They were going around the house looking in every window. Elizabeth was trying to picture and imagine what the room would look like if it was cleaned and polished with all the spider webs washed away, how grand it would look.

All it once Elizabeth screamed out, "That's it." She stared at Danny wide-eyed, "I couldn't figure it out while we were there, but now I know what it was."

Danny looked at her as if she had totally lost her mind as he asked, "What are you talking about?"

"I'm talking about last weekend when we went to that old homestead on that island and we had a picnic remember the homestead?"

"Yes, of course, I remember the homestead. What about it?"

"That place had been cleaned of spider webs. Someone has been in that place, cleaning it. I'm sure of that, and if Linda Kay had needed to stay just one night there, she would wipe down the spider webs.

Danny stared at her as if he was in a trance before he said, "You're absolutely right. We've got to go back; we've got to check it out again. Do you want to go with me Saturday morning?"

"Absolutely I want to go; you know I'm going to be anxious to get through the rest of this week. It'll be hard to wait till Saturday, but we can do it. I'll pack us a picnic lunch, we may end up with just sandwiches this week, but I'll put something together."

Danny smiled at her reached out and put his arm around her waist and pulled her to him. He gave her a tender, loving kiss. As he pulled back and looked at her, he said, "You are absolutely beautiful. Elizabeth, please don't get your hopes up too much. It is promising, but anyone could have done it. If all else fails, at least I've had another day that I get to spend with you. Now let's go before we miss the band."

The band turned out to be absolutely awesome. Elizabeth couldn't have asked for a better or more fulfilling day than the one she had just had. The kiss Danny had to give her at the door would linger on her lips for a long time. That night she dreamed about that old house in all of its glory. She wished there was some way it could be Danny's.

The next day seemed to drag on and on. She was anxious to get off from work. She wanted to run to the store and pick up what she needed for their picnic lunch. She got up early Saturday morning, dressed and quickly went downstairs. She sliced the homemade bread and made ham sandwiches. Then she sliced tomatoes and got a small jar of pickles. She washed and prepared some lettuce leaves. She had fixed a bowl of potato salad and baked beans. Then she had fixed a million-dollar cake. When she got her basket filled with all the goodies, she set it by the door. She went back upstairs to check her appearance. She wouldn't wear any makeup today. Being around all that water, she could just imagine the streaks of makeup running down her face. But that was okay; she was just as pretty without makeup as she was with it. Then she heard the knock at the door, and excitement began to mount. She could feel her heart beating with the anticipation. She just felt like they had to get some kind of clue today about the whereabouts of George and Linda Kay. Danny had told her not to get her hopes up, but she couldn't help it. She had a feeling the first time she saw that place that there was something there. She didn't know, maybe Danny was right, maybe she was just getting her hopes up, but she wasn't going to give up those hopes until she had to.

Chapter 30

George had a hard time sleeping after his talk with Linda Kay. He was filled with too much excitement. He didn't know how, but he knew he had to find a way out of there. All at once, a negative thought ran through his mind. He shook his head trying to get rid of it but the thought just wanted to linger and grow.

He thought to himself that, *Getting out of here is just a pipe dream. I have walked this cave in its entirety, there's no way out behind us and there's no way out in front of us.*

Their food supply was running out, they had one tomato left that they would share today. They were out of the water that they brought with them. He paced back and forth and prayed hard that they would find a way out of here. He was almost hysterical, he felt like the only thing that held him together was Linda Kay. He had to put on a brave front for her. He walked over next to the pond and set down thinking once again how strange that pond was. You could feel the warmth coming from the water. Linda Kay had used the water when she cleaned his shoulder. It didn't seem to hurt either one of them. He had to wonder if that water would be good enough for them to drink. He finally got brave enough to stick his hand in the water, he pulled it back out.

There was no pain in his hand. He smelled the water on his hand, it smelled only of water. Nothing more than that seemed to exist. At last, he put a drop of water on his tongue; it was water, only water. That got him excited; it was all he could do to keep from waking Linda Kay up. They might not have food, but at least they had some water. He finally calmed down and lay down next to Linda Kay. He pulled her close and thanked God for her presence; he loved her more than he had ever loved anything in his life. He drifted off to sleep, dreaming of days ahead for him and Linda Kay.

Linda Kay slowly began trying to get up, being very careful not to wake George. As soon as Linda Kay moved away, George felt the emptiness and immediately his eyes popped open. He smiled up at Linda Kay.

"Good morning beautiful"

Linda Kay looked at him with excitement in her voice as she said, "My foot doesn't hurt at all. I'm able to walk on it again."

"That's wonderful! Just be careful and don't overdo it. If it starts to hurt at all, take a break and prop it up. You don't want to hurt it again, I'm sure it still weak.

"Last night, I couldn't sleep, so I checked out our pond. Linda Kay I can't find one thing wrong with that water. It smells like water, it tasted like water; I don't think we'll have a problem with the water. The food is just about gone but we have plenty of water."

Linda Kay looked up at George, her voice was a little shaky as she said, "You're right, George, there's nothing wrong with the water. I've been drinking it for a while; don't get mad at me please, I wanted to save the water we had for you. I find that the more water I drink, the less I feel hunger, so that's what I've been doing. I really don't think we have anything to fear from the water."

He walked over to the pond and looked into the water. For a few minutes, he stood there, staring at it as if he was in deep thought. At last he said, "Linda Kay, I love you with all my heart, but please don't ever do anything like that again. We didn't know if the water was good or bad. It could've killed you. Please promise me."

Linda Kay came over and put her arm around him.

"I just wanted to protect what we had, to stretch it out and make it last as long as possible. The water's okay, so what seems to be the problem?"

George pulled her close and gave her a kiss telling her how much he loved her. Then he let go of her and stared back at the pond.

"There is something else about this pond Linda Kay. I don't know what it is, but there's something I should be picking up on. I'm missing it, but it keeps playing at the back of my mind. I know the answer is there. It's just waiting for me to pick up the problem, but I don't see it. I've got to figure it out; it's trying to tell me something."

Linda Kay walked over and begin staring at the pond herself.

"George, why would this end of the pond appear be a darker than the other end of the pond?"

He continued to stare in the pond for a moment then he hollered, "That's it, you're a genius, Linda Kay, that's it, I got it. I won't be gone long I promise."

George bent down and started taking off his shoes.

Linda Kay had a tear in her voice as she said, "What are you going to do? Please don't go in the water. I don't want to be left here alone."

"Linda Kay, I promise you I'm not going to be gone long. Look at the water, look at the light in the water; it's getting sunlight from somewhere. I have to go check it out; it could be our only way out of this cave." He kissed her deeply and told her once again how much he loved her. He then turned and dove into the water.

Linda Kay couldn't help it; she was a nervous wreck. She paced back and forth and kept staring at the water until at last she could see George swimming back to her. The anticipation of what George had found was almost more than Linda Kay could stand. The second George started to emerge from the water; Linda Kay was shooting questions at him. She stopped abruptly.

"What happened? Your face is bleeding, let me look at it. It's not very deep, we need some antibiotic, but we'll keep it really clean, I think it will heal okay. Now tell me what happened."

"Well, first of all, I know why you were drawn to this area of the cave. You told me that crystals have positive energy." With that, he took Linda Kay's hand in his. He filled her hand with crystals. I was able to just reach and pick these up, they were laying loose everywhere down there. They are plentiful on the floor of the pond. Look at these walls, you and I talked about the beautiful rainbow they make when the light hits them. So, you see in this section of the cave we are surrounded by crystals and the positive energy that they bring. Now the really good news is that yes, there is a way out of this cave. All we have to do is follow the light in the water, the sunlight will show us the way out. Now for the bad news, when I swam out of the cave and broke to the surface that, entity was waiting there for me. I was shoved back under the water. I felt like he was holding me in place. I couldn't breathe; I thought I was going to drown. I fought with everything I had to get away. Once I got a loose is when I received the scratches on my face. Linda Kay, I don't know if he will ever let us out. Right now, I feel trapped and helpless, to be so close to safety and yet so far away."

"It's going to be okay. We'll figure something out; we're too close to give up now."

Linda Kay laid her head against George's chest and hugged him close.

"Linda Kay, I have no choice, I have to try again. We're out of food; I've got to get us something to eat. You know what we've been eating isn't enough to keep our energy up, we're not getting the vitamins we need. It's better than nothing, but we really need protein. I have no choice, Linda Kay, I have to try to go back to the house and get what I can out of the garden.

"Right now, I need to rest. That thing out there, it drains all my energy. It's as if it tries to draw all the life out of you. After I've rested, I'll try again. Let me sleep about an hour then wake me up. With that. George stretched out on the rocks, shut his eyes, and drifted off to sleep.

Linda Kay sat there watching him sleep. She thought about how much she loved him and how unfair it was that he took all the chances. It's not right; he needed to rest, and Linda Kay thought, *It's my turn to go for food, not his.* She picked up the bag that he carried food in and crisscrossed it across her shoulder before diving into the water.

The water was warm and soothing to her body. She found comfort as the water began to soothe her aching muscles. She had stayed below the surface of the water too long. Now she found herself in need of air. Her lungs were beginning to burn from holding her breath so long. She swam back to the surface where she found there was a wide gap between the surface and the floor of the cave. Allowing her to get the oxygen she needed, she breathed in deeply, enjoying the feel of the oxygen replenishing her lungs. She treaded the water and relaxed her muscles as she looked around and realized there was enough room for her to swim without going back under the water. She remembered that George had told her to follow the sunlight; it would show her the way. From there, she could see the opening at the end of the tunnel.

The water slowly began to shallow until at last she could easily stand at the mouth of the cave. Now she began to fear stepping outside into the open. It would leave her vulnerable to the entity. She remembered how George had looked when he returned from examining the escape route. She didn't know what would be waiting for her. Her heart began to race as panic began to take over. She knew she had to come out of the tunnel at some time. They would not be able to survive without food. As she came out of the tunnel, she began reciting the Lord's Prayer to herself and asked for guidance and help along her journey.

Chapter 31

*Elizabeth had a big smile on her fac*e as she opened the door.

"Danny I'm so glad you're here, I'm ready to get started. I feel real confident about today." She stopped talking and stared at Danny; she knew by the look on his face there was a problem. "I'm sorry, Danny. I was just rattling. What's the problem and how can I help?"

"The word 'help' is music to my ears. I'm sorry Elizabeth I have to cancel our date for today. One of the guys that work on the Saturday crew called in this morning and said that he and his wife were moving to Michigan to take care of his wife's mother who's in bad health. They're leaving today; I have to work at the post office. If you're not too upset with me, maybe we can go someplace when I get off. It will be too late to set out for the river. It would be dark before we could get back in, and that late, the mosquitoes would eat us alive. I'm afraid the float trip will have to be off for today, I'm really sorry."

Elizabeth tried to hide the disappointment on her face as she said, "I understand. What do you say we take our picnic basket to work? We can still eat it for lunch, and I will help you get the mail out."

Danny smiled to himself.

"I knew you were a champ." Danny placed his arms on her shoulders as he said, "I know you're disappointed, but I promise I will make it up to you as soon as possible." He kissed her quickly as he said, "The mail is running late. We've got to go."

Elizabeth handed him the picnic basket and grabbed her purse as they headed out the door in a hurry to get the post office. As soon as they walked in the post office door, they started to work. They worked hard and very fast; otherwise, the mail would be very late. With Elizabeth there to help, it made things go much quicker. Before long, things seemed to settle into a normal day's work. Their timeline was finally on track, and they could slow down to a normal pace.

They had just sat down to eat their lunch when Sheriff Travis came in.

"Sheriff, good to see you, we were just sitting down for lunch, why don't you come join us?"

"It sure looks awfully good."

Elizabeth handed the Sheriff a paper plate and a couple of slices of homemade bread, then told him to build his sandwich the way he liked. "Do you like sweet iced tea?"

"I love it."

Elizabeth poured the Sheriff a tall glass of tea and handed it to him before sitting back down at the table.

Once they were all seated, the Sheriff said, "I come by to talk to the two of you about Terrence. Before I take any steps to do anything, I want to run it by you first. I would like to get Terrence's sentence dropped to a misdemeanor. He only had seven cases of beer left in the cave when we found it. If he goes up on a federal charge, it will be hard for him to ever get a decent job when his sentence is over. Around here, I doubt he would ever be able to get a job. No one will want hire him. Since it is his first offense, I hate to destroy his chances of doing something with his life. Before I take it to the judge and discuss it with him, I first would like to know what Elizabeth thinks about it."

Elizabeth looked rather thoughtful before answering, "Well, I'll tell you what. I think is that would be a great idea. There's no sense in destroying his life because he did something stupid. I say he should have a chance. Danny, I don't mean to step into your business, and this is just a thought. You may not want to go along with it, and if you don't, I wouldn't blame you. I was just thinking you need a new employee, if he could tell the judge that you would hire him it might help his case. What do you think?"

The Sheriff looked at Danny with hope written all over his face.

"Would you consider hiring him?"

Danny stood there as if in deep thought, and at last he responded by saying, "If he's willing to work weekends and evenings and give me his all, I don't see why not. I got to hire somebody; if he's willing to work, I'd like to give him a chance."

Sheriff Travis gave a sigh of relief as he said, "That's more than what I hoped for. If we can get this changed to a misdemeanor, I know it would lighten the load his mother is carrying in her heart right now. This actually gives me something that I can carry to the judge on his behalf. I'm going to talk to Terrence; if he is willing to work hard and do well, I'll go talk to the judge today. If all works out, he should be able to get out on time served. So hopefully by Monday morning you may be hearing from him." Then he put a big smile on his face. "Before I leave, do you think there's a possibility I can have a piece of that yummy looking cake?

Elizabeth cut the Sheriff a large slice of cake and set it before him and refilled his iced tea glass.

"There you go, please enjoy."

They finished their lunch, and Elizabeth immediately started cleaning up, so she could get back to work. At last they were done for the day, and they could lock up and leave.

Elizabeth asked, "Would you mind if we went by and checked on my property before you take me home?"

Chapter 32

"Of course, I'll be happy to take you; it's not out of the way, and besides, I get to spend a little more time with you. I'm also interested in how your cabin is coming along."

"Well, the last time we were there, Trinity was doing something strange to the roof, and I hadn't had a chance to talk to him. I want to find out what that was all about. As you know, I hadn't had a chance to go by the house again. I just want to see if we can figure out what's going on."

As they pulled into the driveway, all Elizabeth could say was, "Wow, wow, wow, look at what Trinity has done, can you believe it wow? I absolutely love it! This place is a dream come true."

Danny had to laugh as he said, "I told you when he gets through with it, this place it will be a beauty."

"Danny, do you realize he is putting an upstairs on this cabin. Do you know how awesome that is?"

Danny laughed, "As a matter fact I do. Can you imagine what your view is going to be like from up there?"

"Oh my goodness, it's going to be awesome, wow. You know what, I made a good deal on this place. No, I made the best deal ever. I really had my doubts, but I am now I'm convinced I got a great deal. Do you realize this is no longer a little bitty cabin? It will be a beautiful home!"

Danny took hold of her hand and said, "Come on let's see if Trinity is still here. If he is, we can get inside and take a good look."

"Trinity is here, and he's redoing the kitchen. I can't tell what he is doing yet. He's got everything tore out; it definitely needed a facelift. I wonder where he is, the door was unlocked so I know he is here."

As Trinity stepped out at the pantry door, he said, "I am right here. Well, what you think? Is it looking okay to you?"

"Oh Trinity, from what I've seen this place is looking great. I love it, love it, I love it. I can't believe you built an upstairs. That is so awesome. What's up there?"

"You're going to have two bedrooms and a bath and awesome view. I know how much you enjoy the veranda at Linda Kay's. I thought you deserved to have your own."

"I just can't believe it; this is so much more than I ever dreamed of."

Just as Elizabeth was about to say something else, a voice came from the front of the house hollering, "Danny, where are you? Wow. This place is looking gorgeous."

Trinity answered, saying, "Thank you, Sheriff. We're back here in the kitchen, come on back."

"I heard that you had bought this old place. Wow, it is looking good. It's hard to believe that Trinity is able to restore it. I love what you are doing, Trinity. I don't mean to intrude, but I really had to see Danny to let you know just how happy Terrence is just at the thought of getting the job. Most of all he's happy because you will trust him enough to give him a chance. He swears that he will never let you down, and he will be the best employee you have ever had.

"I did talk to the judge, and after thinking it over quite a bit, he agreed. Terrence is unaware yet that he will be getting out. It will probably be Monday morning. As excited as he is about the job, you'll probably be the first one he sees. For the first time since Doris died, you can actually see life back into that boy."

Trinity spoke up and said, "Do I understand this right; you're going to hire Terrence to work at the post office?"

"Yes, I am, do you think that will be a problem?"

"I think it's a wonderful idea. Do you have any idea how happy this will make his mom? She is going to be so happy; I've got to call Mary and let her know. I'm sure she will want to go see her immediately and tell her. Mary and I both really care a lot about his mom, she is a beautiful person. She will appreciate the chance that you are giving her son. She won't ever forget you for that. Now I think I'm going to close this place up. I want to get home and tell Mary everything that's going on."

"Well, I just wanted you to know how happy you have made, Terrence."

The Sheriff slowly walked over to Elizabeth and told her, "I knew bringing you into this community would be a great thing. I'm happy that you're part of our clan." With that he gave her slight hug as he said, "Thank you from the bottom of my heart."

He then shook hands with Danny.

"Thanks again, it's really appreciated." And finally he shook hands with Trinity, "This is a great job you're doing on this place. It's going to be the envy of everyone around. It's beautiful and will really enhance the countryside. Now I guess I better get back to work but once again Thank you, guys."

With that, he turned and left.

Elizabeth looked at Danny, "Well that should make you feel good about yourself, it did me anyway. I'm like you. I was a little hesitant at first but now I think maybe it was the best thing you could have done for him. I think he will give you his all."

She gave Danny a big smile before she turned and looked at Trinity, "Thanks, Trinity, for letting us look at what all you've done to the house. I can't wait to get moved in. Right now, I think we need to get out of your way I wouldn't want to hold up progress."

Danny laughed.

"Did you hear that whip in her voice? I think she's ready for you to get back to work. Good seeing you, Trinity, we'll see you soon."

"I think Elizabeth will forgive me. For the rest of the day, I'm going home and talking to Mary. Then I'm quite sure we'll be going to visit Terrence's mother. I promise, I'll be back on it first thing in the morning."

"Of course, you will. You and Mary have a wonderful evening. I'll come back in a few days and see how it looks."

After they got back in the car, Danny asked Elizabeth, "Is there anything you would like to do tonight?"

"Well, I'm kind of tired. Why don't we get something to eat on the way back to my place? Then I'll pop some popcorn, and we can watch a movie, unless you had something else in mind."

"Sounds like a good idea to me. The Mercantile has a few movies for rent if you'd like to stop by there."

"No, we've got tons of movies to pick from at the house. I'm sure you can find something you like. Between what Linda Kay has and what I have, there's a wide variety."

They had just enough time to stop by the diner and enjoy a meal before they closed. The food was all home-cooked and very good. After they finished eating, Danny asked Elizabeth, "Would you like dessert?"

"No, I don't think so. I am stuffed, I couldn't eat another bite."

Danny said, "I was just thinking, I believe you've got some of that million-dollar cake left, and I'm quite sure I'd rather have some of your cake."

"I think there's plenty of cake left. I tell you what; while you pick out a movie, I'll get us dessert and coffee. Then I'll pop some popcorn.

I don't know any way we can eat it as full as we are, but I think we've got to have the smell of popcorn if we're going to watch a movie."

"I have to agree with you. That smell of buttery popcorn is what really makes the movie good."

Chapter 33

As they stepped out of the car, Danny commented on what a beautiful moon there was out that night.

"I don't think I've ever seen one so full with that gold hue. It's beautiful."

"You're right about that it is a beautiful moon; it's also called a 'Liar's Moon,' which means girls beware."

"Just what is that supposed to mean?"

"Well there's an old wives' tale that says when there's a Liar's Moon out, girls beware, the boys will lie tonight. Don't take to heart what they say when you're under a Liar's Moon."

"Well, I guess I've just been put on notice." Although it didn't stop him, he reached out and put his arm around Elizabeth and kissed her deeply. Then he said, "Maybe you better get me out of the moon."

Elizabeth laughed.

"Come on, I'll go fix dessert, and you look for the movie."

Danny hollered out from the living room, "I found a movie; I love this movie, if it's okay with you."

"She hollered back which one?"

"*Blindside.*"

As Elizabeth come through the kitchen door carrying a tray with slices of cake and cups of coffee, she said, "I agree. I love that movie."

Elizabeth had finally popped the popcorn with extra butter, and they had settled back to finally watch the movie.

The movie was about halfway over when Danny's phone began to ring. Danny looked questionably at his phone.

"It's Sheriff Travis. I better take it." Elizabeth heard him say, Yes, okay, right. I understand. I'll be right there." When he hung up the phone, you could see the burden of sorrow written across his face. He looked at Elizabeth. "I'm sorry I have to go."

"Are you okay?"

"I don't know, a friend of mine has a little that girl is missing. She's only three years old. They are putting together a search party. I've got to go help."

"Give me just a minute, so I can put a few things together. I'll go with."

"Are you sure? We could be out all night."

"I am sure. You're talking about a child, even if she's just lost, she scared, she is lonely and wanting her mom and dad. She needs help, yes, I'm going"

She quickly changed into a long sleeve shirt and a pair of cowboy boots before stuffing her cell phone in her pocket. She grabbed her backpack out of the closet and began stuffing it with a small lap throw, her ID, a compass, flashlight, and some money. She then ran to the kitchen and added some packages of peanut butter crackers a few power bars, and three bottles of water and shoved them in her backpack. She also grabbed another bottle of water and a pack of peanut butter crackers before going back to the living room and handing them to Danny, "Okay, I'm ready to go."

"What's this for? I assure you that I'm not hungry."

"That is so if you find that little girl, she may be thirsty and hungry. But you have to be careful before you give her anything to eat or drink, make sure she's not hurt."

"That makes sense, why didn't I think of it? No, don't bother answering that, I really don't want to know. What I want to talk to you about is you going on this search. I'm just not sure that you really need to go. You're not that familiar with the woods around here, and it's already dark."

"I know, that's why I brought my compass I can find my way back I promise. I have a good sense of direction. Besides I'm going to go, with you or without you."

"It makes me nervous, but if you're confident, okay. Please stay close to me, pay close attention to your surroundings and watch your step. There's nothing I can really tell you that you need to know except that she is a beautiful little three-year-old. Her mother's name is Marcy, her father's name is Michael, the little girl's name is Chelsea."

Chapter 34

Linda Kay was ducking behind the bushes and trees as she tried to slither her way through the woods. She was thinking maybe she could hide from the entity as she tried to find her way back to the garden. The reality of just how senseless that idea was dawned on her. After all, she was the one that couldn't see the entity. The entity could see her no matter where she hid. That thing could be standing right beside her, and she wouldn't know it. The entity is the one in charge of everything. There's nothing I can do other than to pray and ask God to walk with me."

She had been walking for quite some time, but her surroundings were still unfamiliar. She had to admit it; she was lost. She had walked for an hour and still didn't know where the garden was. Worst of all, she had lost her bearings, and no longer knew how to return to the cave. She realized what she had done was more than stupid, she had lost George. They should have stayed together. She was really terrified now; she was lost and at the mercy of the entity. Linda Kay knew that finding that tunnel and getting back into the cave was her only safe place and now that was lost to her.

The air began to grow thick, heavy, and hard to breathe. She could feel the presence of the entity; it wasn't bothering her, but she knew it was there. She also knew that evil was up to something; she just didn't know what.

She had gone about as far she could go without a break. She was tired and thirsty. She started to sit on a large rock, when all at once it dawned on her that is was a headstone. It had been put there as a marker for someone's grave. She remembered the burial of that evil entity was among the trees. She knew at once that was Evan's grave. She could feel the evil that surrounded her. She also knew the homestead was very close to where she stood.

Linda Kay's heart began to beat with excitement as she burst through the tree line, and there in front of her stood the homestead. She ran as fast as she could to the garden and began gathering greens, tomatoes, and strawberries. She would give anything for a good meal, but all she did was send her thanks to God for what she had. Again, she was very confused, it was as if the entity was coming and going. It hadn't bothered her in any way, yet it knew where she was. Once she had the bag bulging with all the food she could stuff into it, she was ready to return to her safe haven. She was sure that God had helped her find her way there, and he would help to find her way back to the cave to George, where safety awaited.

She wanted to leave to run, to get back to George, but something was stopping her. As she walked past the shed, she realized something was pulling at her telling her she must go inside. She tried to fight the impulse, but the pull was too strong. She had to give in; the curiosity got the best of her. With caution, she slowly opened the door and slipped inside. It was an old toolshed full of rusty tools. She didn't see anything that would raise her interest. She turned to leave and stopped.

Again, something seemed to be pulling at her to look around; it was there.

She thought, *What is there? What am I looking for?*

She walked back to the old workbench and looked around again. This time, she did notice some old wooden dowels. They looked as if they had been handmade from an old tree branch. She didn't know why, but they drew her interest so she picked them up. There was some old twine lying on the bench for the most part it had rotted with age. Linda Kay wasn't real sure yet what she was supposed to be doing, but she knew she should be doing something with this. She picked up the two dowels and examined them as she mumbled to herself, "It's two old sticks..."

She started playing around with them, turning them this way and that. At last it dawned on her she could tie them and make a cross. Of course, she could use the cross to move the entity back. She went to work trying desperately to tie the cross with twine, but she was having a hard time getting it to hold together. It took a longer time than she wanted to spend, but at last she had the cross tied together. There laid an old hatchet that had been sharpened, and she knew it was the one that George had used. She picked it up and ran the handle through the belt loop of her jeans. She cautiously stuck her head out of the shed door and looked around before she slowly exited.

The very last thing she wanted to do was to go back inside that homestead again, but there was that voice nagging at her to get what she needs. As she entered the house, her heart was beating fast. Fear loomed around her like a cloud. She wanted to get out of there. She grabbed a large pot and stuffed a couple drinking cups and a couple of muslin sheets inside the pot. It was beyond her comprehension, but something made her grab the rags that they had torn into strips when she had hurt her ankle. She thought that was a really dumb thing to grab, but she didn't want to waste any more time. She was afraid to hesitate any longer, she had to try and find her way back to the cave.

Linda Kay ran with the cross held out in front of her as she went. She was hurrying as fast as she could; she knew it was getting late, and

George would be up by now, and he would be looking for her. She didn't realize just how lost she was, nothing looked familiar to her. She should have marked her path, but it was too late to think about marking her path now.

Tears begin to flow from her eyes as the fear of not finding the cave again began to sink in. It was starting to get the best of her. She had no idea where she was. Her vision became blurry from the tears. She had to stop and wipe the tears from her eyes. *This is not helping me find my way… I've got to suck it up and think. It's getting late and will be getting dark in about an hour; I have to find my way back to that cave.* Again, she said a silent prayer and asked God to be with her on her journey. She knew in her heart of hearts that there was something wrong; otherwise, the entity would have been after her.

It was getting dusky dark when Linda Kay burst through a stand of trees to see George there in front of her. He was lying on the ground; blood was pouring from his sides. His head looked as if it had been used for a punching bag. Linda Kay ran to his side screaming, crying for mercy, begging him to be okay. She could hear a faint whisper coming from him.

She told him, "Quit trying to talk. I'm going to get you to safety."

There was no way that she could help him up on his feet. There's no way he could help with her struggles to get him back into the tunnel. She was going to have to figure this one out on her own. She was scared; she knew he was hurt and hurt bad. She didn't know if there was anything she could do to help him survive, which caused her to have squeezing pain around her heart. The thought of losing him was more than she could endure.

All at once, she felt nothing but anger. Her heart was filled with anger at the entity for what it had done to George. The anger seemed to fuel her with energy and give her strength. She refused to believe that George wouldn't live through this. She had to get all the negative thoughts out of her head. With God's help, she would defeat that entity. She laid the cross across George's chest, grabbed him under the arms and began to drag him toward the tunnel where they could find some safety. She hadn't realized just how big he was. It was no easy feat trying to get him back to safety. She fell on her bottom twice, jarring everything inside her, but she had no choice; she had to keep trying. Slowly, she began to gain headway, and she was getting closer to the tunnel. Linda Kay's arms were giving out; she was tired and exhausted. Darkness seemed to be creeping around them quickly; she had to get him in the tunnel while she had the last drop of light of the day. The anger Linda Kay felt for the entity seemed to give her strength. Once again, she wrapped her arm under George's arms and began to pull until at last they were entering the tunnel. Now the biggest problem of all lay ahead of her. How would she get him through the water and up into the cave?

Linda Kay knelt down next to George. she ran her hand across his forehead; he felt a little warm to her, and she was scared that he was getting a fever. She talked softly to him as she said, "George, I need your help, can you hear me? Do you understand what I'm telling you?"

George nodded his head slightly, as if it pained him to move.

He mumbled in a very low voice, "I will try."

Linda Kay took the cross off his chest and dropped it down the front of her blouse with all hopes of not losing it once she got in the water. She grabbed George under his arms once again and slowly began dragging him into the water. He was easier for her to handle once she had him in the water. She no longer had to try and carry his weight.

What she had to do next was to get George on the ledge and back in the cave. That was the part she was really concerned about; she didn't know how she would get him out of the water. She turned him to where he was facing the floor of the cave. She got his arms propped on the ledge.

She then told him, "Hold on to the ledge. I'm going back in the water, and I'm going to shove you up as hard as I can. I need you to help me to get you on that ledge."

He did as she told him; she pushed and shoved up as hard as she could. She knew she hadn't gotten him all the way on the ledge, but she had no choice she had to come up for air. She was surprised and stunned when she saw him. She had managed to get from his waist up lying on the ledge. She ran her hand across his forehead, feeling the heat that radiated from him. She knew she had to get him help, and she had to get it fast; his fever was rising.

She whispered, "I love you so much, George. You're going to be okay I promise."

With that she dove under the water, and she pushed and she shoved up as hard as she could on his legs, pushing and shoving them back on the ledge. She climbed out of the water, and once again grabbed him under the arms and began to drag him until she could lay him close to the pond.

CHAPTER 35

ELIZABETH PAID CLOSE ATTENTION, as everyone congregated together making plans. They were told where to start the search and when to give it up and head back. They were also informed that the family dog, named Chet, had disappeared at the same time as Chelsea. The dog was very protective of Chelsea. If anyone finds them, be careful if they tried to pick up Chelsea without the dog's approval, he would bite you. She checked her watch to make sure her time corresponded with everyone else's. Everyone had to have a partner for safety reasons, and they were told to stay together. They were also assigned areas to search. Elizabeth and Danny were partners and took off to work their assigned area. When they first started walking, they could hear other people calling Chelsea's name. As they walked on, other people's voices became fainter as everyone began to spread out.

Danny told Elizabeth, "We will spread out, but do not get farther away than what you can see my light or hear me calling you. I sure don't want to lose you."

"Believe me; I want to be close enough to you that if I holler you will hear me."

With that, they begin to veer apart from one another in order to cover more ground. The plans were to only stay out a couple of hours tonight and get up at daybreak and start again if no one had found Chelsea by then.

Elizabeth carefully walked along trying to take in everything she could with the flashlight. She was glad that they had handed out cans of bug spray before they left because she could hear the mosquitoes buzzing loudly around her head. With that, her thoughts went to that small child out in these woods somewhere without any protection. The thoughts of that broke her heart; they had to find her quick, or she would be eaten up with mosquito bites. Who knew about snakes? They would also be out crawling. She knew there were wolves in the woods because she had heard them howl at night. Yes, this child was in a lot of danger, and her heart broke for her. She prayed that they would please find her quickly and get her home to safety. She had let her mind drift too long on what could be instead of paying attention to what was. She brought herself back to reality and started looking around for Danny's light, but she couldn't see it anywhere. She called out for Danny a couple of times. She realized that she had messed up, and now she was lost. She was alone, and it was her fault.

Elizabeth told herself not to panic but to keep calling for Danny, maybe he would hear her. Then she could get back on track. She hollered and hollered for Danny to no avail. As she walked, she began turning one direction and then another trying to locate Danny's flashlight. She couldn't see his light anywhere, her heart began to pound, she didn't want to be out here alone she was scared, she really wanted Danny. She finally told herself quit being such a wimp.

There's a little three-year-old girl out here somewhere, and she's probably not acting this badly. She needs my help. Now go find her and stop being a wimp. Besides not only do you have a compass, but you know good and well Danny is not going to leave you out here. He won't stop until he finds you. I've got a little bit of food and some water; I'll be okay.

She decided to make a trail for Danny in case he came looking for her. She broke some branches on low bushes. She picked up a big stick and scratched in the dirt as she walked. Sometimes she would call for Chelsea, and sometimes for Danny. What she got in return were the sounds of the night, all its little creepy crawlers letting her know that she was in their domain.

She knew she had been walking for a long time. She punched the button on her watch, it lit up, and she saw they should've been heading back 30 minutes ago. She set her backpack on the ground and started digging through it in search of her compass. She was just fastening her backpack when she heard a noise. She wasn't sure if it was a cry or a whimper. She didn't know.

Her ears perked up, straining trying to hear more. It could have been the crying of a child; she wasn't sure. She listened hard, afraid to move from the spot she was in. Afraid she would not be able to hear the noise again; it was so faint that she wasn't sure if she heard it at all. She didn't realize she was holding her breath until her chest started to burn. She stood there for what seemed to be forever, but she was sure it wasn't more than a minute when she heard a faint cry again. She slipped back into her backpack trying to stay very quiet. The noise was so faint that she was afraid if she moved in the wrong direction, she would no longer be able to hear it. She very slowly started trying to move towards the noise. She had to be careful with every step she made because the crumpling of the leaves under her feet drowned out the cries and made it impossible for her to hear. As she slowly moved toward the cries they gradually grew louder. It became music to her ears when it became loud enough that she knew it was the cry of a child. She didn't want to startle Chelsea; she started singing hoping to soothe and comfort the little girl. As she got closer, the beautiful sound of the cries changed to the growl of a dog.

She knew she had found Chelsea but had to be very careful and not frighten the dog. She stopped in her tracks and shined her light around until the child and the dog were captured in the beam of the light.

She very calmly said, "Hi Chelsea, my name is Elizabeth. You don't have to be afraid. Your mother asked if I would help find you, she misses you and wants me to bring you home".

With that Chelsea stopped crying and stared at Elizabeth as if she was in a state of confusion. The dog continued to growl and let her know to keep her distance. Chelsea began looking around calling for her mama.

In a very calm voice, Elizabeth started talking to the dog. She was trying to convince him that it was okay for her to be there.

"I want to help Chelsea, okay?"

She struggled out of her backpack and set it on the ground. Without making any sudden movements, she slowly opened the backpack and pulled out a pack of peanut butter crackers. She held the cracker out toward Chet and said, "Come on, boy, this is for you, Chet."

The dog slowly, very cautiously walked toward her; she talked to Chet in a very calm and soothing voice, she knew she had to convince him that she was not the enemy. Chet very cautiously took the cracker from her hand quickly and backed away to eat it. She then took another cracker out of the pack held it out toward Chet; he immediately headed for the cracker, only slightly leery this time when he took the cracker. Next Elizabeth took out two crackers and moved a step closer this time when she knelt down, she held the crackers out one to Chet and one to Chelsea. Elizabeth had to smile at Chelsea; she looked so excited to have a cracker, and she could tell that her and the dog were beginning to feel more comfortable.

This time, it who Chet that walked up to Elizabeth and began sniffing, checking her out, just to make sure she was going to be okay to trust. Elizabeth slowly reached into her backpack and pulled out a bottle of water she took off the cap and poured water into her hand. Chet immediately started lapping up the water. Then Elizabeth moved over and gave Chelsea a drink.

She sat next to Chelsea and talked to her, and Chet in a very calm and soothing voice until Chet came and sat down next to her letting her know that he now fully approved of her.

Elizabeth then pulled her cell phone out of her back pocket and punched in Danny's number. She was very skeptical of whether or not the call would go through because she only had one bar.

Danny answered the phone.

"Where are you? We have been looking everywhere. Are you okay?"

Elizabeth tried to tell him that she was okay. She had found Chelsea and Chet, and they were okay. She told Danny to use the find my iPhone app in order to find her. Suddenly, the phone went dead; she had lost connection. The only problem was, while she was talking, her conversation come across on the other end sketchy and distorted.

Chapter 36

Danny couldn't make out half of what she was saying. He was trying to relate to everyone what she had said. Most of what she said did not make sense to him.

"I think she may have found Chelsea, I'm not sure. She may have just been asking about Chelsea, I really don't know. Please don't get your hopes up; I'm not sure of what she said. She was saying something about finding my phone, but I didn't understand that either. I still don't know where she's at or how were going to find her."

One of the teenage boys stepped up and said, "Let me see your phone, sir."

Danny looked at him questionably and reluctantly handed him his phone. The teenager immediately started punching keys. It wasn't long before he pulled up the coordinates for the location of Elizabeth's phone.

The boy handed the phone back to Danny and said, "Let's look on the map find these coordinates."

Danny shook his head in disbelief.

"What are you talking about, I don't get it."

"I traced her phone location. That is exactly where she's standing right now."

Danny took off to search the map for the coordinates; once he located the coordinates, he told the teenager, "Okay, here it is, now what?"

"I would say that it shows her phone to be approximately three miles that way. If you follow that path, it will take you to her phone."

"That's wonderful, thank you so much; I really do appreciate it, and I owe you and your girlfriend supper when I get her back. We will make plans I promise."

"Wait a minute my name is Mark Sharrette, I think you know my mom."

"Of course I do, my name is Danny, I haven't seen you since you were small child, sorry I didn't recognize you."

"That's okay, what I want to tell you is that my friend and I are here on our motorcycles, we can get you there a lot faster than you can walk it. Would you like a ride?"

"I would love it, thank you so much for the offer."

Mark turned around and hollered, "John, get your motorcycle and come on." He turned around to Danny and said, "I'll get my bike, be right back for you."

Chelsea's mom was standing there with tears flowing from her eyes, saying a silent prayer that Chelsea would be with Elizabeth. Danny slipped an arm around her and hugged her close, he told her they would be back as soon as possible.

"I wish I could tell you definitely that she has Chelsea, but I really could not make out what she was saying for sure. I'm sorry; I don't want to get your hopes up too high in case she didn't find her. I can only promise I will let you know as soon as possible."

Mark was back with his motorcycle raring to go as Danny hopped on the back. Mark took off, heading for the woods as fast as he dared to go. John's motorcycle was fast on Mark's heels as he took off following Mark through the woods. They bounced and jerked as it hit ruts that ran across the ground. Truthfully, Danny was scared, but he wasn't saying a word; he just wanted to find Elizabeth.

Chelsea's mom continued wringing her hands, pacing and watching for any sign of their return. Time seemed to stand still for Marcy as she stood there with fear and hope filling her heart with mixed emotions. She couldn't stand the pain another minute; she was falling totally and completely apart. Michael was trying to get her to calm down when the roar of motorcycles could be heard above her cries. She stopped her sobbing immediately as if everything had been sucked out of her as she waited anticipating the results.

Mark pulled his motorcycle up next to Marcy and come to a stop. Elizabeth uncovered Chelsea and handed her to her mother. There were so many cries of laughter and joy.

Tears of relief flowed from Marcy's eyes. She gave Elizabeth a huge hug, saying, "Thank you, thank you so much." She hugged Chelsea tight as she cried, "My baby, oh my baby, my beautiful baby, I love you so much."

Elizabeth smiled as she looked at Marcy and said, "She's safe, that's all that matters. When you get her to the hospital be sure and tell them I gave her a peanut butter cracker and a drink of water. I didn't want to give her too much before she saw the doctor. I also rubbed bug spray on her; she is covered from head to toe in mosquito bites." Elizabeth then leaned down and gave Chelsea a kiss on the cheek and told her, "I will see you later."

She then told her mom, "Okay, you can take her to the hospital and have her checked out I think she will be fine other than needing antibiotic cream for those bites. And a good meal topped with ice cream of course."

John pulled up next to Mark, Danny and Chet got off the motorcycle. Chet began barking and dancing around, excited to be back with his family once again.

Danny slipped an arm around Elizabeth as he said, "I am so proud of you. You did a beautiful job in handling your situation. If it hadn't been for Mark, I probably would not have figured out your conversation. He's a lot more computer savvy than I am. People talk a lot about the young kids today, well let me tell you Mark and John really stepped up to the plate when I needed help to find you. Thank God for them. God is really great. And by the way I promised to take Mark and his girlfriend out to eat, I would also like to include John and his girlfriend, and I hope that you will join us. I thought we would go to Harrison and have a good meal and then maybe go listen to one of the local bands. Anyway, I'm going to call Mark's mom tomorrow and make sure we can all get it together for maybe next Friday, and I will try to take off a little bit early from work. I think that'll be doable for us. And then let's plan our float trip again for next Saturday.

"Now it's awfully late or early morning, whichever you choose to call it. I think it might be a good idea to get you home and let you go to bed. You can sleep in tomorrow if you wish. I can promise you that's what I'm going to do. Maybe we can do something tomorrow afternoon. We can make all of our plans then. Especially, I want to make the plans for our trip to float the Buffalo once again. If Linda Kay and George are there, we will find them."

Elizabeth had a smile on her face as she said, "Honestly, I have been pretty hyped-up on adrenaline all night. Now I'm ready to crash. Nothing sounds any better than being able to sleep in. I could probably sleep most of the day tomorrow. Why don't you give me a call when you wake up; maybe we can plan something then."

Danny led Elizabeth back to the car and helped her in.

"You know Monday I will probably have to work late."

"Why is that?"

"Terrence is supposed to be in Monday remember, I need to start training him as soon as possible."

"Yeah, you're right, I guess I had forgotten. I will do anything I can to help. I also agree with you, I think he really wants to do a good job. So therefore, I believe with all my heart he is going to be a great employee."

"I really appreciate the offer, but honestly, I think you've been through enough; you get some rest. Besides you could be spending time planning the meal for our next picnic. As soon as things settle down, we're going on that float trip. I agree with you. Things need to be checked out a little more."

Before Danny got Elizabeth back to her house, she leaned her head against the window and fell fast asleep. Danny couldn't help but to look at her and think just how peaceful and beautiful she looked. He really wished he could wrap her in his arms and keep her safe from all the nightmares that haunted her from the loss of her friends. He pulled into the driveway and turned the car off, and with regret, he woke her up and walked her to the door. Once again, he told her how proud he was of her. He also told her just how beautiful he thought she was.

"You're a very special person, and I'm a very lucky person that I finally met you. He lowered his head and kissed her deeply. "I would give anything if I didn't have to let you go, but for now you better get to bed."

With that he took her key and unlocked the door. He lifted her head up to face him and kissed her softly before seeing her safely inside.

Elizabeth couldn't believe what had just happened. She didn't know what it was about Danny, but every time he touched her a shock ran through her body. She lost all sense of time and reality. This time, she was left in a state of shock and a little lightheaded as she seemed to float up the stairs as her thoughts dwelled on Danny and his electrifying touch.

Chapter 37

Linda Kay felt some relief now that she had George back inside their safe haven in the cave. At the same time, she was scared; she knew that George was in serious condition. She had dropped the pot with the muslin sheets and rags that she had been carrying when she saw George lying on the ground. She had left the hatchet where she found George. She now knew why she needed those things. She knew she had to go back out and retrieve the pan and all of its contents. She had also seen some wild yarrow growing in the woods during her excursion. She would need to retrieve the hatchet in order to help her dig up the yarrow. She had always heard that the Indians had used yarrow as a medicine. She hoped that it was true because she had no other choice; she was going to have to try and use it. She had high hopes that she could remember all the ways in which it was said that they used the medicine from this plant.

The worst part of it was, she needed that stuff, and she needed it now. It couldn't wait until she had daylight. The first thing she had to do was stop the blood flow from George's sides. She needed to get George's tee shirt off over his head. She was going to apply pressure to the cuts with his shirt to stop the blood flow. George had passed out, and there was no way he could assist her. She struggled, trying to be as easy as possible while she rolled him from side to side as she removed his shirt. What was making it so difficult was that the shirt was still wet. It clung to his body like some kind of a suction cup. She was not going to give up; she continued to tug until at last she had managed to pull his arms through the sleeves. She gave a big sigh of relief; she knew the hard part was over.

She wrung all the water out of the shirt that she could before she began applying pressure to his wounds. It took longer than she wanted but at last she did stop the blood flow. As long as he lay still, he would be all right for a little while.

Now she had to try and retrieve the large pot with all of its contents. Most of all, she had to come back here with some yarrow that she had seen growing wild outside. If the evil entity would let her, that is. She knew it was out there lurking, waiting to cause them harm or death. She couldn't help but feel like that whole trip yesterday was a set up just to let her know what can be taken from her.

Linda Kay laid her hand on George's forehead; he felt hotter to the touch than he had earlier. She knew his fever was rising, and she was running out of time. She had to retrieve the things she needed now. There was no more prolonging the time; she would have to do it in the dark.

She felt in her heart that she was probably walking into a trap. The evil entity would be waiting just outside their safe haven for her to once again step into the open. What choice did she have? She had to try and save George. She refused to dwell on the negative; she was going to get what she needed and return as soon as possible. She picked up the cross and put it into her blouse once again trying to keep it safe while she swam through the tunnel. The tunnel wasn't quite as dark as she had feared; there was enough of the moon out that she could follow the light to the end.

Before she stepped out into the open, she removed the cross from her blouse and held it out in front of her. She could feel the pressure in the air. It was as if she was pushing her way through the night air. She thanked God for the moon that helped to light her way. This was going to take a lot longer than she had thought; everything looked totally different in the dark of night. She felt vulnerable out in the open as she continued searching for the hatchet she had left next to where she had found George. She turned in circles, but nothing looked like it did in the light of day.

Her only choice was to walk forward in the direction that George had been laying and hope she would come close to that area once again. She stumbled along holding a wooden cross out in front of her, asking for God's protection as she walked along.

She saw something ahead of her that glittered in the grass. She let her hopes soar; maybe, just maybe, it would be the head of the hatchet glittering in the moonlight. She moved forward as swiftly as possible, holding onto the hopes that this would be the right place. Her heart beat fast with excitement as she bent down and picked up the hatchet and once again shoved it into her belt loop. Now if she could just find the pot with the muslin sheets and rags, she knew there were a lot of the yarrow plants in the same area. She would dig them up as quickly as possible and get back to George. Excitement filled her; she wanted nothing more than to get back to George and feel the safety of that cave. The air was still heavy around her, so she knew the entity was close to her. She held her cross high trying to protect herself as she recited the Lord's Prayer as she walked. She continued to say the Lord's Prayer over and over, which gave her a lot of comfort and the strength to go on.

She knew that she had dropped the pan as soon as she caught sight of George. That meant it shouldn't be very far from where she stood now. She had to think exactly which way did she run to reach George.

She did her best to try to guide herself in the right direction, anxious to get the job done and get out of there. She honestly did not see the pan until she accidentally kicked it, walking through some of the taller grass. She picked up the pot and all of its contents and hugged it close to her, whispering her thanks.

She was so thankful for the white blooms on the yarrow plant. It helped her to spot where the plants were located by the light of the moon. The only problem was, she couldn't dig them up with one hand. The dirt was packed hard and filled with rocks, in order to get to the roots of the plants she would have to use the hatchet. She had no choice but to lay the cross on the ground as she began whacking at the ground with the blade which caused sparks to fly.

Linda Kay had just started to dig up a plant when something slapped her hard and knocked her backwards. She knew at once that the entity had gotten to her. She couldn't reach the cross, even though it lay only a few feet from her. She needed to get to the cross fast, otherwise, she would be in the same shape as George, and they would both die.

She tried to get up, but to no avail; blood was pouring from her lips as she was knocked right back down. She did not want to give up; she had to fight with everything she had. She had to get back to George. This time when she tried to get up, she felt the sharp claws dig into her side. She flung herself forward as far as she could. She still could not reach the cross to help protect her. As she struggled to get back to the cross, suddenly her head was yanked backwards by someone or something pulling her hair. Linda Kay still would not give up. She started as loudly as she could to recite the Lord's Prayer. She continued praising God as she used all the strength she could muster to go forward. The entity continued to knock her back every time she tried to go forward, but she could tell its strength was waning.

She continued reciting the Lord's Prayer as loud and as strongly as she possibly could. Her strength was also giving out. She could feel the blackness wanting to surround her as her body became weaker and weaker. She put everything she had into her prayers as she continued to struggle forward trying to reach the cross. At last, she felt the end of the cross against her fingertips. If she could get just a little closer, she could get a grip on it and once again be able to push the entity back. There was one more knock, but it was more of a slap, the strength of the entity was being drained. She lunged forward one more time and got a grip on the cross and shoved it out in front of her continuing to recite the Lord's Prayer. Once again, she could feel the heaviness in the air. She knew it was still around but he had backed off once again. It was waiting for the next chance to attack.

Linda Kay had just learned a valuable lesson; she knew better than to lay her cross down again. It was going to make it harder trying to dig up the yarrow. There was no way she could go back without it. She feared that without this medicine, she would lose George. The thoughts of losing George sent a shudder down her spine and hurt her to the core. It also gave her the strength to fight harder to get through this because above all cost, she had to save George. She knew she needed some of the roots of the plants, and they would have to be dug up one way or the other, but she was going to do it. She knew in some cases, you used the flowers, and in others you used the leaves and stalks.

Linda Kay continued to work diligently going from plant to plant digging with one hand and holding the cross high with the other hand. Once she had the large pot filled with yarrow, she placed the muslin on top of the plants and put the hatchet back through her belt loop. She wrapped one arm around the big pot and held it close to her body. With the other hand she held the cross high and headed back toward the cave. As long as she had been busy digging the yarrow for George, she hadn't realized how sore and hurt she was. Now she could feel the pain with every step she took. The entity had caused her more damage than she had originally thought. She was beginning to feel a little lightheaded.

She tried to hurry back to the safety of the cave. She could feel herself getting weaker, and she began stumbling as she walked. She fell once, hitting the ground hard and knocking the wind out of her. She spilled all the contents out of the pot, but she had managed to hang onto the cross. She realized the reason why she was getting so weak was because blood had been flowing from her side where she had been cut. She couldn't stop herself from crying as she crawled around on her hands and knees retrieving the things she had spilled. The pain was excruciating, but she knew if she didn't make it back to George, he would die alone. That was enough to give her power to push forward. She knew she had no shame, but if she was going to die, she wanted to be there next to George. There had to be a way for her to get through that tunnel carrying the supplies; she needed to help both her and George. They now both needed medical care. She wasn't going to worry about that right now. She could only take on one problem at a time, and right now her problem was getting back to the tunnel.

Moving forward wasn't easy; Linda Kay's energy was spent. She thought, *I'm so close to George and yet so far away.* She felt as if her life was draining away from her bit by bit, but in her mind, she knew she did not want to die without George in her arms. If they were going to die, she wanted them to be together.

She began to crawl on her hands and knees; she would not give up that easy. If she was going to die, she wasn't going to go down easy. At last, she could see the entrance to the tunnel in front of her. It was only a few feet away, but it felt like miles to her she continued to crawl and push herself forward. The rocks were cutting her hands and knees. Making them bloody and sore, it was almost impossible for her to withstand the pain as she crawled forward one more time. She had to make frequent stops and try to take in a deep breath; breathing was becoming harder and harder for her. George wasn't far away.

She continued her struggle until she found herself at the tunnel's entrance. Excitement filled her heart; she wouldn't be stopped now. One way or the other, she would make her way back to George. She slipped inside the tunnel and immediately the air became lighter and easier for her to breathe. Linda Kay sat down on a rock taking air into her lungs and feeling her body beginning to grow stronger. Now was the time for her to figure out how she was going to swim with the hatchet and a large pot full of supplies that she needed for George. She decided to leave the hatchet inside the tunnel. She was going to try to hold the pot on top of her head with one hand and dog paddle with the other hand. She had no idea if such a thing would be possible. She just knew she had to get the pot through the tunnel without losing its contents.

It wasn't working out very well dog paddling with one hand, didn't really get her anywhere. She was just going around in circles. She tried to relax and just float and think of what she could do next. Her arm and hand were tired from holding the pot over her head. She had no choice; she just didn't have the strength to hold the pot up any longer. She lowered the pot in order rest her hand and arm a minute. When she did, she realized that pot would also float in the water. This gave her another idea; she pushed the pot as far out in front as she could then she swam to it then pushed it forward once again. She felt a slight sense of accomplishment as she had made her way through the tunnel and back to the cave, where she felt safe from the entity, and she felt the loving arms of the Ozarks as they encircled her safe haven.

CHAPTER 38

ELIZABETH WOKE UP WITH A SLIGHT MOAN as she struggled to roll over. She had managed to sleep away nearly all of Sunday. It seemed like only the blink of an eye before Monday morning was here, and it was time to get up and go to work. She sat up on the side of the bed, trying to make a decision. Did she go to work today, or just go back to bed? She debated with herself before at last she rose and dressed quickly before she changed her mind. She was tired and sore. She didn't think there was a spot on her that didn't hurt. She felt as if there hadn't been a weekend; it went by in the blink of an eye. There really wasn't any time to rest. It all started when one of the employees quit and then it didn't stop once they received word that little Chelsea was missing.

To tell the truth, Elizabeth was very proud of the fact that she was the one that found Chelsea. She was such a cute little child and was so happy to be found. All she wanted was her mama. Elizabeth's heart swelled with pride when she handed the child over to her mother. It sure made Elizabeth the talk of the town, which that made her feel a little embarrassed, but she knew it would soon pass. This little town would move on to the next problem. She was thankful that she was there when they needed her. When she had needed help, everyone had been there for her. At the same time, she felt like maybe she was cheating Linda Kay and George; maybe she should have been searching for them. Then she wondered, *What would've happened to that beautiful three-year-old little girl if I had not been there to find her?* Right now, her mind was a jumble. She decided to let it go because she did believe that she was where she needed to be at the time. The only thing she needed right now was the strength and the energy to get through today.

Danny walked up to Elizabeth as soon as she walked in the building.

"Why are you here today? You look to be totally worn out, why don't you go back home? We will handle this. You deserve a day off."

"Don't encourage it too much. I already had that discussion with myself and decided I needed to come to work. I'll be all right. I don't know why I'm so tired; I slept nearly all day yesterday. No one needs that much sleep. But I just feel tired and sore all over… Maybe I just need to work it out.

"Danny, I feel so bad because I really wanted to go look for Linda Kay this last weekend, but it wasn't meant to be. I can deal with that; I understand that things come up, but I'm afraid that I won't be able to go this coming weekend either. I don't know why I think that. I just do. That is what hurts it's because of me I'm too tired, I'm sore, and by the time we put in a week's work, I need to rest. That makes me feel really selfish. I don't know what's wrong with me today. I just don't feel good. Don't pay any attention to me.

"I've got to meet with Trinity this afternoon when I get off from work about the house. The exciting news is the house is about done. Then I will have all the moving to look forward to. I guess all I want to know is where I am going to fit Linda Kay back into my life. Who is going to look for her if I don't? I've got to go look for Linda Kay, that's why I'm here. She would never turn her back on me, and I just feel that she is out there waiting to be rescued."

"I understand how you feel it's going to be okay. I also understand that you're really tired; you had a very rough weekend. I think maybe you should go home and rest for the rest of the day. Maybe tomorrow everything will look different. As soon as you feel better, no matter what else comes up, we are going to spend our weekend looking for Linda Kay and George. Not just one day of the weekend but Saturday and Sunday. Then, when you feel like you have time to move, you have nothing to worry about. That is going to be no problem; you will have all the help you need getting your stuff moved out of the storage and into your home. You have done nothing but made friends here and given of yourself. Trust me, these people will give back."

With that, he bent his head and gave her a quick kiss, making her promise not to worry.

"I'm sorry; I guess I'm just feeling overwhelmed. But as far as going home today, I think I'd rather stay here and work. I'll be okay, you'll see."

CHAPTER 39

LINDA KAY HAD MADE IT BACK, but she was weak and tired. She didn't know where she was going to find the strength to do what needed to be done. She took one look at George, and her heart melted. She knew she would fight until her last breath to get him the help he needed. After getting out of the water, the cut on her side was bleeding heavily, and the first thing she had to do was to stop that bleeding. She took a piece of muslin and held it against the cut while applying pressure. She took the rest of the muslin and the drinking cups out of the pan, leaving only the plants. She walked back to the water and added water to the pan, she took the plants out one by one and washed them the best she could. She dumped the dirty water out of the pot. She refilled the pot once again and repeated the process. Once she had completed washing the plants, she filled the pot with water and carried it back next to George. She cut some of the roots of the plant and began chewing as she walked. She gathered a couple more torches and began gathering some of the old wood that was thrown around the cave. Once she had the roots chewed into a mush she spit it out into her hand. She took the paste and placed it on the cut at her side.

She lit another one of the torches. The old one didn't have much life left in it. The light was dim and just about to go out. She was so thankful that she had been able to light another off of it before it had gone out. She ripped off splinters of wood from the old boards and placed the smaller pieces around some of the larger ones and lit it with the torch. When she had a good flame going, she placed the pot of water on top of the fire to start the pot to boiling. She placed some of the plants in the water.

She now had another mouthful of chewed up roots; she spit it into her hand and begin spreading it over George's cuts. Then she wrapped his sides was strips of muslin cloth. Once Linda Kay had let the plants boil down and they were steaming heavily, she moved the pot close to George. She then opened the muslin sheet and covered the steaming pot and George's head so he could inhale all the steam possible. It was supposed to help with infection and help him to be able to breathe better.

Linda Kay strained some of the plants that she had cooked down to make a tea, and then filled the canteen with yarrow tea. She poured a small amount in one of the drinking cups. She lifted George's head and got him to sip a little of the tea. She then laid him back down and covered his head once again, so that he could breathe in the steam. That was about all she could do for now. She was so tired and sick herself, she crawled under the sheet with George in hopes that the medicine from the yarrow plant would help them both.

Linda Kay had just laid down when she felt as if the life was draining from her body. She felt a sense of nothingness. When all of the sudden, she saw someone there with her; he said, "I am the angel of death. I am here to see you through your journey."

Linda Kay knew at once she was going to die. That was okay because this angel of death that was sitting beside her had brought with him more peace and comfort that she had ever known. It would be hard to explain to someone just how relaxed she felt. She had no worries about anything as she began to feel herself slipping out of her body. It wasn't as if she was really walking but gliding along effortless. She could feel herself rising higher and higher until at last she come to a stop. That's where she was met by her grandmother, grandfather, her mother and a strange good-looking man that was introduced to her as her father. They each gave her a quick hug and a kiss, then her mother stepped forward and said, "Baby girl you've got to go back now. It's not your time yet. God said there's something else you need to do. First, we love you, and we'll be waiting until we will see you again."

Immediately Linda Kay could feel her spirit start to descend and once again land in her body. The angel of death smiled down at her with the sweetest and most gentle smile that she had ever seen as he started to fade away. Linda Kay had always feared the angel of death, but now she knew he had to be the gentlest angel of all. It was something that she would never fear again. No matter how much she stretched her imagination, she could never imagine the amount of love that she had just felt. She knew now that she was going to live, that she would be all right, and she would take care of George.

Linda Kay had no idea how long they had slept. She could tell by the light in the water that the sun was high in the sky. She crawled out from under the cover and immediately started building another fire. Once again, she sat the pot on the fire and brought it to the boiling point. She then set it carefully under the sheet so George could get more of the steam.

She was still very sore and hurt with every move she made. She had no choice; she had to keep moving, George needed her, and she would not turn her back on him. She placed more of the yarrow root in her mouth and began chewing it into a mushy paste. While she was chewing, she lifted George's head once again, getting him to drink some of the yarrow tea. Even though he did not drink much, she thought maybe he drank a little more than he had the night before.

Linda Kay then uncovered his sides revealing the ugly cuts the entity had made. Puss was oozing out of the cuts. She wasn't sure if that was good or bad, but she was happy to see that his body was repelling the infection. If that's what it was doing. She cleaned the cuts and then spit the rue out into her hand and once again began smearing it over his cuts. She wrapped his wounds with clean muslin cloth. She then washed out the old muslin the best she could in case she needed it later on. She was wishing that she had another pan that she could boil the linen and make sure it was sanitized. For now, she would make out the best way she could and make sure that everything she did for George was as clean and sanitized as possible.

Once she had George doctored, she repeated the process on herself. The tea she drank, she thought was awful to taste, but if it would help with infection and keep the fever down it was worth the awful taste. She wished now that she had paid more attention about how to use the yarrow, but she was applying everything that she could remember. She went over to the food supply and picked out a tomato and ate it. She wished she could get George to eat something, but she hadn't even been able to get him to stay awake. He'd been out of it a lot more than he'd been aware of anything that's going on. She still wasn't feeling well, so when she had cared for their needs, she crawled back under the muslin sheet with George and fell asleep.

When she awoke again, it was because George was thrashing about, she immediately got up and got the fire going once again. She could tell it was dark outside by the color of the water in the pond.

She felt of George's forehead. He was drenching wet; apparently his fever had broken, and he was fighting to get out from under the cover. She took the sheet off of him and began to wash him down with one of the muslin cloths. He was very weak. She could hear him mumbling about something. She really couldn't understand what he was trying to say.

She told him, "Just relax, and let me take care of you. You're going to be okay; I gathered some plants that will help you to heal. I will be right here with you, George, I love you I'm not going to leave you."

Linda Kay could see his body starting to relax as he drifted back off to sleep.

Linda Kay began her ritual of chewing more of the root while she poured some more tea to give to George. This time, when she lifted George's head, she told him, "This is yarrow tea. It's good medicine for you. You need to drink all you can. I know it doesn't taste good, but it's good for you."

George drank heartily this time, as if he was aware of what was going on. He seemed to be extremely thirsty, which gave Linda Kay high hopes of his improving. Then once she cleaned his wounds and put fresh paste of the rue on his wounds, she said, "George, would you like to try and eat something."

He shook his head no. That was disappointing, but Linda Kay understood how he felt. She then asked, "Would you like me to boil you some water to drink?"

He nodded his head yes.

"Okay you just rest; when it's ready I'll wake you up."

She brought a small tin of water to boil and then set it aside to cool. While the water was cooling, she proceeded with doctoring her own side. The cut was still red and swollen and very tender to the touch; she didn't know if it was wishful thinking, but maybe, just maybe, it was getting better.

Linda Kay leaned back against the wall of the cave and let her mind wander back in time. Her mind went to that beautiful cabin that her grandfather had built out of love, the love for her grandmother. She dreamed about the times she looked out at the mountains and pictured and imagined the arms of the Ozarks enclosing around them at night, protecting the people from danger that lurks in the night. All of a sudden, she realized that she was inside that protection now. Love and joy filled her heart because now she could understand the real beauty of this mountain. She had a smile on her face when she lifted George's head and helped him to drink the water. She didn't hesitate this time when she told him they would make it, they would be safe, and God was good.

Linda Kay had been making marks on the wall to keep up with the days that they sought shelter in the cave. She had lost count of the days while they were sick. They would wake up and go back to sleep so many times through the night. She would get up on several occasions to doctor her or to doctor George. There was no way she could keep up with whether or not it was the same day or the next day. Time became too confusing for her. She had no choice; she was going to have to give up trying to keep track of the days.

Exhaustion was beginning to take her over once again. She kissed George softly on the forehead and whispered how much she loved him. She hadn't realized just how weak she was, but she had no choice, she lay back down next to George and was soon fast asleep.

CHAPTER 40

ELIZABETH WAS ONLY ABLE TO WORK a few hours before her throat started hurting, she ached all over, and her temperature began to rise. She now understood why she had not wanted to come to work that morning. She thought at first it was just fatigue from the hectic weekend. She now knew better; she was sick.

Danny walked out of the back room and took one look at Elizabeth.

"Girl, you've got to go home. I don't know what you've got, but I don't want it."

"I understand. I'm feeling bad enough if I had a doctor, I would go see them first. Since I don't, I think I'll try to find something over the counter and then go home and go to bed."

"Wait a minute, I'm going to call my doctor and see if there's any way I can get you in to see him today. If I can, I will."

"I really don't even want to take the time to get something over the counter I just want to go home and go to bed. Don't worry about it, I'm just going to go home for now. When I get to feeling better, I'll try to go get something. Right now, I just need some sleep. Hopefully I'll see all of you in the morning."

Danny gave her a sideways glance as if to say maybe you've lost your mind. What he said was, "You can see a doctor today, or the hospital tomorrow, you pick it."

"Okay, I'll go. I don't like it, I just want to get it over with, so I can go home."

"I'll go make the call, and I'll be right back. Sit down right there, and wait for me." Danny disappeared to the back room again, so he could make his call. When he returned, he was happy to tell Elizabeth, "The doctor will work you in if you come right on."

"Okay, tell me where he is located, and I'll go."

Danny looked rather sheepish as he said, "He's located in Harrison."

"Are you out of your mind? I don't feel like driving to Harrison. I'm sorry; I can't do that. I'm going home and going to bed. I'll see you when I get to feeling better."

She started toward the door. Then she came to an abrupt stop, aggravation and frustration was written all over her face. She began looking around the room for her purse.

"No, I'm going to drive you to Harrison myself. You can lay down and rest in the back seat on the way. Now that that's settled, let's go." He handed her purse to her, took her arm, and guided her out door.

Elizabeth thought this day would never end. She knew that it was because she felt so bad that she looked at everything from the negative side. The trip to Harrison seemed to take forever, and she just wanted to go home. She sat in the doctor's office for what seemed to be forever before her name was called. She still didn't want to be there. Why wouldn't Danny just take her home and let her go to bed? She didn't know he could be so stubborn.

Now her only choice was to sit back here in this little room by herself for God only knows how long. She was feeling so miserable and thinking about climbing up on the doctor's table and lying down. She was ready to cry and thinking seriously about leaving. Suddenly, the door opened and the doctor walked in with a big smile on his face asking, "What can I do for you today?"

That made Elizabeth even angrier; she felt like telling him she had just come by to discuss old times. What in the world did that man think she was doing there? Instead, she took a deep breath and began to tell him what was wrong with her.

At last she emerged from the doctor's office with prescriptions in hand and a pain in her arm where she had been given a shot. The doctor had diagnosed her with the flu. This time, she was happy to get back in Danny's vehicle because at last he was going to take her home, where she could go to bed. Elizabeth was lying on the backseat sound asleep when Danny stopped at the drugstore there in Harrison and had her prescriptions filled. She was still asleep as Danny climbed back in the car and proceeded to take her home.

Danny had called Trinity and told him that Elizabeth had been diagnosed with the flu. Trinity had assured Danny that Mary would be there to help Elizabeth. Sure enough, when Danny pulled into Elizabeth's driveway Mary was there waiting for them. Mary immediately took charge helping Elizabeth up to her room and getting her prepared for bed. She then went downstairs and got her prescriptions ready, got her a glass of water and returned to the bedroom. She told Elizabeth what each one of the pills was for before having her to swallow it with some water. Once she had taken her medicine, Mary told her, "Lie back to rest. If you need anything else, just call out for me, and I'll be here to help you.

Danny went in to see Elizabeth one last time before he left her in Mary's capable hands. Danny assured Elizabeth that everything would be just fine at work.

"I don't want you to worry about anything. Just take care of yourself, and I'll be checking on you every day, I promise. Mary will be here to take care of you and make sure you get your medicine on time. If you have a problem or need me just, give me a call and I'll be right here. I'll be by tomorrow to check on you."

He bent down and kissed her on the forehead and turned to leave. Elizabeth stopped him as she called his name.

"Danny, do you realize that will probably mean another weekend that I won't be able to go look for Linda Kay and George? No one has found the bodies and unless that happens, I will never give up my thoughts that she could still be alive. I think she's out there and needing my help, and I'm letting her down. What am I going to do? I can't just keep leaving her out there and not even going to search for them. Don't you understand? When I sleep, I dream of her calling my name. I dream of her asking for my help. Yet for one reason or another, I haven't been back to search for her. I'm just getting on with my life and letting my friend suffer alone in need of my help."

"As soon as you get to feeling better, we will go out and look for Linda Kay. I promise we won't forget Linda Kay or George either one. They both mean a lot to us, and I understand exactly what you're saying, but you have to take care of yourself and get well so we can do that. Now you get some rest, and I will check on you later."

As Danny turned to leave, his head was hanging low because he really did understand the heartache she was feeling. She had been trying to carry the heart ache all on her own. But no more; he was going to be there for her and to help her carry that burden. He wished there was something he could do to bring Linda Kay and George back. Personally, he doubted if they would ever find them. He felt like if they were there, they would've been found already, if they were okay. That was the one thing he did not have the heart to tell Elizabeth, but he would take her out to search for them as long and as often as she wanted to go.

Chapter 41

Linda Kay woke up, and she immediately reached over to check on George. His fever had broken, and at last he was cool to the touch. She sat up slowly and looked over at George and smiled when she saw that he was awake and alert.

"Hey you're looking good, better than I have seen you in a while."

"I was trying to lay still and not disturb you. I'm sure you could use the rest."

"To see you looking better is all I need. You have been very sick; I was very worried about you. I'm glad to see you doing better. Do you think there's any way you could eat something? Your body really needs some nourishment.

"I really think I'd like to try. I do feel awfully hungry. I feel like I haven't eaten in days. I'm sure that's why I feel so weak."

Linda Kay got up and started walking over to the food; as she did, she told him, "That's because you haven't eaten in days."

George began to struggle as he tried to sit up. You could see the pain in his eyes as he struggled not to cry out in pain.

"How long have I been in this shape?"

"The shape you're in right now not very long. You're looking great now compared to what you did. If you want to know how long you been sick, I wish I could tell you, but I lost track of the days. I tried to keep up with it, but I was sick, too. There was too much sleeping and waking up, I couldn't keep up if it was the same day or not, I'm sorry. I can only tell you it's been a long, hard road. So, let's see what you can eat."

She laid out before him some strawberries, greens, tomatoes, and some yarrow flowers that had been dried. George pointed to the flowers and frowned as he asked, "What is this, am I supposed to eat it?"

"That is why you're feeling better. It's called a yarrow plant. You really need to eat some of the blooms. It will help to get your strength back. While you eat that, I'm going to pour you some yarrow tea. You really need to drink it. It doesn't taste great, but it's very good for you. You have lost a lot of blood; we've got to get your strength built back up. We're not getting the vitamins we need out of what we've been eating. I'm not saying that foods we've been eating aren't good for us, because they are. I'm just saying that we need more vitamins in our diet. We've got to get our strength up. We need to be in good shape the next time we go out."

"I don't understand what's been going on. I don't know what happened. The last thing I remember was that I woke up, and I couldn't find you. I went outside to start searching for you. The next thing I remember is, I wake up, and I'm here, and I don't know how I got here. Or anything else that's happened in between."

Linda Kay took her time and tried to explain everything that had gone on from the time she left until she got them both back in the cave to safety. She tried to tell him as much as she knew about the yarrow plant. She also related the fact that they needed to exercise and build up their strength before they went back out. Then her eyes lit up, and you could hear joy in her voice as she told him how the cross had helped her to get back to safety.

"I'm sure we can use some of the scrap wood in the cave to make a cross for you. I don't think either one of us should ever leave this cave again without the cross. One way or the other, we've got to get off this island. I know you're still very sore, and so am I. I'm going to check our wounds, and then we're going to eat. We're going to start working on some light exercises. Then we will work our way up until were strong enough to get out of here. I'm not going to let that thing beat me. In a few days, I will have to go back out and get some more yarrow. As you know, what food we've got is not going to last forever. I saw some fishhooks in that old shed. I should've got some, but I didn't know we were going to have to find a way to fish. We need the vitamins they provide. So, eat up—whether it tastes good or not. We're getting better, and we're getting out of here.

George just shook his head in agreement and sit in silence for a few moments before he said, "I agree with you. I will do everything I can to get us out of here." Then his eyes filled with a pleading look as if he was almost begging her. "Please promise me that we will never be separated again. Without you by my side, I have no reason to go on."

Linda Kay knelt beside him as she leaned over and kissed him softly.

"I could never regret anything more than I did trying to get food on my own. I agree with you, I never want to be separated like that again. Now that that's settled, let's eat and go to work."

Instead of rationing their food, today they ate their fill. Then they went to work and assembled another cross. It was difficult considering what they had to work with. It held together mostly on the wings of a prayer, but hold together it did. Then they got into the water and began to swim until they were tired. Then they climbed back out of the pool. They rested for a little while before climbing back into the water, this time to do some water aerobics. They continued this process of swimming and then aerobics until they were both exhausted and climbed back out of the water.

Even though their wounds were healing quite well, Linda Kay still begin the process of chewing the roots and making a plaster to cover their cuts. Once again, they ate another meal and ate until they there were full. They knew they needed to conserve food, but by the same token they needed to regain their strength and their energy. They had decided to fight, and fight they would until they found a way off this island. Tomorrow was another day, and they would go out again and retrieve more food. They would look for different food that grew wild on the island. Linda Kay swore she would retrieve the fishhooks from the shed, and they would be doing some fishing. The land would provide everything they needed to grow stronger and healthier.

Even though Linda Kay was tired, she went to sleep with a smile on her face because her heart was filled with confidence once again. She still didn't have any idea how they were going to get off the island; she just knew they would.

As soon as she woke up the next morning, she realized just how sore she was from the exercise they had done the day before. She still wasn't going to give up. She had high hopes that walking today would work out the soreness. Their food supply was diminished. They had no other choice they had to go for food today.

She gently woke George, encouraging him to get up. They would eat the remainder of their food then they would head out once again in search of a variety of edible plants and berries.

George groaned as he sat up.

"Wow, I didn't know I had so many places that could be so sore. Do you think we're really going to be able to swim out of here? I don't know how you feel, but it hurts for me to even blink."

Linda Kay softly laughed at his comment.

"Blinking is about all I can manage right now. I'm hoping as we start to walk, we'll be able to walk out some of the soreness. We have no choice but to go today. As soon as we eat breakfast, there will be no food left. We will make it, I have faith. Besides I'm almost dreaming about those fishhooks; getting those is about all I can think of. Just thinking about it, has me tasting fish over and over again. So, eat up and let's get ready to go."

Trying to swim wasn't the easiest thing they had ever done. They could really feel the muscles stretching and pulling they can feel the pain as they glided through the water. They had no choice they had to keep swimming now or drown. They would not give up on life and their chance to finally be together.

Once they climbed out of the tunnel, George stopped Linda Kay.

"Wait just a minute." With that George reached down and got some mud in his hand and made a cross on Linda Kay's forehead. "Turn around." He then proceeded to apply the mud to the back of her blouse, making a large cross on her back. He then took what mud he had left and proceeded to put a cross on his own forehead.

"That is a wonderful idea I'm sure of one thing it won't hurt. Now turn around so I can put a cross on your back. As they started to walk in search of food Linda Kay began saying the Lord's Prayer. George soon joined in reciting the Lord's Prayer. The words began to sound musical as if the notes were floating in the air.

They hadn't walked too far when the air around became heavy and hard to breathe around Linda Kay. She knew the entity was now close to them, waiting to attack. She just held her cross a little higher and began reciting the Lord's Prayer a little louder. George followed her lead. He had learned the hard way that she knew what she was doing.

They stopped periodically for George to dig up some yarrow. They had also stumbled across some blackberry vines that were loaded with plump juicy blackberries. They not only picked what they could carry but they also ate their fill off the vine.

Just as Linda Kay thought everything would be okay; she felt the air get even thicker and dust started flying around them so hard and so strong it made it impossible for them to see where they were going. It stung their arms and faces; it felt as if their faces were being sand blasted. Linda Kay ducked her head trying to keep the sand out of her mouth as she continued the Lord's Prayer in a loud and predominant voice. There seemed to be streaks of lightning flashing in the air all around them. There was an angry noise like the yell of an injured animal that filled the air with a piercing noise. Linda Kay and George both had to put their hands over their ears trying to drown out the piercing noise; it was such a high pitch that it seemed to drill into the eardrum. It was down to the battle of strength and who could hold out the longest. Linda Kay and George continued reciting the Lord's Prayer, although their voices were losing strength. Linda Kay knew if they were to quit, the entity would win, and they would die. At last, she could feel the entity losing control, and the sand begin to slow down until at last it had settled once again.

George and Linda Kay were left with pit marks over their bodies. Linda Kay felt as if she had really been sandblasted. Blood seeped from their faces and arms. Yet Linda Kay told George she would not go back without the fishhooks. They continued trudging toward the old homestead. Once it came into sight, Linda Kay's heart began to race with excitement. They both begin to run, anxious that they finally had their goal in sight. Without thought or concern about what punishment lay ahead of them or how much more they would have to endure they continued to march forward. They just knew they had to grab the fishhooks and the old fishing line.

As he turned to leave, George grabbed a couple of dowels that were lying on the workbench. Now they would grab what food they could from the garden and try to race back to the cave and their safe haven.

Their hearts pounded with fear as they begin to run back toward the cave. They were expecting at any moment to be attacked. It was as if the entity was toying with them. Linda Kay and George once again started their musical song of the Lord's Prayer. The only problem they had going back was the heaviness in the air that made it hard to breathe. It was as if the oxygen was being sucked out of the air. The loud, shrill sound of agony that was piercing on the eardrum continued. The sounds causing them to endure pain and agony, their heads were pounding in pain, but they were almost back to the cave where they could find safety.

Once they entered the tunnel things seem to quiet, and they were at peace once again. They both had a bad headache. Dried blood was spread over their bodies where the sand and dirt had scoured them. Linda Kay was fighting back tears trying not to show the anguish she felt. George slipped an arm around her shoulders and pulled her close telling her that everything was going to be okay.

"After all is said and done, we still have each other. What better day could you ask for?"

Linda Kay couldn't handle it any longer she burst into tears.

"I just want to go home. I don't wish any hurt nor harm to anyone or anything. I just want to go home."

"I understand, and together we'll make it home. Once George had gotten Linda Kay to settle down, she proceeded to make them some yarrow tea with hopes that it would take care of the damage that they had suffered that morning.

CHAPTER 42

ELIZABETH HAD A TERRIBLE WEEK. She stayed in bed with chills and fever. Mary was a faithful friend; she saw to it that her medicine was taken on time and that she either ate or drank a health drink that insured she would get the vitamins that she needed to regain her strength.

Elizabeth rolled over just as Mary entered the room.

"I'm glad you're awake, I need you to take your medicine. I'm happy to see you looking better today. You'll be on your feet before long."

Elizabeth sat up in bed and took her medicine and swallowed it with some water. Then she handed the glass back to Mary and fell over in bed. She was ready to go back to sleep. While she was asleep, the aches and pains were tolerable. She didn't know the flu could ever make you feel so bad.

Mary tapped Elizabeth on the shoulder.

"Stay awake, I need you to eat first."

"I don't want anything; I not hungry I just want to go back to sleep," she mumbled.

"That's fine, as long as you drink this first."

"What is it? I don't want it. I want to go to sleep."

"If you want to go back to sleep, you pick it: You either eat, or you drink this nutritious drink. You can't go back to sleep until you do one or the other."

Elizabeth quickly sat up in bed and took the nutritious drink and drank it down as fast as possible.

"Now please let me go back to sleep." With that she rolled over, shut her eyes, and within moments, she had fallen back to sleep.

That was pretty much how Elizabeth's week went by. She barely talked to Danny when he came by every day to check on her. He reassured her of the promise he had made; as soon as she got to feeling better, they would go look for Linda Kay and George.

The week seemed to creep by; Elizabeth felt like it had been a month, but at least she was out of bed today. She was a little weak, but getting around. It was Friday, and Danny couldn't wait to get off from work; he was going to see Elizabeth. It had also been a long week for him. Not only had he missed her at work, after all she was a good employee, he had also missed her personality, her presence, laughter, and joy that she brought into his life. Once again, he had a big smile on his face knowing that he could spend some time with her this weekend. She would be able to come back to work Monday morning. Maybe then their lives could get back to normal.

Danny was standing at Elizabeth's door with a dozen yellow roses when he knocked. He didn't really know what her favorite flower was, but yellow roses always seemed to be a hit. He had news to tell her, and it was all he can do to hold his excitement in check.

Elizabeth opened the door and let Danny in, she was excited to see him.

"Oh my goodness! It is so good to see you, and I feel like talking to you at the same time. I know you came by the whole week, but honestly, I didn't feel like talking. I'm sorry. but I'm ready to make up for it now."

Danny had a big smile on his face as he gave her the roses.

"I have always heard that roses will make you feel better. I sure hope that these will put a smile on your face. I've got news to tell you. To tell you the truth, I'm nervous as a cat and so excited at the same time. I hope and pray I haven't made a mistake."

"Well, don't keep me in suspense tell me all about it."

"You know that house in Harrison that I've always loved? I bought it. The next day after we saw it was for sale, I went after it. I just found out today that it's mine."

"Oh, Danny! I'm so excited for you. In my mind's eye, I can already see it in all its grandeur."

"I knew you would be excited for me. To tell the truth, I'm scared to death and at the same time I'm so excited. It has been my dream home for so many years; there was no way I could just walk away and let it go. After all, you bit the bullet and took a chance, and now your place is looking beautiful. I figured it was about time that I take a chance."

"Come on, have a seat, and I'll get us a coke. We can discuss all your plans; every minute of working on that place will have to be done with excitement and skill."

As Elizabeth handed Danny a coke he told her, "I haven't talked to Trinity yet, but you know there's no one else I would want to work on that house but him. I know that everything he does there would be done with love and care."

"I'm sure fixing that place up would be the highlight of Trinity's life. He loves the work and can pull beauty out of thin air. It's amazing at the magic his hands can work. I totally agree with you; he is the only one I would want to work on the house. There's no doubt in my mind that he can bring back all of the original beauty."

"I sure hope you're right. I think with Trinity's help I have a good shot at it. There is one more thing I wanted to ask you; do you think you will feel like going on a canoe trip this weekend? I promised you we would go and look for Linda Kay and George, and I intend to keep that promise."

"Yes, that's the one thing I definitely want to do. I'll need to go to the store to get some groceries in order to pack us a picnic lunch."

"No, not this time. This time I furnish the picnic lunch. I don't want you wore out before we ever start."

"Are you sure? I really don't mind doing it."

"Yes, I'm sure I've already talked to Mary about it. She promises it will be ready in the morning."

Elizabeth had to laugh.

"That's terrible! You said you were going to take care of it."

"I did. I asked Mary to do it so therefore I took care of it. What do you say we watch a movie and make it an early night? I want you to have plenty of rest before we leave."

"That sounds like a good idea to me. You pick out the movie, and I'll go pop the popcorn."

Danny picked out *Alaskan*; it was a great movie that they thoroughly enjoyed. But most of all, they enjoyed each other's company. They stuck to their word and called it an early night. Danny was going to pick Elizabeth up at 7:00 the following morning. Elizabeth went to bed that night and had sweet dreams of Danny.

Elizabeth was anxious to get up the next morning. She had such high hopes that maybe; just maybe they could find Linda Kay and George. The odds may not be very good, but they only needed one, they needed the right one. As long as there was no body, no one would be able to convince Elizabeth that Linda Kay had passed on. She would not give up her hopes that easily.

She dressed in comfortable clothing, but she did not apply her makeup. She learned from her first canoe trip that makeup was not a good idea. She had black streaks running all over her face from that canoe trip. She knew right away it wasn't a look she desired to repeat. Besides, she was someone who really didn't require make up, her features seem to stand out on their own.

She hurried downstairs fixed her a piece of toast and a cup of coffee. Her timing must've been perfect because just as she had finished eating, there was a slight knock at the door. She opened the door with a big smile on her face.

Danny said, "I have our lunch already in the car and all I need now is you. Are you ready to go?"

"Oh yes, I'm definitely ready"

Elizabeth's heart beat with excitement as Danny pushed the canoe away from the shore they were actually on their way once again. This time, when she found that old homestead, she was going to check it out lot better than she had before. In her heart, she really felt as if there were some answers there, and she intended to find them.

Chapter 43

Linda Kay and George finished eating their fill of fish and berries. They had spent this week working out, fishing, and trying to build up their strength. They had been eating better, and they were feeling stronger and healthier. They didn't have steak or a big pot roast, but they ate good, healthy foods. They had decided that today was the day that once again they would fight their way back to the homestead. The only thing they were taking with them was their crosses and their food bag. Once they filled the bag with food, they swore they would get off the island. They had no idea what would be thrown at them. Therefore, they really couldn't make plans. They had to decide everything on the spur of the moment, but one way or the other, today was the day they were going to leave this island. They refused to be held hostage for the rest of their lives.

As soon as they stepped out of the water, George picked up a handful of mud. He highlighted where he had made the cross on the back of Linda Kay's shirt the last time they had left the cave. Once he had completed working on Linda Kay's shirt, she had George to turn around, and she did the same to the back of George's shirt. With that ritual completed, he turned Linda Kay to face him he looked at her with love in his eyes as he began fixing the mud cross on her forehead. At the same time Linda Kay added a cross to George's forehead. George then kissed her deeply before taking her hand and walking out into the open. They were met with that heavy feeling of dread.

Linda Kay knew immediately that the entity was there, waiting for them and refusing to let them go. It was as if the entity felt like they were its hostage. It would never let them go until it killed them, in its own time and at his leisure. The air seemed even heavier than usual, this time making it where they had to struggle in order to breathe. She knew that the entity had no intention of letting them walk away. There was a loud piercing cry in the air; it was made up of anger and violence. It seemed to be even stronger and angrier than before. As Linda Kay and George started to chant the Lord's Prayer, the cries of the entity seemed to grow louder and stronger. Just for a second, Linda Kay's faith began to dwindle. Out of nowhere, she started to shout, "Never will I give up my faith, never. Now go to the light, give up the anger, and give up the hostility, God waits for you. Now go to the light in peace and tranquility, it waits for you."

Once again she starts reciting the Lord's Prayer, but the entity's anger just seemed to grow louder and meaner than ever before.

Elizabeth and George rowed up to the bank and docked the canoe. Elizabeth began looking around.

"Look Danny all the footprints are gone, it's as if no one has ever stepped foot on this island before."

"I'm sure the rain washed them away. You don't need to worry. We will put some new ones down."

"What I was talking about, if they had been Linda Kay's and George's, there would still be some footprints around. I don't care; I still want to look around at that homestead again."

Danny wrapped an arm around Elizabeth and looked deep into her eyes.

"That was my sign; I had all the other footprints washed away. So, we can call this our island. We can run wild between the trees and answer to no one but each other."

Elizabeth laughed, "Yeah, I'm afraid that picnic basket will run empty before long. Then we'll be ready to go back, so don't get too attached to this island. Hunger will win out every time."

"Well it sounded good for a minute until you brought me back to reality. Right now, I'm going to pretend and have all the fun I can while I'm here. Now are you ready to pretend with me? Remember I use the word pretend, so pretend, and that is what I'm going to do as long as we're here. I get enough reality every day at work. So today is my day to play."

Elizabeth laughed.

"Well, since we're pretending, let's leave the picnic lunch until later. I wouldn't want our pretending to end too soon because we ran out of food."

Danny bent down and kissed her on the nose, put his arm around her waist, and said, "Come on, let's go check out that old homestead."

They walked slowly, enjoying the scenery, and most of all, they were enjoying each other's company.

Danny looked at Elizabeth as he said, "I'm afraid to ask if you have decided to stay here? I don't mean to pester you. I'm asking for personal reasons; it has nothing to do with the job. I'm afraid I'm beginning to get a little too attached to you. I would hate to see you leave."

"You know, Linda Kay always talked to me about the beauty of the Ozarks, and I didn't really understand what she was trying to tell me. Now that I'm here, I understand exactly what she was telling me. Sometimes I miss the hustle and bustle of town. I miss the grocery store being within a few blocks of my house. No matter what I need, it's close to where I live. I drop my clothes off at the cleaners, stop by and pick them up on the way home. I never gave it a second thought of how convenient everything was to me. So yes, I do miss city living in a lot of ways. But now I don't know if I could ever sacrifice the beauty that's here in the Ozarks. At night, I can listen to God's creatures scurrying about. They're living free and taking only what they need from the land that God has provided for them. During the day, I meet people who really care about one another. They have time to ask about you and your family. It's a whole different world here in the Ozarks, but it's also a wonderful world, and I don't know that I'll ever be able to live without its wonder ever again."

"I hope that you decide to never leave here. If you were to leave now, it would really mess with my world. To me, you are one of the wonderful wonders that God put here on Earth. I don't know what will happen, but I'm hoping that maybe he put you here for me."

Just as Elizabeth was about to say something else to Danny there was a loud shrill cry that seemed to come out of nowhere.

"What was that?"

"I don't know. It's a sound I've never really heard before, but it sounds like the cry of a wounded animal."

"Do you think we should still go to the homestead? I'm not really sure where that noise came from; it was almost as if it was surrounding us. I know one thing: it's making me awfully nervous."

"Yes, I think we should keep going. I'm not sure either of where the noise came from, but if it's up that way, maybe we could help it. If we can't help it, maybe we could find some way to get it out of its misery. It was a frightening sound, one like I've never heard before. It sent a shiver down my spine. If there's something in that much pain and in need of help, I need to do what I can to help it. I say, yes, we need to try and help, let's go on and see what's up there."

"Okay, but please stay close to me. I may be in need of your help if I see something that could make that kind of noise."

Danny just smiled at her and hugged her close as he said, "My pleasure."

Chapter 44

Linda Kay whispered to George, "There's the homestead let's run for the garden."

She went back to her chanting, and they took off running. George started picking tomatoes and strawberries and greens as fast as his hands would move. Linda Kay held the cross over his head while she continued reciting the Lord's Prayer in a voice that was filled with confidence.

Elizabeth and Danny just stepped in sight of the homestead when Elizabeth started shouting, "Linda Kay, Linda Kay! Hey, it's Linda Kay!"

She took off running as fast as her legs would carry her. Elizabeth and Linda Kay grabbed each other with tears running down both their faces, they were so happy so excited to see one another again. Danny and George were shaking hands talking about how proud they were to see each other.

George told them that he was so thankful to see them.

"I was afraid that we would never get off this island. Can you please take us home now? We don't have time to talk, we've got to get off this island, please get us off now.

Elizabeth said, "Of course, we will take you home right away. We brought a picnic lunch if you would like to eat before we leave."

Linda Kay immediately spoke up: "No! Get us out of here now."

Elizabeth was fixing to answer, but instead, she let out a loud scream. Blood began pouring from her side. Dust and dirt blew up all around them. Dirt blew in their eyes before they had a chance to protect themselves, causing their vision to blur. Danny cried out in pain as he was slashed crossed his chest. Blood poured from his chest. They couldn't see to run, and they didn't know which way to go. They were in agonizing pain. They had both fallen to the ground, Danny felt as if he was being kicked. They couldn't see what was attacking, but it was unmerciful what they were trying to endure.

Out of nowhere, just as it had started, it came to a halt. In the distance they could hear that horrid cry once again. You could feel the anger and hatred in the air around them. Across the grounds, lightning crackled and popped all around them.

Arms reached down and helped Elizabeth and Danny to their feet. Elizabeth heard Linda Kay's voice as she shouted out, "Get them inside the homestead!"

All Elizabeth knew for sure was that they were being moved to a safer area. They were being hurried away as someone's arms pulled them in the direction they wanted them to go. Elizabeth and Danny were both having a hard time seeing, so they let themselves be guided away. Lightning danced around their feet as they moved, Elizabeth had never been so scared in all her life. She was beginning to freak out, losing all signs of reasoning when she heard Linda Kay say, "Snap out of it, girl, we need your help. Freak out later, you don't have time now."

Tears began to flow from Elizabeth's eyes, and dirt began to run down her cheeks.

"Help me, please, I can't see."

Linda Kay took Elizabeth's hand and guided her to the sink. She primed the pump until water began to flow evenly and clearly. Then she had Elizabeth to run clear water over her eyes until the dirt and debris was washed away. Her eyes were bloodshot and looked very irritated, but at least she was able to see again. Danny followed and cleaned his eyes; when he finished, his eyes burned and stung, but at least he could see. They all hugged each other thankful that they were together. Now the problem was to try and find a way out of there.

As quickly as Linda Kay could, she began trying to explain what was going on. At the same time, she began getting ashes out of the stove mixing it with water making a paste out of it. She then put the sign of the cross on Danny and Elizabeth's foreheads. She then had them to turn around and put the sign of the cross on the back of their shirts. George was busy making them a cross that they could hold out in front of them as they tried to run for safety.

Linda Kay explained to them about the entity that existed on the island. She also explained the danger that they were all in. She explained to them how very important it was that they held the cross in front of them at all times.

Linda Kay then took some of the yarrow plants that they had gathered out of the food bag and washed them at the pump. She then cut the roots off and started chewing them. When she had the consistency of a paste, she spit it out into her hand. She began rubbing the paste on Elizabeth's cuts. She repeated the process and did the same to Danny. She also explained that they really were not safe in the house. That the entity was just gathering up more energy and would return with a vengeance.

"Now we've got to figure out how to get out of here, fast," she told them.

Their dilemma was whether to try to make it back to the cave, or should they make a run for the canoe? Had the entity already destroyed the canoe? If they decided to go in the direction of the canoe, and it was destroyed, it would make it more difficult to get back to the safety of their cave. By the same token, if the canoe was still in good shape, it would be their only chance to get off this island. They decided to check on the canoe and take their chances.

They opened the door ready to make a run for it. The entity was there to meet them; it started screaming as if in agony as they continued reciting the Lord's Prayer as they were heading as fast as they can toward the canoe, but suddenly, rocks were being thrown at them—heavy rocks. One hit Elizabeth in the ribs, and she doubled up in pain, screaming. Danny wrapped his arm her, trying to help her to dodge the rocks that kept coming. They continued dodging them by darting this way and that. It was hard for Elizabeth to breathe; she was sure her rib had been broken.

Linda Kay knew they would never make it this way. She turned and looked straight ahead, as if she was staring the entity in the eyes. She continued reciting the Lord's Prayer in a loud and defined voice. The others stopped and stared at her not knowing what to do. She finally told them to keep reciting's the Lord's Prayer. Linda Kay stood there as if she knew she was going to break the entity down. She would send him to the light.

She began saying, "Go to the light; go to the light now. You will find peace and tranquility in the light, get rid of your anger, let go of all the ugliness, and go to the light. Peace and happiness wait you there, go now. Go to the light."

The entity raised his anger higher than anyone could ever imagine. He began throwing everything he could at them with a vengeance. Lightning flashed; dirt and rocks whirled around them. Linda Kay did not falter she stood her ground. You could see the bruise marks and the scratches where she was being attacked, but she didn't falter. She continued telling him to go to the light. There was a long and agonizing cry as if the entity was in mortal pain.

When everything stopped, the air became lighter, and once again it was easier to breathe. Linda Kay knew the entity had gone into the light, and they were now free to head home to safety and their loved ones that awaited them.

Chapter 45

Once the canoe had moved away from the island and everyone began to relax a little bit, George and Linda Kay were anxious to get into that picnic basket. The food was wonderful to them. It had been so long since they had eaten good food that had been seasoned with spices, it was hard for their systems to consume. They ate only a small portion but raved about how wonderful it was.

Linda Kay told them, "Once you do without food, you understand and appreciate the value of what you have."

Yet when Linda Kay thought back on the time she spent on that island, a shiver of fear ran through her body. All at once, Linda Kay began to fall apart, and she became hysterical; it was as if she had held everything inside her for so long that when she saw safety on the horizon, everything within her blew, and she was completely out of control. George held onto her and let her cry it out. Finally, total exhaustion took her over, and she fell asleep.

Elizabeth thought the most beautiful sight she had seen was when they pulled the canoe back on the bank from where they had started. There were times that she had her doubts that they would see their homeland again. She was having a very difficult time breathing, the pain was excruciating. She just held tight to her ribs and tried hard not to complain. Every one of them had been through enough. She could only imagine what George and Linda Kay had been through.

Danny was very sick at his stomach, and his chest was causing him horrible pain. He knew that all of them needed medical care as soon as possible. They all climbed into Danny's car he immediately headed for Harrison to the local hospital, so that they all could get the professional care they needed.

News spread very quickly that Linda Kay and George had been found. The hospital rooms began to fill with flowers and get well wishes. As their strength began to return to normal, they were anxious to leave the hospital and go home. One by one, they were being discharged; things begin to look on the brighter side. There were times that each and every one would have their flashback of memory of that horrible entity. They were all trying to put that terrible time in the back of their memories and not have to relive it from time to time. They all just wanted to get on with their lives and see what their futures would bring.

The town got together at the Buffalo River to celebrate their homecoming. There was a big cookout to celebrate their return. The whole town was there. There were mountains of food, a lot of fun, laughter, and games. There was a large area roped off where a live band was set up, and people were able to dance. It was a memory that Linda Kay, George, Elizabeth, and Danny would never forget. The celebration lasted all day and into the night. What made the celebration even better was when George announced his engagement to Linda Kay.

Danny and Elizabeth had not forgotten their promise to take Mark, John, and their girlfriends out to eat. They decided to also include George and Linda Kay. They wanted to make a wonderful night of it for everyone, especially for the boys and their girlfriends. This was to be their special night. They made reservations at the Tallgrass, the most exclusive restaurant in that area. Their intent was to make memories for the teenagers, something special that they could carry with them through their lifetime. They wanted to round the evening off by taking everyone to the Lyric, so they could listen to the local band. It turned out that it didn't just make memories for the teenagers; it made memories for all of them. It was one of the most beautiful times that they had together.

Isn't life grand with all of its twists and turns, you never know where it's going to take you next? One minute, you seem to be on top of the world, and in the next you can crash and burn. So, we have learned to try to live life to its fullest and at the same time live a simple life searching for fun, laughter, and love as we walk through this life.

CHAPTER 46

ELIZABETH WAS NOW MOVED INTO HER BEAUTIFUL NEW LOG CABIN that she was so happy with. It was hers, and she felt a sense of belonging. At the same time, Linda Kay was home now, and it was time for a decision. Will she stay or will she go? Could she leave this wonderful new life she had built for herself? Did she want to go back to the hustle and bustle of the city? She had a beautiful, calm life here. If she left, she would have to leave her beautiful cabin and put it up for sale. She could definitely make a profit off of it. No, she would not be able to sell her cabin; she loved it too much. Most of all, the question was would she be able to leave Danny? She knew that she had fallen in love with him. What she didn't know for sure was how he felt about her. If there was any kind of future for them or not, she didn't know. Her decision now was whether or not she should stay and see what the future brings, or should she go back to town before she got hurt and her love was rejected? She was supposed to meet with Linda Kay that afternoon to go over her wedding plans. She intended to discuss her dilemma with Linda Kay at that time. She only felt it was fair that Linda Kay knew she was thinking about going home.

Elizabeth pulled into Linda Kay's driveway and took the key out of the ignition. She gave a big sigh and sat there for a moment; her indecision seemed to have her planted in place. Now was the time for her to discuss her future. When she left here today, her plans were to have her mind made up whether to stay or whether to go on a new journey and see where life takes her next. She slowly got out of the car slamming the door behind her and walked to Linda Kay's door, her head hanging low in deep thought. She tried hard to have a smile planted on her face as Linda Kay opened the door hugging her and inviting her in.

"Have a seat, I'll be right back. We have so much to discuss today, and I am so excited."

As Linda Kay walked back into the room carrying a couple of iced down cokes and placed them on the coffee table. She said, "Girl you've got my curiosity up, what's going on? You said there was something you wanted to discuss with me. All good news I hope." She laughed as she said, "Maybe some good juicy gossip…?"

Linda Kay looked at her and smiled.

"None of those things, it's just something I want to tell you about what's in my heart and what I've been thinking about. I would like your honest opinion. I need your help in making a decision. I haven't mentioned this to Danny yet, but I'm going to soon. I thought maybe you could help me figure it out first." Then she took her time and explained to Linda Kay how she was in such a dilemma. "I feel as if my life has been put on hold, and now, I have no choice but to make a decision and make it right. It's time now that I get my life back in order."

Linda Kay looked at Elizabeth with a tear in her eye.

"I thought you were happy here and your decision to stay was already made. That was just my assumption. I understand that you have to live your life in a way that seems best for you. You have to be where you're the most comfortable and everything fits you. If I'm not being too selfish, I would like to ask you to wait on making that decision until after my wedding, it's only a couple of months away and whatever decision you make, I will stand behind you all the way."

Elizabeth sat there for a moment as tears formed in her eyes, but at last she said, "I will stay here until after your wedding. Linda Kay, I have to make the decision on what I'm going to do today. I can't continue to have my life in limbo. I want to be here for you as you make your wedding plans. You're my best friend, and I always want to be a part of your life. Linda Kay, I hope you don't think I'm being too selfish. I need to tell you how I feel about Danny. I love him more than I can put into words. He has never told me how he feels about me. He may not want anything more than what we have now. If it's not meant to be, I don't want to continue being here with hurt staring me in the face. So, if I come crying to you, please forgive me and help me make it through the next couple of months."

Linda Kay gave Elizabeth a hug.

"Of course, you can come to me anytime, we'll work things out. I know that Danny really cares a lot about you. You can see it in his eyes every time he looks at you. Although I cannot say what's in his heart or what he wants. However, things work out it's going to be what's best for you and what makes you happy. You deserve happiness, and no matter what happens I will be there for you. You also know that's a personal decision, one that I can't make for you. No matter what decision you make, I will always be there."

"Thank you, Linda Kay, that means an awful lot to me. As long as you're on my side, I'll make it. Whatever decision I make, I'll do the best I can to make it right. There's no way I can put into words how hard this decision is. I don't know that life will ever be the same without Danny. I don't know that I can continue to live in this state of limbo."

Linda Kay squeezed Elizabeth's hand, reassuring her that everything would be all right.

CHAPTER 47

IT WAS A BEAUTIFUL AND SUNSHINY DAY, and Linda Kay couldn't contain herself any longer. She had to call Elizabeth and let her know that she had finally made the decision to open Mama's room up.

Elizabeth seemed to be as excited as Linda Kay. There could be a treasure trove of memorabilia in there. Things that you want to treasure your lifetime or even hand down to your children someday.

"That's what I was thinking, plus I want to make use of the space. It's time to let go, to let Mom's spirit be free. So, I was wondering since you are coming over tonight, would you mind spending the night with me? I would really appreciate it if you would help me clean that room out. I would like to get up early in the morning and get started cleaning. It's been locked up for so many years, there's no telling how deep the dust will be. If you can stand it, I would love to have you with me."

"Of course, I'll spend the night. It would be my pleasure to help you clean out that room. I don't know if you thought about it or not, but I'm sure the room will have to be repainted. So, if you wish, once you get the room cleaned up be prepared to paint. Myself, I love to paint, so if you need help with that, I'll be happy to help you."

"You're a champ. Thanks a lot! I knew I could count on you."

"Okay, what if I gather my stuff and come on over? We could go shopping. Pick out the paint that you like and get all the stuff we need. Then I will help you prepare supper for tonight. I'm kind of looking forward to a good meal."

"That sounds like a wonderful idea to me come on over. I hope we can come up with a good strategy to beat the guys in a game of cards. It seems like they always beat us."

"Do you need me to pick up anything at the grocery store on my way? I'll be happy to stop."

Linda Kay kind of snickered.

"Well if you don't mind, there are a few things I'd like for you to pick up…"

She gave Elizabeth the short grocery list, and they hung up. Linda Kay was excited and happy that Elizabeth would help her with the room. She knew that any day now Elizabeth would be making her announcement to the others about whether or not she would be moving back to town. That was something that Linda Kay dreaded. She had gotten used to Elizabeth being close at hand. If she left now, it would really be heartbreaking, but she would stand by her and wish her the best.

Linda Kay and Elizabeth had had a wonderful time shopping for paint. They were in a hurry as they returned to Linda Kay's; they had spent too much time shopping and were running a little late. They were full of excitement over all the plans and having a wonderful time working together, preparing supper for their two favorite men. They began cooking, and everything seemed to be absolutely wonderful when Elizabeth looked at Linda Kay.

"Tonight, just before everyone goes home, I'll be giving my decision."

Her eyes begin to fill with tears, and she ran from the room. Linda Kay didn't follow her; she wanted to let her have some time alone to compose herself. This was her decision, and she needed to deal with it in her own way. When Elizabeth returned, she had a smile on her face and once again began chatting joyfully.

It turned out to be an absolutely wonderful night. Their supper was great. They all laughed and told jokes as they played cards. Then Elizabeth and Danny went for a walk in the moonlight. As they returned to the house, Elizabeth felt as if she was floating on air, she was overfilled with joy and excitement.

They hadn't been back in the house long when Linda Kay shouted out, "What is that on your finger! Let me see."

Elizabeth squealed in excitement as she stuck her hand out for Linda Kay to see her engagement ring. They both begin to squeal in excitement as they begin discussing wedding plans.

With that Danny stood and said, "I think I better go home and get some sleep. I've got a lot of work to do and a house to finish, so I can make a beautiful lady happy." He bent and kissed her softly as he told her, "I'll see you tomorrow. Besides you girls will want to talk about wedding plans and all that girl stuff. I hope you have a lot of fun doing it." He gave her one more kiss before he turned to leave.

George was in agreement it is getting late.

"I've also got work to do tomorrow." He gave Linda Kay a kiss and told her good night and the guys left. Linda Kay and Elizabeth were so excited, they stayed up for a while chitchatting about their weddings to come.

"Do you realize I was going to tell y'all tonight that I would be going back to Little Rock? My head is too high in the clouds to pay attention anyway. My life decisions have just made another turn, and I couldn't be happier. What do you say we go to bed, get up early in the morning, and see what life has to offer tomorrow?" She was almost dancing as she headed for the bedroom.

Linda Kay smiled. Her heart was full of excitement for her best friend.

Chapter 48

Linda Kay woke up early, went downstairs and prepared breakfast. Elizabeth could smell the coffee brewing and the aroma of sweet bacon being fried up. She immediately hopped out of bed and dressed quickly and went down meet up with Linda Kay.

"Pour yourself a cup of coffee and have a seat, breakfast is almost ready. We'll eat, and then I'm ready to get started on that room. How about you? Are you ready?"

"Sounds like a great plan to me. I heard you mulling around last night, but I didn't get up. My heart was too full of excitement, and I was afraid that if I got up, you might've come up with more bad news. I don't ever want to go through that again."

"Yes, I was woken in the early morning hours by a voice from someone; I don't know who it was. She sounded like a little old woman who seemed to be quite grandmotherly. She had a singsong voice that seemed to be of no threat; it was full of love happiness and promise. There seemed to be something that was causing her discomfort. Or maybe she was feeling anxious about something… I don't really know. The only thing she told me was, 'You will know it when you find it.' I made her a promise that I would spend today putting a real effort into trying to find the source of her discomfort. I just hope we come up with some kind of a solution. I think it would be a lot easier if I knew what the problem was. Sometimes I wonder if this is just a distraction. My goal when we returned home was to try and find out about those little girls that were on that island. I believe in my heart that they really existed, and I would like to know if they really made it to safety. I don't know how to explain it, but I fell in love with those little girls. I would like to know what happened to them."

"I can understand what you're saying. I probably wouldn't have if I hadn't seen for myself what was going on. That was the scary, and the worst place I had ever been in my life. That was an experience that no one should ever have to endure. I tell you what, after we get through fixing up your mother's old room, let's go spend some time at the library. We'll try to do some research and see if we can find out something about those little girls. It sure won't hurt to try."

They hurriedly ate their breakfast and cleaned up the kitchen. Then they headed for the bedroom with high hopes in their hearts of finding things that would be near and dear to Linda Kay.

Who knew what that woman wanted last night who came to Linda Kay, but maybe they would find something in there that would help the old woman to find the comfort she sought. They would see if they could find anything that they could connect with the woman's voice that woke Linda Kay in the night. She had to come to her for some reason, but she really didn't know who she was.

Linda Kay took a deep breath and held her hand out to Elizabeth.

"Would you do the honors?"

Elizabeth looked down, and there in Linda Kay's hand laid the key for the bedroom that had been locked up for all these years.

"Are you sure you want me to be the one to unlock it?"

"Yes, I would appreciate it. I'm just too nervous."

Elizabeth took the key from Linda Kay's hand and slowly turned it in the lock, releasing the door so that it was free to open. Elizabeth slowly began pushing on the door. Elizabeth was reluctant; it felt more like they were opening an ancient tomb. A shiver ran down her spine. Once the door was open, it revealed the sight of years of dust and neglect. It covered a room that had once been beautiful and filled with personality.

Linda Kay was nervous at the thoughts of touching her mother's things after all these years that had gone by. It brought back memories of the time her mother had spent playing with her, reading to her, and teaching her new things. Most of all, she recalled how beautiful her mother was. She actually recalled that wonderful smell from the cologne her mother wore. She had to put a big smile on her face as she whispered, "I love you, Mom."

Linda Kay let out a sigh as she said, "I hope we can salvage some of the stuff, but it may be to rotten. We have no choice; we've got to clean the room before I can think about looking around for memorabilia. Would you mind getting the vacuum cleaner out of the hall closet? I'll start taking down the curtains. There's no way we can salvage them. I guess I will be going shopping next week. You were also right; we're definitely going to have to paint. I will also have to buy new bedding for the bed, what's on here is rotten.

"Sure, you go ahead with that. I'll get the vacuum. Be right back."

Elizabeth returned with not only the vacuum cleaner but a box of trash bags which they immediately began to fill. They spent hours vacuuming, dusting, washing down walls, washing years of grime off of the furniture. They went through dozens of clean rags. They retrieved mop bucket after mop bucket of clean water before they were satisfied. Then at last they waxed the furniture and brought it back to its original beautiful shimmer.

"Where would you like to start?"

"Let's start with the dresser."

"Okay."

With that, Elizabeth pulled the first drawer open; a musty odor smell mixed with the scent of old cologne hit her in the face.

"Linda Kay, why don't we clean out these drawers as we search the room? Anything that's too old to salvage we can get rid of. Things that you want to keep, we'll just leave in the drawer."

"That sounds like a good idea to me. As musty as its smells, I'm afraid I will have to throw a lot of it away."

"You start going through things, and I'll go get more trash bags."

When Elizabeth returned to the bedroom Linda Kay was rummaging through a jewelry box.

"Look at some of mama's old jewelry, there is some beautiful pieces here. Especially this ring, look at the diamonds, how they sparkle."

"It is beautiful, that mounting is exquisite. And it's something you need to be enjoying not having locked up."

"You're right, but I think I need to get out of this old jewelry box and start looking for something that would have to do with the voice in the night."

They went about cleaning out all the drawers and leaving only the sentimental items and things that Linda Kay wanted to keep. They cleaned out the chest of drawers throwing away most of the old clothing that was in there. When they started on the nightstand that's where Linda Kay found her gold mine. It was letters that her daddy had written to her mama while he was in the service. Tears rolled down Linda Kay's cheeks as she read the letters of how much he proclaimed his love for her mother and for her, even though she wasn't born yet. Linda Kay thought the letters were the biggest and best treasure she could have ever found. At last, Linda Kay rebound the letters and laid them gently back in the drawer. She pulled a Kleenex out of the box, wiped her eyes, and blew her nose before she smiled up at Elizabeth.

"Well, we've gone through everything in here except that old cedar chest at the foot of the bed. I guess we might as well get started on that."

"Look at all that. There is a ton of pictures in here. Oh look! Here these are pictures of Mama when she was a baby. There's a whole photo album of her baby pictures. This is awesome. I hope there's some of my dad in here; I was always told he was a very handsome man.

"Hey this is my grandma and my grandfather; this is a picture of their wedding. There are tons of pictures in here of people I don't know. Maybe I can trace down and find out who some of them are, that would be pretty awesome. Wow, look at this this is a family tree album; look how great it is set up. It tells you exactly who married who, what year, where, and then there's a picture of each couple. And then all of their children and who they married. Elizabeth, can you believe this page? It's a page of all my grandparents for several generations back. This is my grandma and grandpa. That would be my great grandmother and grandfather. And my great, great grandmother and grandfather it's got their names and everything right here my great, great grandmother was named Nell…" Her voice began to fade as she kept reading. "My great, great grandfather was named Benjamin. This is awesome."

"Yeah you think that's awesome take a look at this. This is your great, great grandmother Nell's Journal."

Linda Kay screamed, "What!" as she grabbed the book from Elizabeth. She seemed to be thinking aloud as she said, "Do you think there's a chance that could be the little girl Nell that was on that island?"

"My grandmother seems to have kept everything didn't she? Do you think she ever read this? I'm a little confused because I really want to read it; I would love to know what she had to say. It's as if I could get to know her as a person not just the name. By the same token, I was always taught to never read someone else's journal. It's private and personal, and you should never invade someone's privacy."

"That is a hard decision, and I understand exactly how you feel. If I was in your situation, I would feel the same way you do. On the other hand, have you thought maybe the voice you heard last night could be hers? Maybe this is what she wants you to find."

"You're right it very well could be, or do I want to use that as an excuse because I really do want to read it? There's still a check in my soul on whether or not it would be right. I tell you what let's go eat a sandwich and drink a coke in order to give me time to think about it. Then we'll both come back and read it, or I will lock it safely back up."

Linda Kay gently laid the journal back in the cedar chest and shut the lid. She stood there just for a moment staring the chest as if it would give her permission to read the journal.

She slowly turned and headed for the kitchen. "Wow, I didn't realize it was this late. It's way past lunch time. Do you want me to start supper?

"No, I really don't I'm more interested in getting back to that room. A sandwich some chips and a coke will be fine with me. I will be more than happy to call that supper."

As they prepared their late lunch or early supper, Linda Kay talked about wedding plans. She talked about how she wanted to arrange the house so that she and George both would have their own offices in order to write their books. She talked about some of their plans for their future. Elizabeth knew she was simply stalling, so she didn't have to talk about the journal—not yet, let it rest just for a while. So, Elizabeth joined in, and after they had cleaned the kitchen 45 minutes had slipped by. Elizabeth would not bring up the journal she was just letting that subject rest as long as Linda Kay needed.

Linda Kay finally stood up.

"Okay I've wasted enough time. If I'm wrong, I'm sorry, I'll pray for forgiveness. Right now, I feel like I need to read the journal let's go and see what it has to say."

Linda Kay and Elizabeth both had tears running down their faces as they finished reading the journal. Linda Kay grabbed herself a couple of tissues and passed the tissue box to Elizabeth saying, "Help yourself."

"Do you realize what this means? Those beautiful little girls were all related to me, and Nell was my great, great grandmother. What she said in her journal was exactly what I saw in my dreams. I know now why I had to be on that island. I had to clear that island of the evil entity that was there. Evan should now be at peace. I hope he is. For when he lived here on Earth, he was an evil man who had planned to bring evil on to those beautiful little girls. Do you realize if he had killed them, I would not be here today? Now I know my family is finally at peace. I, too, can go forward with my life and live in peace.

That night when Linda Kay lay down to sleep, she heard that musical voice one more time say, "Thank you, my beautiful great, great granddaughter. I loved being with you."

With that, the voice faded away into the night. Linda Kay knew it was all finally over, a sense of peace and happiness washed over Linda Kay, and she went to sleep with a smile on her face. Everything was well in the Ozarks once again.

THE END

Printed in the USA
CPSIA information can be obtained
at www.ICGtesting.com
LVHW010409090824
787694LV00001B/56

9 781646 106783